I0545198

Hartz String Theory

Ken Coffman

Other books by Ken Coffman

Fiction

Steel Waters
Alligator Alley, Ken Coffman and Mark Bothum
Twisted Shadow, by Ken Coffman with Mark Bothum
Glen Wilson's Bad Medicine
Toxic Shock Syndrome
Immortality, LLC
Endangered Species
Fairhaven
Mesh, Ken Coffman and Adina Pelle
Fiona and the Black Faerie Prince, Ken Coffman and Kristen Lolatte
Fianchetto

Nonfiction

Real World FPGA Design with Verilog
Buffoon: One Man's Cheerful Interaction with the Harbingers of Global Warming Doom

ISBN 978-1-941071-42-7

Hartz String Theory copyright © 2016 Ken Coffman
All Rights Reserved

Cover design by Guy Corp
www.GrafixCorp.com

STAIRWAY⫶PRESS

www.StairwayPress.com
1500A East College Way #554
Mount Vernon, WA 98273

Dedication

For Carver Mead.

I only understand about 11% of what he says, but he's still an inspiration.

Fortunately, there is, within our culture, an evolution of knowledge over and above the addition of facts and the specialized understanding of those facts. Many phenomena that in the past were seen as separate are now understood to be the same: fire is a chemical reaction, not a separate element; temperature is energy; light is electromagnetic radiation; molecules are aggregations of atoms; mechanical forces are electromagnetic in origin...each of these equivalences represents a major *unification* and *simplification* of the knowledge base. Ideas formerly occupying separate conceptual spaces now occupy the same conceptual space. Each unification was made possible by a deeper understanding of existing facts, often triggered by the discovery of a crucial new fact.

It is this unification and simplification of knowledge that gives us hope for the future of our culture. To the extent that we encourage future generations to understand deeply, to see previously unseen connections, and to follow their conviction that such endeavors are noble undertakings of the human spirit, we will have contributed to a brighter future.

— Carver A. Mead, remarks on acceptance of the 1999 Lemelson-MIT Prize.

CHAPTER ONE

Rob Perry

Gusty wind ripped at Rob Perry's umbrella, nearly yanking it from his cold, wet fingers. His tasseled shoes and pant cuffs were soaked with freezing rain and spelled fashion disaster by the time he reached the executive parking area. Gazing at the gleaming cars, he admired a Volvo SUV, a Hummer H4 and the blingy Lincoln the company leased for the VP of Sales. His heart yearned for the president's tricked-out Audi A8.

One day, senior management will notice me. Then, a new Audi and executive parking permit will be mine.

From the corner of his eye he noticed a laboratory notebook standing in the gutter. Its pages fluttered in the brisk breeze, but in its sodden condition, it was too heavy to take flight. Annoyed, he picked up the notebook and tucked it under his arm. One of the researchers would be reprimanded for losing it. These notebooks were numbered and logged. They held proprietary information and the company frowned on breaches of security.

What if corporate spies from TekBio found this notebook?

By the time he reached the front door, he'd mentally composed the letter of reprimand which would include references to reckless disregard for company property and negligence in handling trade-secrets. A warning letter would be entered in the personnel file and the employee could be placed on probationary status. With properly documented warnings, an employee—even a female or minority—could be terminated. Then, team members would learn respect for company policy and management authority.

A soft company is a weak company.

What if Pacific ElectroMed was removed from the next revision of Tom Peters' *In Search of Excellence?*[1] Wall Street's masters-of-the-universe would not like that. Executive management's underwater stock options would submerge further and there'd be no additional executive parking places or shiny new Audi sedans for anyone.

---

[1] The Robert H. Waterman, Jr. and Thomas J. Peters' book *In Search of Excellence: Lessons from America's Best-Run Companies* includes luminary examples of *excellent* companies that include People's Express Airline, Digital Equipment Company (DEC), Wang Labs, Braniff, Data General, Pan Am Airlines and Atari—all now defunct. In the December, 2001 issue of *Fast Company*, Tom Peters says: "Confession number three: This is pretty small beer, but for what it's worth, okay, I confess: We faked the data." This footnote may seem critical of Mr. Peters, but, truly, he seems like a cool and interesting man.

Under cover at the employee entrance, Rob shook rain off his umbrella. After opening the entry door with his security badge, he sloshed down the hallway to his office. His dripping overcoat found its place on a coat tree. After arranging the lab notebook over his heating vent, he fanned the pages so they would dry quickly. The lost notebook would be dealt with after he checked his email, responded to voicemail and finished editing his staff meeting minutes.

The matter would be dealt with severely.

After the nine o'clock engineering meeting, he used a letter opener to gently ease apart the damp pages of the lost notebook. He tented it over his heating duct to finish drying before hurrying to his ten-thirty Safety Committee meeting.

At four o'clock, the meetings were complete and Rob was back in his office. The notebook was dry. Though the pages were crinkly and the handwriting faint, most of the pages were legible. He flipped to the inside cover. There, in accordance with company policy, the notebook owner's name, department, email address, desk phone number and mail stop should be recorded. However, this section was blank—lacking even initials. He examined the front and back covers and scanned every page for a clue to the owner's identity, but found nothing. Irritated, he made note of the book's serial number and walked across the building to the Document Control Center cubicle.

"Hey, got a minute?"

To mark her place, Polly Patterson placed a yellow sticky note in the bulky document she was reading.

"Uh, sure."

Polly, despite her youth—she was in her mid-twenties—hid her figure under layers of old-fashioned wool. Plaid. Tiny reading glasses were attached to a golden chain draped around her neck. Her nails, trimmed short, gleamed with clear polish. Subtle make-up did not over-emphasize her green eyes and prominent cheekbones. At first glance, Polly was unremarkable. Her dress and demeanor, hinting at religious cat-lady fervor, discouraged unwanted attention.

"I found a lab book out in the parking lot. I need to find out who it belongs to so I can write a reprimand for the security breach. The serial number is 2744."

"Okay, I'll look that up." She pulled a three-ring binder off her bookshelf and scanned through the pages. "Oh my," she said, "there's no name, just scribbled initials. I can't read them."

"All the researchers have crappy handwriting. Let me see." Polly rotated the book and put her finger on the page to mark the spot. "Well, shit. I don't recognize it either."

Polly shrugged. "Let's see if there are other entries that look similar," she suggested.

They examined each page, but found no handwriting that matched.

"Well, that does it for me. The company handbook is clear on this topic. Lab books must be filled out in detail. This sloppiness is intolerable. Why didn't you catch this problem?"

"Look at the dates, Rob. This assignment was before my time. Look at all the ones entered under my watch."

Rob scanned the entries. "Okay, I see what you're saying—you've done a good job. I commend your attention to detail."

"You're welcome."

"I'll hunt down the owner. When I find him or her, there will be grave consequences."

"Unless…"

"Excuse me?"

"Well, it's possible the book belongs to Harris."

Harris Stanwood, the youngest son of company founder Preston Stanwood, was a legendary screw-up. Company lore included an episode where he'd been discovered by the late-night cleaning crew smoking marijuana and screwing one of the Vietnamese production line workers in the freight elevator. Any other employee would have been terminated immediately, but Harris was untouchable. The mention of Harris's name caused Rob to clench his fists and grind his teeth.

"Wouldn't that be typical? I can see him scribbling indecipherable initials in a log."

"Isn't he coming down the hallway now?" Polly asked, gesturing furtively with her index finger.

Rob turned quickly.

"No, that's not him." He leaned over the desk and peered into Polly's eyes. "Was that your idea of a joke? Now that I think on it, I've never seen Harris use a lab book."

"You're in charge of engineering—ask around. Someone might recognize the handwriting."

"One way or another, I'll get to the bottom of this."

"I believe you, Rob," Polly said.

She bore a look of studied innocence on her face. Rob tilted his head and looked at her sideways before briskly walking away.

Back in his office, Rob pulled a bottle of Ritalin from his jacket pocket. He broke a pill in half and washed it down with a swig of warm Red Bull. He needed to suppress a growing rage—self-medication often helped.

Sitting at his desk and scanning his email, he tried not to hyperventilate. His mouse refused to move smoothly— it was a supreme act of will to avoid throwing it on the floor and stomping it to pieces. He stifled the urge to heave the heavy computer monitor through the window and rip his flesh with the resulting shards of glass. One day, someone would say exactly the wrong thing at exactly the wrong time, and he would explode with fury and rage. This could derail his career. Gradually, his pulse rate slowed and the red fringe around the periphery of his vision faded. With cruel efficiency, he delegated tasks to staff members and finished his workday.

By the time six o'clock rolled around, it had been dark outside for an hour. Most of the engineering staff punched out at exactly five o'clock on an unauthorized time clock. The clattering clock was not company equipment; to irritate Rob, a group of unruly engineers gathered contributions and a bought a used one off eBay. It was a black mark against his management that most of his staff, denying the company free overtime, clocked in at precisely eight A.M. and clocked out at precisely five P.M.

This situation started with a misunderstanding over a memo Rob published early in his tenure. It would have been better to wait until his authority was fully established before charging from the chute by publishing a scolding memo about professional corporate attire and dressing for success. Now Rob was known throughout the building as the manager of the Time-Clock crew (or TC Crew, for short). This subversion by his team of unruly engineers was not fatal to his career, but was unhelpful. He'd insist the time clock be removed (or better yet, he'd rip out the ugly thing and smash heads with it), but, under employee handbook rules, it was allowed as a personal cubicle decoration. The President of the division—who read a *Forbes* article encouraging employee frivolity to increase productivity—found it amusing.

Trying to ignore the click-clicking of the noisy clock, Rob looked through the errant lab book. His lips moved as he read incomprehensible formulas and studied sketches. He read and reread a four-page section titled *Multidimensional Analysis of Gravi-Chrono Plasmas*.

Charles 'CB' Barthre, one of Rob's design engineers, poked his head in Rob's doorway. CB worked on the company's neural stimulator family and ran regression analysis software on data collected from hundreds of chimpanzees with sensors surgically implanted in their temporal lobes—though it was well-known he spent much of his day playing Everquest while analysis software ran autonomously on remote servers. Rob liked CB well enough—in fact, they were buddies—but Rob could barely tolerate the pungent odor of primate musk that surrounded CB no matter how often he showered.

"Hey, CB. Take a look at this." Rob tossed the notebook onto his desk. "It's giving me a bitch of a fucking headache. This stuff looks like a psycho coughed up algebraic hairballs."

With an index finger, CB rotated the book. He leaned over and casually glanced at the pages.

"Hmmm, tiny handwriting. Where'd you find it?"

"Out in the parking lot. I can't figure out who it belongs to. You have the PhD; what does all this shit mean?"

"Beats me. I can take it home and look it over if you want. In the meantime, let's get a beer. The Trailblazers are playing tonight."

CB folded the notebook and slipped it in his jacket's pocket.

"Let's truck the fuck out of here," Rob said.

While the Trailblazers beat Boston in overtime, Rob lost track of how many pitchers of beer they'd consumed. Slowly the bar emptied and the pub got quieter. He rested his head on his arms for a brief moment before the barmaid tapped him on the shoulder.

"No sleeping," she said.

"I was resting my eyes for a minute."

"Maybe it's time for you switch to coffee."

"Yeah, that's a good idea. Get me a Baileys and coffee."

The barmaid, with a critical expression on her face, made a note on a scrap of paper and ambled off. CB, with his head six inches from the notebook pages, studied the fine handwriting in the dim bar light.

"Hey, Rob, I know what we should do with this."

In response, Rob spoke slowly to enunciate his words with artificial precision.

"I'll bite. What should we do?"

"Type up the Gravity Plasma section. Make it all pretty and typeset with MathCAD, and send it to one of the Physics journals. It's crazy enough to make a good April Fool's joke. It would be awesome-funny."

"What are you talking about? Shut up and have another beer."

"I'm just saying, man, it would be a great prank. We can collect rejection letters. Stanford is always bugging me for papers. If the true author comes out of the woodwork, it will teach him a lesson."

"You have brain damage," Rob said. He stood and held his beer glass up high. "Go Trailblazers!" he shouted at the top of his lungs.

Mike Thomas

The alarm clock was set for two A.M., but Mike was already awake. He listened to the wind in the trees and the creaking of his house. With acute hearing, he followed mice running through piles of magazines—shredding paper to make nests. He thought of prancing electrons, pirouetting proton-neutron quarks, sashaying gravitons, flitting sonichrons and reclusive wallflower chronotrons. The particle menagerie: a choreography of molecules, atoms, photons, neutrinos, bosons and muons. Secret patterns in constellations and interrelationships hinted at a magical blueprint before drifting away.

As much as he enjoyed the warm comfort of his bed, there was work to do. To perform his experiments, he used laboratory equipment at Pacific ElectroMed during the very early hours of the morning. Day after day, he staggered around, sleep-deprived and exhausted. His cozy bed held him captive in a cozy cocoon, but he forced himself to get up.

The radio came to life and he listened to the paranoid ranting of a late-night talk show.

I'm not doubting your veracity, Caller X, but how could the government stifle an innovation like that? Surely, it would be impossible to keep such a thing a secret forever?

Caller X was a regular who phoned from a secret location in the Nevada desert. His voice was an urgent whisper—his words tumbled over each other like rocks in a polisher.

Follow the money, Caller X said with exasperation, *a trillion-dollar economy would be disrupted overnight. The power grid, petroleum infrastructure, automobile manufacturing, airline industry—instantly obsolete. The established powers can spend billions in return for sucking the system like vampires. Follow the money!*

Big business and government collude to enslave the people of the world. What do you think radical Islamic terrorism is?

Without the money from our oil purchases, those mullahs and Imams would dry up and blow away.

It's a Faustian bargain! Without petrol dollars, the Middle East would be irrelevant. No advanced technology, no modern medicine and no future. They use our money to kill us. The oil industry puts up with it because it's easy business. Don't watch the magician's handkerchief. Keep your eyes focused on the coin. People, wake up.

Mike's thoughts drifted. He *did* need to wake up. Rotating out of bed, he stabbed at the radio power button until the voices stopped. Randomly, he pulled on clothes and walked to his bathroom to rinse his mouth and drain his bladder. The trail wound through a convoluted maze of trade magazines. Thousands. He needed to do something about the disorder. One day, a pile might topple and bury him. However, the thought of discarding magazines made him feel ill. They were his most loyal friends, though he knew the line of thought was insane. A magazine was inanimate; it couldn't be anyone's friend.

Maybe radiation from the lab affects my brain?

From his refrigerator, he grabbed his favorite technological miracle: yogurt that could be squeezed from a plastic packet directly and efficiently into his mouth. Simple, easy—no mess. Pure genius.

Why weren't more foods packaged like this?

He imagined plastic packets of Thai noodles or fried chicken that could be heated in a microwave. He dreamed of squeezable packets of beef stew and cake. Until modern science caught up with his desire, he'd settle for the yogurt.

Sometimes, his thoughts scattered. When he should be thinking about the sub-atomic properties of hexavalent Cesium, his mind drifted toward hyper-efficient food delivery systems.

I'll tell you something funny. One morning, early, when my brain wasn't working well, I evacuated a glass sphere to near-vacuum, purged it with nitrogen and refilled it with inert argon. With high-voltage electrodes connected on each side, I dispersed a very fine powder of hexavalent Cesium—suspended in the bulb like a copper-colored fog. 2.4 Gigahertz magnetrons, scavenged from microwave ovens, were installed at right angles to the probes. This created a standing wavefront in the center of my containment vessel.

I slowly increased the power supply voltage to 33,000 volts. The Cesium aerosol hovered on the ragged edge of ionization. Here's the funny part: I visualized ionization and it happened. The bulb filled with lightning-like blue tendrils—dazzling filaments of plasma.

I jumped to the conclusion that thinking of ionizing— caused ionizing.

I cleared my mind of the image and the ionizing stopped. I revisualized and it appeared. I did this five times and it worked every time. It was impossible and surreal. Then I realized, when thinking of ionizing, I leaned forward ever so slightly; the slight pressure on the electrodes triggered the reaction. When I cleared my mind, I relaxed and leaned backwards. The pressure eased and the reaction stopped.

I had a good laugh when I realized what was happening. The idea of creating an electro-quantum reaction with my mind, that's dumb. But, for a minute, that's what I believed. There's an object lesson in this story. Be careful—your mind will play tricks. During my minute of madness, I thought up a name for this phenomenon: Spooky Remote Mind Activation, SRMA. It's sneaky, so one must always watch for SRMA.

He found his laptop computer buried under a talus of yellowing *Byte* magazines. His wool hat, hanging on a nail by the front door, was easy to find. He did an inventory: car keys, wallet, notebooks, and shoes—one for each foot—check. After checking the zipper on his pants, he was ready to go to work.

Lorenz Hartz

"I warned you, my friend," Lorenz whispered.

He was tempted to close Doctor Wang's dead, staring eyes, but he knew they would not stay closed. The Doctor was duct-taped to a leather desk chair and seated with his head resting at a sharp angle. The murder weapon, an insultingly-cheap Czech-made .25 caliber revolver, was discarded on the carpet.

As far as Lorenz knew, Doctor Wang was the first Asian on the East Coast to get a top secret security clearance. Later, he was the primary lab assistant for Fermi and Szilard at Pupin Hall during the early stages of the Manhattan Project.

Lorenz looked around—the room was much as he remembered it from a visit earlier in the year. Manuscripts and books, mostly written in Chinese, were arrayed in heaps around the dark study. Doctor Wang had refused to wear Lorenz's gift, a silver medallion adorned with the snake-eating-tail Ouroboros and hourglass. It hung by its glittery chain across the corner of a photograph of Hans Bethe, Edward Teller and a shockingly young Doctor Wang.

In the photo, Doctor Wang's expression was silly— an absurd, toothy grin. He wore an explosion of thick black hair on top of his head. His slight body was stuffed into a too-small suit and his arms protruded from the sleeves like a bumpkin. The picture had been taken in front of a thicket of trees. Lorenz assumed the location was Morningside Park in lower Manhattan in the early 1940s. He could only imagine how tough things had been for a young Chinese student in those times.

Lorenz thought back to their last conversation.

"Wear the medallion. If you're in trouble, press the center for a few seconds and we'll find you."

"How does it work? Does it use cell phone towers?"

"Satellites."

"Ah," Doctor Wang mused, "I don't think anyone will bother an old man," he said while draping the chain over the photograph hanging on the wall behind his desk, "but I thank you for thinking of me."

"You always seem to get here first."

Startled, Lorenz turned. Steve Stephens was a large black man wearing an expensive overcoat. His mostly-gray hair was trimmed close to his skull. Now semi-retired after a long career in the military and the DEA, he did freelance work for an obscure department of the National Security Agency—and indulged a new-found individualism with a wispy, non-regulation goatee.

"I'm sick of this, Steve," Lorenz replied. "It makes me goddamned angry." He shook the big man's hand. "Do you guys track my Escalade?"

"Of course. Care to guess who did this?"

Lorenz sighed. "I don't know. The Agents of Karnage could have accepted a termination contract from one of the Seven Sisters. Or a whacko Wahabi fundamentalist financed by the Saudi royal family? One day…"

"I know, one day the house of marked cards will topple. But, not today."

"Right. Not today." Lorenz lifted the medallion and slipped it into his coat pocket. "Soon, I hope."

"From your mouth to God's ear. There's talk in the corridors at Fort Meade about reigning in you SUVs." [2]

"That talk goes on all the time."

"The increased intensity is notable."

"Would you suggest another demonstration?"

"No, not yet. The higher powers-that-be are neutral, if not supportive."

"Professor Wang was a good man."

---

[2] Sovereign Union of Vagabonds. A secretive organization financed by the reclusive billionaire, Andrew Wyatt.

"It wasn't our guys."

"Don't bullshit me, Steve. You guys do this all the time."

"Only with good reason. Fundamentally, we're on the same side."

"Hmmph," Lorenz grunted. He turned his gaze back to Doctor Wang's corpse. "He must have been close to something important."

"Clearly."

Lorenz stretched his back, which popped alarmingly.

"What's this world coming to?" he mumbled.

He smoothed his leather jacket and plopped his fedora on his head.

"Same old shit, same old shovel," Steve said.

"It sounds more serious when you say it in Latin," Lorenz said with a wry smile. "Idem fimus, idem rutila. I'm sorry if I seem testy—it's been a long day. If you change your mind about signing on with us…"

"I know. Wouldn't that frost a few asses at Foggy Bottom? But, no thanks. The day may come, but not today."

Lorenz took a last look at Doctor Wang's corpse.

"Goddamned murdering fucking bastards," he said.

Barry Rothschild

Barrymore Rothschild was tired of Cherie. Her body was perfectly-toned and fashionably thin from a daily two-hour session with a personal trainer along with the liberal consumption of medical-grade cocaine. She'd caught his eye as he perused a Victoria's Secret catalog. Modeling a sleek silk camisole, she captivated him with a saucy smile and perky breasts pressed against the sheer undergarment.

He called the modeling agency and hired her for a private photo session. Unfortunately, she was never without two little dogs—Clem and Buster—each clutched under an arm. They yipped and skittered on tiny claws, and there was so much licking. He found it disturbing—the way she kissed them and let them lap her face with tiny, pink poodle tongues. He could make her wash her face, but she'd spend forty-five minutes reapplying makeup and his desire would evaporate. With doggy goo on her face, he could barely stand to let her fellate him. Face-to-face sex was inconceivable.

They drove her microscopic Mini Cooper to Majestic Motors, a private auto showroom on the second floor of a Dallas skyscraper. Unmarked and unadvertised, it was known only to the moneyed class. Cargo elevator doors swept open and she drove forward. Excited, the dogs licked his ears, but he pushed them away and got out of the car. His salesman, Enrique, scurried to greet him.

"Monsieur Rothschild, what a pleasure to see you again."

Something is wrong.

Barry detected a chill in Enrique's tone. By tradition, Enrique should have been carrying a cold Bimbo apricot drink, but his hands were empty. The first time Barry visited—during happier days before the most-recent financial meltdown—he'd bought a Maserati. They'd toasted with apricot nectar poured over ice in a tall, crystal tumbler. He preferred the drink topped off with a dollop of Crown Royal, but they would not serve alcohol—though they would look the other way if a drink was fortified from a private supply. The only bottle Cherie carried was a nearly-empty quart of Jim Beam. That would not do.

"Hello, Rikki," Barry said.

Under banks of LED light fixtures, the cars gleamed with promise. The floor, polished to mirror-like perfection, reflected bright, stunning colors—a king's garden of earthly delights. The collection included new European imports alternating with older cars, fully restored and gleaming. A Jaguar, a Duisenberg—and for more specialized collectors—one of Adolph Hitler's squat, black Mercedes sedans. Incongruously, a tiny Metropolitan, like a toy, rotated on a spotlighted pedestal.

"I need a car for the Oscars. I'm taking Renée this year. I want something old-school and classic, but different. This year I'll drive her myself instead of hiring a limousine. Perhaps, I don't know, a 1963 Corvette?"

Enrique waved his hands as if he was an umpire and Barry had been thrown out at home plate.

"I'm sorry, Monsieur Barrymore, but your father's accountants called last week and specifically denied you corporate funding. So, unless you have cash…" Enrique allowed his sentence to trail off hopefully.

Cash?

What's this nonsense?

Barry didn't have cash, he had something better—an unlimited corporate expense account.

"I don't follow."

"Your father is cutting back expenses."

"Twaddle-pee. Surely something can be done?"

Enrique frowned as if smelling something overripe.

"There is a 1997 Porsche we took in on trade…"

"A Carerra?"

Enrique shook his head with regret.

"Turbo?"

More sad regret.

"I can't drive a garden variety Porsche!"

"It only has eighty-thousand miles and is in very nice condition. It was owned by…"

Enrique stopped. It was obvious that Barry did not care who had owned it.

"I bought three cars here and you're telling me I can only get a used Porsche? *Me?*"

"The economy is weak. This happens. Last week I had to put Mark Cuban's girlfriend in a secondhand Lexus. Perhaps you could trade the Bugatti for something nice."

Barry clenched his teeth. The Bugatti was in the boneyard after an encounter with a light pole. Barry was unhurt, but his girlfriend-of-the-moment spent a week in Intensive Care. Barry's shoulders slumped. He was beaten.

"Okay, I get it. But, don't expect me to be back when I get this straightened out with my father. I'll take my business elsewhere."

He turned on his heel. In the car, the dogs licked Cherie's face while she giggled. He dropped into his seat and slammed the door.

"Let's get out of here. They don't have anything I want," he said.

AK-149

The Agents of Karnage believed the new age of God would begin when society collapsed and chaos reigned. The A-K's were conceived in 1979 after AK-47, Wallace Henry Jackson, was released from prison. He'd been arrested, convicted, sentenced, and served six years at the Atlanta Federal Penitentiary for robbing a Circle-K store and beating a female clerk nearly-to-death with a golf club. The net of this robbery was $117. Before the police caught him, he stuffed this cash in a pipe at the edge of a Mechanicsville parking lot. The money was never found.

Wallace, though he'd done stupid things in his life and was a textbook example of a psychopath, was not stupid. He grew up in a normal, middle-class family. The convenience store robbery was an accident—he'd been high on animal tranquilizers. The clerk called him a loser when he fumbled with change to buy a candy bar.

It was coincidence that he had a set of golf clubs in his car and happenstance that he took the money from the cash register after *punishing* the clerk. On the surface, this was just another everyday brutal robbery, but strong forces roiled in Wallace Henry Jackson.

In prison, he had time to think about doing things differently.

How could he maximize other's pain and suffering while minimizing his risk of returning to incarceration?

He'd been killing cats and railway bums since he was 13; he'd never been caught. Then, ironically, after losing his temper with a no-account convenience store clerk, he was thrown in the slammer. There was a lesson embedded in this experience.

Wallace might have evolved into a garden-variety, mass-murdering creep, except for a stroke of blind luck. After being released from prison, he recovered his $117 and, at the same site of his brutal crime, purchased a quart of milk, two fried cherry pies and twenty five-dollar Powerball tickets. One of these tickets was a huge winner. His net—after the jackpot was split with two other winners and taxes were deducted—was eighty-three million dollars.

Wallace recognized this as a message from God; it meant God approved of his work. Heeding the signal, Wallace founded the Agents of Karnage to embark on a mission—to destroy human civilization.

The A-K Academy was established in an Atlanta church put up for sale after the pastor was convicted of having sex with a 13-year-old Sunday school student. The sale price was a bargain and Wallace paid cash. At the academy, the A-K doctrine was planted in the heads of young Agents. Only from anarchy and bloodshed would the new Son of God appear. Spreading pain and destruction was a sacred duty.

Wallace did not like to cause devastation directly. The A-K method increased the *likelihood* of mayhem and allowed God's destructive will to emerge.

To fill the Agents of Karnage Academy, Wallace searched for other intelligent psychopaths. Using Google, they were easily found. The academy program did not have a fixed term. Each Agent studied until he or she pleased Wallace. On graduation, each was assigned an AK number and permitted to reenter society.

Before being discovered by Wallace, Trent MacNeal lived in a group home after being convicted of killing a thoroughbred racehorse with a fire axe. He was a perfect candidate: young and handsome, but morally corrupt. Step ladders and bowling balls were the keys to Trent's transition. He found a pedestrian overpass where, each afternoon, black students from Martin Luther King Secondary School walked over the I-85 freeway. The protective fencing was low. Trent, wearing an orange transportation employee jumpsuit and a fake beard, positioned bowling balls and a step ladder. When the kids walked home after school, some naturally picked up the balls, climbed the ladder, and tossed them into oncoming traffic. Three motorists were killed in the traffic bedlam. As an added bonus, a furious racist cracker from Charlotte pulled a deer rifle and killed one of the kids. Further chaos was unveiled. Wallace was well pleased. Trent—AK-149—was born.

AK-149's first assignment was in Seattle and he was eager to get started.

CHAPTER TWO

Mike Thomas

WHILE STANDING IN the hallway outside his boss's office, Mike gazed through a window. Rain poured from low clouds and, standing on tiptoes, Mike could see his mustard-yellow Maverick in the last row of the parking lot under a sopping canopy of overhanging alder branches. The driver's side window gaped open a few inches. The swirling wind guaranteed a cold, wet seat for the ride home. Concentrating and calculating, he futilely estimated the cost to get the heater fan fixed. He had ten dollars in his wallet which was enough to survive on if he ate ramen noodles and canned tuna until payday. It was no immediate comfort, but, because he had assets, he was not poor, just broke.

"How long have you been standing there?"

Mike's boss, Madison Howard—in her late twenties—had been with the company for two years, though, to Mike, it felt like twenty. She used a manila folder to direct him to her visitor's chair. Dressed a stark, black wool skirt and blazer over a white blouse, she wore a gold ankle chain glimmering under her nylons—her skirt hitched when she sat back in her chair and flopped her feet on the desk. Mike's eyes were drawn to the old-fashioned seams of her stockings.

"What are you staring at? Haven't you seen a woman's legs before?"

Mike shifted in his chair and searched for something safer to look at. The office was clean and sterile, but, in a corner, a strand of cobweb hung from the ceiling. It undulated in the air's Brownian quest for harmony.

"Are you uncomfortable with women in the workplace? If so, you'd better get over it. The good-old-boy glass-ceiling is obsolete. Read me?" She stared at him for a few moments. "Do you talk?"

"I…"

"Never mind. My afternoon is booked solid—let's get this done." She opened the manila folder and leafed through the contents. "Did you bring the self-evaluation form?"

Mike's mind flashed on the image of the waterlogged document sitting on the front seat of his car.

"I filled it out, but I left it in my car."

"Wouldn't it be perfectly natural to bring your self-evaluation form to your biannual performance review?"

"I…"

"Forget it. That was a rhetorical question. Remind me—what do you do for the company?"

"I'm a materials coordinator and I'm in charge of incoming inspection of rivets, screws, bolts, nuts, washers, metal shielding materials, inserts and foils."

"And you've had that job for seven years?"

"Eleven years."

"Right, you rolled over tenure when Allied Medical bought the company. Eleven years. That's a long time inspecting bolts. You're probably pretty good at it by now, am I right? Zip-zip with a caliper and stamp them off?"

"There's a bit more to it than that. I check plating and anti-corrosion finishes."

"I'm messing with you. I know you're a hard-working screw inspector and company operations would grind to a screeching halt if you fell down on the job."

"I wouldn't go that far."

"Of course," she said. Lifting her feet off the desk, she swiveled to face him and waved a sheaf of spreadsheets. "Throughput is off twelve percent. To keep up with off-shore suppliers, we have to improve productivity every quarter—relentlessly and without fail. Your department is going backwards. I stopped senior management from transferring your job to the team in Bangalore, but with numbers like this, you can't blame them for looking for more cost-effective options."

"We had a shipment of bad rivets from Hungary. Counterfeit. The plating flaked off. It took a long time to get that straightened out."

"You can't argue with numbers. To be competitive, efficiency must increase. Do you think the board wants to hear that we can't pay a dividend because we spent too much time messing with ten-cent rivets? Do they want to hear we missed a revenue forecast because we couldn't deal with a routine supply-chain issue in a timely manner?"

"No, ma'am."

"So, you understand why I have to give you a *three* in *finishes work assignments in a timely fashion* and a *four* in *reacts well to unexpected business challenges*. Overall, your performance *needs improvement*. Sign the last page and we'll be done for now."

Mike scribbled his name and pushed the papers across the desk.

"Bring in your self-evaluation and we'll go over it, okay?"

Mike nodded and walked to the door.

"One last thing, Mike."

He turned. The top buttons of her blouse were open. Creamy breasts oozed over the lacy trim of her black brassiere. Mike steered his eyes back to the safety of the dangling cobweb.

"Yes?"

"An invoice crossed my desk for something called hexavalent Cesium—a radioactive rare earth. Seventeen thousand dollars a gram. Someone ordered it and someone received it, but no one knows who. Seventeen thousand dollars. Someone privately covered the bill with a PayPal transaction, but it's inappropriate to use company resources this way and someone will get canned, possibly prosecuted. It won't be me. So, if you have anything to say, this would be a fine time to enlighten me before senior management gets involved and things turn ugly. So?"

Mike shook his head.

"Nothing to say? You don't talk much, do you, Mike? You're the quiet, mousy type creeping through the corridors with an optical loupe and a micrometer. I'll be watching. In fact, pass the word along, I'll be studying the whole team very carefully. I have ambitions and this job will not leave a black mark on my record. Anyone thinking differently should think again. Are we on the same page, Mike?"

"Yes, ma'am."

"Okay, run along then. I believe I hear a rivet calling your name. *Mike, come inspect me. You're the best, Mikey, inspect me good.* Can you hear it?"

"No," Mike said.

"Another rhetorical question. Carry on. And, have a great day. Thanks for stopping by and close the door on your way out."

Outside, Mike pulled the door shut and exhaled. He took a moment to allow his heart rate to settle. A coworker, Steve Walters, sat in the guest chair, fidgeting as he waited for his turn in the hot seat. Steve was in charge of inspecting capacitors, inductors and transformers.

"I overheard. Bad?" Steve asked.

"Yeah," Mike replied.

He took a deep breath and walked down the corridor that led toward his workstation.

"Very bad," he mumbled.

Polly Patterson

Polly did not report directly to Rob Perry, but she stood in line with other subversive employees to clock out on the unofficial time clock at 5:03 P.M. Someone printed a plot of data showing a slight upward trend in work hours and posted a fake company memo scolding employees for working extra hours. *Severe consequences* were in store, it warned, if free overtime continued to be recorded.

Polly took an indirect route to the exit, passing through the engineering section—exchanging goodnights with people still working. She mixed well with the social retrogrades of the design groups. The introverted engineers were tongue-tied and bashful with women. She felt comfortable and safe with them.

After unlocking the doors of her Mazda Miata and letting the engine warm up, she headed home. As rain splattered the roof, the CD player picked up where it left off—Frank Sinatra urged her to put her dreams away (for another day). It was a perfect soundtrack for the chilly evening. She shook off melancholy—feeling sorry for herself was not her style. After turning off the stereo and adjusting the heat, she focused on driving home.

Two cats waited in the window of her little house. After hauling in the garbage can, she fed and watered the animals, then sat and stroked them in gathering darkness. Fighting lethargy, she rose and stalked through the house—making sure the drapes were tightly closed before flipping on bright studio lights installed in her living room. After peeling off her staid work clothes, she folded them neatly and stacked them in a pile on her dresser. This left her wearing form-fitting lavender leotards that covered her slim body from ankle to wrist and neck.

Shuffling through songs on her iPod to find something to match her mood, she settled on an avant garde arrangement of Stravinsky's *Rite of Spring* performed by a München string ensemble. From a stack of loose paper, she found notes on a dance that accompanied the music. Idly, she reviewed cryptic notations before starting her warm-up routine. Slowly and deliberately, she stretched muscles tight from a sedentary day. With a patina of sweat on her forehead, Polly worked her feet into her oldest and most-comfortable ballet slippers and, with the cats as her audience, began to dance.

With eyes closed, she pressed into a *plié* before executing a series of slow leaps and *pas de chats* across the floor. She focused on keeping her knees high and turned out while seeking the elusive simulation of weightlessness. When her muscles were loose, but not yet rubbery from exertion, she imagined time and gravity relaxing; the sensuous release of the earth's binding force.

Having trouble finding the rhythm of a complex passage, she programmed the iPod to repeat and practiced a pirouette until the spin was perfected. As time passed, she achieved an unconscious, meditative state—a tranquil alignment with the cosmos.

Two hours of spinning, leaping and adding pages to her dance notation passed quickly and left her mentally and physically exhausted. After toweling sweat from her hair and weighing herself on her bathroom scale—107 pounds—she turned on the TV with a remote control and walked to her compact kitchen to select a low-calorie dinner from a selection in her freezer. Her one caloric indulgence was a pint of Guinness Stout poured into a frozen mug. Beautiful, heavenly mud. There were better Irish stouts, but none readily available from the Larry's Market where she shopped.

She nibbled dinner and savored beer with cats sprawled at her sides. They watched daytime dramas Tivo'd during the day. Though sleepy, she forced herself to stay up until 9:30. After peeing and brushing her teeth, she dropped sweaty tights into the laundry hamper and slipped her nude body between her bed's crisp cotton sheets.

While sleeping, she invented gravity-defying dances. The dreams would be unremembered in the morning, but were multicolored prayers offered to the gods that watched over the night.

Rob Perry and Charles 'CB' Barthre

Rob sorted through a stack of mail—mainly trade magazines and credit card offers. Buried deep in the stack, he found two letters addressed to Dr. Charles Robert Perry; one from *Modern Physics Letters* and the other from *The New Journal of Physics*. While reading, he was momentarily confused before grasping that both journals accepted *Studies in Multidimensional Spherical Algebraic Analysis, Particularly Sub-Quantum Chaotic Gravitational Chronotrons* for their online publications. The MPL letter included an honorarium check of $250 and the one from NJP explained that their typical request for a $50 donation was waived for this particularly interesting paper.

A month had passed and he hadn't been completely sober when CB dreamed up the idea, so it took a minute to remember the paper they extracted from the sodden laboratory notebook.

Shit.

He picked up the phone and dialed CB's extension.

"Get your ass over here."

Sixty seconds later, CB poked his head through Rob's doorway.

"What's up, chief?"

"Sit down and look at these letters."

He handed them across.

"Ha, that's cool! Our paper got accepted. That proves it—these online journals will print any goddamned thing if it looks complicated."

"I don't like this."

"Come on, it's a joke. What are they going to do, arrest Dr. Charles Robert Perry? Earth to Rob, there ain't no such person. All they have is a phony name and the company address. They'll never pin anything on us."

"Well, I'm getting the fricking mail."

"So what? That doesn't mean anything. You're the engineering manager—you get all the lost letters. Just relax, will ya?"

"I suppose. How am I going to cash this check?"

"You're not going to cash it. Stab it on your corkboard for laughs. Look, it's almost four. Can't we sneak out and grab a couple of beers? It's been a long day. I could use a tall, cold one—how about you?"

Rob fished a pushpin from his desk drawer and skewered the papers on an empty spot on his corkboard.

"Sure, but you're buying the first round for coming up with the stupid idea for that paper."

"You're on. I'll grab my jacket and meet you."

Rob swiveled in his chair and stared absently at his wall of fame. It consisted of snap shots from a sturgeon fishing trip, cross-country skiing adventures, an old girlfriend holding up a beer and making the 'devil horn' sign at a Kiss concert and now, the letters and check.

What in the name of the holy Jew is a Gravitational Chronotron? These crazy journals deserve to be spoofed for publishing such utter nonsense.

He slipped into his jacket and, with a furtive glance toward his manager's office, headed for the remotest exit so he wouldn't get caught sneaking out early.

Caller X

While sipping coffee from a USAF 53rd Tactical Fighter Squadron mug adorned with arrowhead and *Prepared to Prevail* logo, Caller X multitasked. His trio of desks was arranged so he could efficiently roll his chair between them. Each desk bore three monitors. Each monitor had several windows open so he could keep an eye on worldwide news feeds pulled in from multiple satellite dishes pointed skyward outside his aluminum Airstream trailer.

When a website-of-interest or blog updated, a chime would sound. The chimes were a constant fabric audible over the industrial air conditioning system that kept the place cool despite extreme outdoor temperatures. Power was generated by a massive solar array and backed up by an Army-surplus diesel generator buried in a concrete bunker. The Airstream's plumbing was fed by a water tank mounted on the back of a flat-bed truck. He drove the water truck to Elko once a month for a refill.

His compound was located on a rocky shelf with a flat expanse of desert visible for many miles to the East. Clouds of dust from the gravel road appeared a half hour before any vehicle could reach him. A lookout tower, accessible through a hatch in the Airstream's roof, was equipped with a 50-caliber water-cooled machine gun. With many choices for ammunition—armor-piercing depleted-uranium rounds, tracer, thermite and explosive core—he was ready. When the New World Government Fascist goons came in their matte-black helicopters, he'd take many to hell with him. For fun, he could lock his sights on a coyote and, in seconds, turn it into a bloody spray of scattered chunks. But, he was generally too busy for this crude entertainment.

He made a living selling videos and running a members-only web empire. His current video project had the working title *Storm Troopers at the Gate: The Secret History of Bill Clinton, the American Stalin*. He had sold 7,023 copies ($39.95 not including $7.95 for shipping and handling) of his last video, *String him from a Lamppost: The Real Barack Hussein Obama, Modern American Mussolini*. His

BanaMex account balance was impressive, but most of his wealth consisted of palladium bars buried under a yucca at secret GPS coordinates.

He was a regular on George Noory's *Coast to Coast* radio program. This week, George scheduled him for a full hour. Caller X took a sip from his mug, cleared his throat and dialed the show's private line. He chatted with the producer while the introductory commercials for short-wave radios and freeze-dried emergency rations ran in the background.

"Did you catch last night's program?"

"You mean the one where the guest channeled Pharaoh Ramses-two?"

"No, the one about the Incans and the aliens. It was a great show. We had callers by the bushel."

"Sorry, I missed that one. It's been busy around the Outpost. Aliens? Do people really believe that stuff?"

"We don't ask questions like that around here," the producer said with a hearty laugh. "What's on the agenda tonight?"

"There's breaking news from Brussels about a global warming tax to enslave the sovereign peoples of the world."

"George would like to get to callers sooner if that's all right."

"Sure. Anyone new on the line?"

"Let me look." The producer clicked on his keyboard. "Stan from Nogales, Patricia from Colorado Springs and Karl from Little Rock. The usual menagerie. Wait, here's a good one. Lorenz is checking in from Seattle; he's always fun. He wants to talk about zero-point energy."

"Like the corporations will allow that. Give me the usual forty-five second warning?"

"Sure, Caller X, stay on the line. George wants to mention a Bigfoot sighting in British Columbia, and then he'll introduce you."

"Thanks."

With half an ear attuned to his headset, Caller X scanned updates from computerized spybots trolling the Web. Random pieces of information slipped through cracks in the mainstream media's bubble. They killed most of the real news, but good stuff slipped through. There were real-time news feeds coming from North Carolina where thirty-six people had been killed in a chemical plant *accident*. Caller X suspected an attack by Islamist radicals. Reading between the lines, it looked like Sarin gas was likely rather than any biological agent, but it was too early to jump to a conclusion.

Pesticide tank leak?

Bullpucky.

"Okay, X, my friend, you're up."

"Thanks."

Caller X listened to George Noory's sonorous voice.

"We'll get an update from Doctor Chandler with the latest Bigfoot sighting in Hope, BC. This could be the cryptozoology breakthrough we've been waiting for. Tune in for that next week. Now, I have a special treat. Caller X is calling from his secret desert headquarters. Caller X, thank you for joining us."

"You're welcome, George. It's always a pleasure to be with you. There are monumental events looming and I'm delighted provide an update. World War Four with Islamo-Fascist terrorists is heating up and World War Five is visible like a black cloud on the horizon."

"We have callers on the line. Do you mind if we go right to them?"

"Not at all, George. Your callers are knowledgeable and interesting—I'm always happy to chat with them."

"Great. First up is Patricia from Colorado Springs in the shadow of NORAD headquarters on the front range of the Rockies. Patricia, what's on your mind this evening?"

"Caller X, have you followed the news? My neighbor's son was killed by a freeway sniper in Los Angeles. He was a good kid driving a Miller Beer truck. The police say it was a random act of violence, but it was near a Moslem neighborhood. Something doesn't smell right. Is the government covering up murder by Islamic sleeper cells?"

"Yes, what about that, Caller X? Does the government play down domestic terrorism? If so, why?"

"Patricia, you ask a great question. My sources tell me there are an average of five killings per day caused by Islamic terror cells. For example, remember the propane tanks that exploded in a U-Haul truck near Malibu? Seven fatalities if I recall correctly. Did you think that was a tragic accident? For another example, the mainstream news reported an accidental Botulism poisoning in Minneapolis, but did you know the FBI arrested a *person of interest*; a former convict who converted to Islam in prison?

His Muslim name—I have it here somewhere—yes, he legally changed his name to Ahmed Mohammed Hassan. They killed that story, but I have it documented in my video called *World War Four at Your Doorstep*, where you'll be shocked to learn how much killing happens on our soil, in our neighborhoods and under our noses. There are many more cases since the video was released and you can get the latest information from my subscription site with daily updates from the front. The war is here and it's real."

"Excellent answer, Caller X, thank you. Stay alert out there in Colorado, Patricia. Next we have Lorenz calling on the Left Coast line from Seattle. Lorenz?"

"Yes, George, thank you for taking my call. I'm a member of the Sovereign Union of Vagabonds—"

"Yes, the SUVs. We know of your organization. What's on your mind tonight?"

"We're on the cusp, the veritable threshold of a new age of zero-point energy—free energy from space—but the transition will be hard for common folks. Metamorphing into a free-energy society is inevitable, but the change will be brutal for the unprepared. And let's not underestimate the fury and brutality of world forces addicted to oil revenues."

"I'm fascinated by this topic," George interjected. "Do you have a question for Caller X?"

"No question, just a warning. Caller X is bravely spreading the word, but the multinational corporations will stop at nothing to milk a few more years of exploitation from the souls of the people. Caller X should be cautious."

Caller X chuckled. "Lorenz, you make great points, but we disagree on one thing. Zero-point energy will *never* be allowed. How do you profit from something that is free? The corporations will kill it. In the seventies I knew a man who modified his Cadillac carburetor to get greater horsepower and one-hundred and fifty-three miles per gallon. Before his discovery was released he died mysteriously. The police said it was a tragic accident, but would an experienced horseman fall off his horse and break his neck? The plans were lost and his patent applications vanished. If gas mileage goes up, how much does gas tax revenue go down? Would the governmental-corporate complex allow that?

"As to my safety, Lorenz should rest assured. I am well-protected. They may try, but they will not get me. On that topic, folks should download my eBook, *How to Protect your Family from the new Slave Masters*. Nine-ninety-five, and if you order now, I'm throwing in, absolutely free, a copy of my white paper, *Democrat or Republican, Who Cares who Holds the Whip?*"

"Excellent, Caller X, that's a great deal and must-reading for our listeners. Don't go away, we'll be back with Caller X after a word from our sponsors. The Ultimate Survival tool is the genuine Swiss Army Knife, now with corkscrew. Order now and you'll get a pair of free LED flashlights. That's right, friends, I said free with your order. Just call the toll-free number…"

Mike Thomas

My dad, after working on the Bomb in New Mexico, was a professor at Caltech where he worked with Mead, Bethe, Gell-Mann and Feynman. Truth be told, he made most of his money buying shitty little duplexes out in the orange groves and holding them for twenty-five or thirty years. It would be great to recognize him as a financial genius, but he slipped a few gears later in life and lost everything with a sure-fire horserace handicapping method based on stochastic, multi-dimensional vector math.

Me? I have a diploma adorned with the California Institute of Technology flame of knowledge. I followed dad's footsteps for a while, but got sick of LA traffic and smog. Plus, I couldn't deal with his drinking and slow decent into senility, so I packed my stuff and moved to Seattle.

I like my job and didn't need to change companies to work for many different employers—I stayed in one place, and the companies changed around me. First, Pacific United Electronics until the founder sold the company to Felton Electro, which was absorbed by General Electric, then spun off into a separate division with the current name, Pacific ElectroMed under GE's subsidiary: Allied Medical.

Most of the old-timers are gone, so few remember I invented the algorithm for the products that established the company's initial reputation and fortune. Those products are still in production—occasionally a problem comes up and someone thinks to ask me about it—but institutional memory fades. Most people don't even know the company's founder still wanders the hall like a spectre.

I don't mind. I like my workspace by the receiving dock—the forklifts and to-and-fro of trucks don't bother me. I do my job and think my thoughts. It's relaxing and undemanding as long as I ignore the corporate bullshit.

Someday, someone will notice I didn't sign the non-compete agreements and that I haven't attended the diversity and corporate ethics training sessions. As long as my friend Baltazar works in the personnel department (he threatens to retire), I stay under the radar and avoid stimulating the corporate immune system. I'll go on like this for the foreseeable future. I could make more money by going back into product engineering, but they expect you to work long hours in exchange for the substantial engineering salary. It's not worth it.

Einstein was uncomfortable with Bohr and Heisenberg's uncertainty principle; I share that discomfort. We visualize matter's building blocks as particles or waves. I dreamed of a universal model in terms of waves and wavelets—standing waves of gravity, magnetism and even stranger, temporal packets stacked like playing cards to form a continuous anti-clockwork stream of quantum states. That's what I think about while inspecting threads of stainless steel screws.

I won't be satisfied until my theories are demonstrated and repeated. The men building the first atom bomb were not completely sure it would work. Some worried the Earth's atmosphere would be ionized and set aflame. There was a statistical chance that all life on earth might be destroyed. Sure, the math and simulations were promising, but until that first beautiful explosion, there was doubt—doubt annihilated by the heat and energy of that lovely conflagration in the remote New Mexico desert. It silenced nay-sayers and skeptics. My version of that day is what I work toward and what I dream of when I sleep.

40

CHAPTER THREE

Mike Thomas

STRETCHED ACROSS HIS bed, Mike stared at red light reflecting off his ceiling. This light appeared to come from his clock radio's flashing red display. However, from a subatomic perspective, all processes are reversible. It wouldn't violate the laws of physics if, rather than being emitted from the clock display, the light was emitted by the red cones of his retina and beamed to the ceiling to reflect back into the display. Like a photonic vacuum cleaner, the voracious display could theoretically suck light from the room.

He wished he could switch off the parts of his mind that housed such nonsense. As a diversionary tactic, while a headache kindled, he turned his thoughts to gravitons and chronotrons—the elemental particles of gravity and time and pondered the conservation of time and simultaneity's illusion. He leaned over to see the time reference of his inertial frame. It was nearly midnight and he'd had his sleep allotment. Three hours was all he allowed himself. It was time to go to work.

Lethargic, he listened to the ever-present murmur of the talk radio station. It was the usual refrain about evil Islamic terrorists attacking the West.

"World War Three—the Cold War—ended when the Berlin Wall fell in 1989," Caller X explained earnestly. "It overlapped World War Four, which began when the Baathist Arab Sirhan Bishara Sirhan killed Robert Kennedy in revenge for the United States supporting Israel in the Six-Day War."

Caller X patiently listened to a challenge from Jerry, a caller from Pasadena. "That's nuts, everyone knows our conflict with the Muslim world erupted in 2001 when crazed Saudi Arabians and Egyptians hijacked commercial aircraft and turned them into flying bombs."

Caller X responded impatiently. "We were under attack long before 2001. The first attempt to take down the World Trade Center came in 1993 when Ramzi Yousef detonated a Ryder truck filled with fifteen-hundred pounds of explosives and killed six people. Have we forgotten the attack on the USS Cole and the two-hundred and twenty Marines killed in Lebanon when Reagan was president? What about the embassy bombings? You people need to pay attention.

"Think about the mysterious Iraqi connection to the Murrah Federal Building bombing on April 19, 1995. Do you think morons like Tim McVeigh and Terry Nichols designed that shaped-charge bomb on their own? How many Iraqi phone numbers do you have in your address book? McVeigh had several. After leaving Oklahoma City, the alleged John Doe #2 in the

bombing investigation, an Iraqi named Hussain al-Hussaini, took a job as a cook at Logan Airport in Boston. You know, the airport where—on September 11, 2001—American Airlines Flight 11 and United Airlines flight 175 originated? Unlikely coincidence? Wake up, America.

"Let me address you directly, Jerry. From your vocabulary and accent, I'll make some assumptions. You're young, perhaps in your early twenties. You're in college or maybe you dropped out. You like to smoke weed, practice your chops on Guitar Hero, meddle with bar girls and watch sports on television. If Islamic Fundamentalists got their hands on you, they'd try you for Sharia crimes and cut off your head. The only thing that holds them back are barriers of geography and the military might of this country. Our defenses were built by an unprecedented free market engine. So why in God's name do you march in the street and side with our evil enemy instead of the country that grants you the constitutional right to mouth off without consequence?"

George interrupted the rant. "We have to go to a break now. Thank you, Jerry, for calling in from Pasadena. We'll be back with more from the always fiery and fascinating Caller X after this brief message from our friends at Metalife Supplements. Are you feeling run down and tired? Bee Good contains only pure and natural plant pollen—"

Mike switched off the radio and rubbed his eyes while walking through the magazine maze to his bathroom. As he ran an electric razor over his chin, he tried not to visualize fragments of whiskers going backward in time— flying from the razor to implant themselves in his face. After a shower, he grabbed his coat and walked up the street to his car. He couldn't park in his driveway because the battery was shot and he needed a hill to coast down for a compression start.

He arrived at Pacific ElectroMed on his normal schedule—planned so he slipped quietly into the research lab while the security guards changed shifts. From scattered locations, he hauled test equipment to a borrowed section of lab bench. The research gear created an esoteric mélange. A Gallium-Heisenbach X-ray Diffractometer, a Varian cold-vapor atomic absorption spectrophotometer, a high-voltage plasma generator, a Hewlett-Packard 5071A Cesium frequency standard with custom-built interface fixtures and finally, a twenty-dollar Radio Shack volt-ohmmeter.

The point of his experiment was to create a plasma where magnetic fields could modulate graviton fluxes. It was frustrating because he didn't have the proper equipment and was forced to make-do with a crude assemblage of gear designed for different purposes. Just a few days with the CERN particle accelerator in Switzerland would quickly prove or disprove his theory about the gravitronic linkages between strong, weak and electromagnetic forces. If verified, worldwide acclaim and certainly a Nobel Prize would be his.

He shook his head. He'd wasted an hour dreaming of how the world would react to his radical theory once the basic concepts were demonstrated. There was no time to waste; he needed to allow time to stow away equipment and clean up the lab before the earliest-arriving researchers discovered him doing unauthorized work.

After connecting cables and flipping switches, he booted the computer that controlled the lab equipment. Looking over his bench, he documented the test setup in a ten-cent college-lined one-subject spiral-bound notebook.

He was ready to attempt forming the world's first manmade gravitron plasma. Gas hissed as he filled an evacuated glass carboy with Xenon and an aerosol of powdered hexavalent Cesium. Unconsciously superstitious, he crossed himself before actuating a switch applying 33KV to terminals arranged around the glass vessel.

For an eternal instant, like other innumerable experiments, nothing happened. Then a pinkish-purple glow emerged from a bright point in the bulb's middle and slowly expanded. Before Mike's awestruck eyes, the glowing sphere hesitated at the perimeter of the glass, and then spread through the room like a smoke ring. It was possibly his imagination, but he thought he felt a tingle as the wavefront passed through his body. Then, with a sharp snap, the vacuum bulb disappeared, leaving behind a gray nodule the size of a pea. Mike flipped off the power supply and touched the pea with the tip of his finger. It dissolved into a pile of dust. In a few seconds the dust dispersed in a nonexistent wind—drifting away like motes in a sunbeam.

That was cool.

He lost track of time while frantically scribbling observations in his notebook. By five o'clock he'd pressed his luck as far as he dared; he started disassembling the setup. Satisfied that all the equipment was back where it belonged, he retreated to a janitorial supply storage area for a nap before work.

On waking, he popped out of the storage room and nearly knocked over Polly. She pushed a cart loaded with documents to be distributed in the production area for the day shift.

"Sorry, Polly," Mike said. "I—"

"It's okay, Mike. I've seen you come from there before. What is it you do? Sleep?" She pushed the door open and flipped on the light. It was obvious that Mike had fashioned a crude bed from plastic-wrapped rolls of toilet paper. "I thought so."

She turned off the light and allowed the door to close.

"Don't tell anyone, okay? I could get in big trouble."

"Your secret is safe with me," she said over her shoulder as she rolled the cart down the corridor. Looking back, she favored him with a sweet smile which made his knees weak. "I'll talk to you later. I gotta get these documents distributed so I can get clocked-in by eight."

Unable to form words, Mike waved at her, but she turned a corner and his gesture was wasted.

Rob Perry

The Brain Stem Implant project was three months behind schedule and $8.44 per unit over budget. Using a pencil eraser to probe an itching ear, Rob reviewed a preliminary bill-of-materials. Surely something could be removed or made cheaper to avoid explaining the discrepancies at a product review. Perhaps the EMI filter could be cheapened, then, they could save a few cents on magnetics. He was tired of lecturing his team—they should recognize the importance of hitting cost and schedule targets. After all, the management team's annual bonus program was tied to these metrics.

He was jolted from reverie by the telephone. Though the phone was muted, the receptionist could override.

"I'm sorry to bother you, Rob, but I have a persistent man on the phone. Yours is the closest name I can find in the employee directory. Would you take the call? He says he'll keep calling until someone talks to him. I tried to block his number, but that didn't work."

Anything but creating $8.44 in savings out of thin air.

"All right, Jenny, I will talk to him. Put him through."

Rob cradled the phone on his shoulder.

"Hello, this is Rob Perry."

"I am calling for Doctor Charles Robert Perry."

Rob's eyes flicked to the letters stabbed into his cork board.

I'm going to kill CB.

"We don't employ anyone by that name—perhaps I can assist you."

"I'm calling about a paper published on The Modern Physics Letters website."

"As it turns out, I'm familiar with that paper," Rob admitted.

"Good. It's important that I speak with the author. Doctor Perry is in danger. It may be too late, but he should withdraw that paper."

"Excuse me, who am I speaking to?"

There was a long silence on the line.

"My name is of no particular importance, but I will tell you. Lorenz Hartz. That's Lorenz with a 'z'. Please tell Doctor Perry to search the web for information on Doctors Chi Wang and Harr-Abbasi. That's C-H-I W-A-N-G," he spelled. "Figure out how to spell Harr-Abassi on your own. Tell Doctor Perry to proceed with caution."

Hartz broke the connection.

"Why?" Rob said into dead air.

He took a deep breath to calm himself.

A crackpot.

He brought up a search engine and typed in: "Doctor Chi Wang" and glanced through the results. After clicking on a few search hits, he unconsciously picked up the phone and called his friend.

"CB, get your ass in here, you need to see something."

MIT Physicist Found Slain

ZBS News – North American Herald-Star Online Edition

Dr. Chi Wang of the MIT High Energy Physics Department was found slain in his home on Monday morning. The body was discovered by his housekeeper. Police refused to comment, but bystanders suggest Dr. Wang had not been seen for several days. Unconfirmed reports indicate Dr. Wang's hands and feet were bound and death was caused by a small-caliber bullet wound to the forehead.

Doctor Wang was a prominent researcher in high energy and particle physics. His work, with Doctor Harr-Abbasi (see related story, *Tragic Accident Claims Life of Popular Princeton Professor*), was widely acclaimed. Doctors Wang and Harr-Abbasi were best known for a *Scientific American* article titled *Toward a Theory of General Temporal-Gravitational Relativity*.

A public memorial for Dr. Wang will be held at the Apostolic Faith Church in Boston on Friday.

CB read the article over Rob's shoulder.

"What was the dude's name?"

"He said Lorenz with a 'z' and I guess his last name is Hartz—like the flea collar."

"It could be some nut job messing with your tranquility. Let's search on *his* name."

Typing "Lorenz Hartz" into the search engine led to several dozen hits—most in German, but two came up in English.

"Click on his book," CB said, pointing at a link titled *Low-Temperature Microwave Alloy-Fusion*. "What's his Amazon rank?"

"745,933."

"Shit, he sucks," CB mocked. "No one buys his book. What should we do?"

"Well, we'll start by shredding the letters," Rob said, motioning toward the items pinned to his corkboard.

"Good idea," CB replied.

National Institute of Standards and Technology

Boulder, CO, USA

Elmo Bohr slapped his notebook loudly on the table to get the attention of the arguing crowd.

"People, please sit down. Let's get started. I have more accurate data and if you'll shut up and listen, I'll share it with you. Okay?" He glared at each employee in turn until they were silent. "At local time 5:47:0397 a temporal anomaly spread across the world. From our readings, the propagation velocity was on the order of point zero one percent of the speed of light. We don't know how this happened, but our electro-mechanical clocks skipped backwards by 0.0177 seconds. As a result, the electro-mechanical clocks do not match the time given by the Cesium atomic clocks."

"Elmo, you don't know if the Cesium clocks skipped ahead or if the mechanical clocks skipped backwards?" Dr. Pefley said.

This created another uproar among the scientists. Dr. Snow threw a cup of tea in the face of Dr. Kishin Bhagat Singh.

"If you don't compose yourselves I will order the National Guard to shoot you. Cease this mayhem."

The command was ineffective. Dr. Bohr whispered in the ear of an armed guard who brandished his .45 ACP pistol.

Everyone sat down except Dr. Yamahatsu. "Doctor Bohr, we don't know what the Coordinated Universal Time is," he said hoarsely.

"That is correct, Dr. Yamahatsu. We do not. Let's compose ourselves and define a rational course of action."

"Is it true about Dr. Bayers-Walters?"

Elmo sighed and rubbed his forehead.

"Yes. Dr. Bayers-Walters committed suicide by jumping off the roof by the heliport. This is unfortunate, as we could use her help in this crisis, but we must deal with the situation as we face it. The first order of business is to create a brief for the President and a press release for the public."

Dr. Singh stood up.

"Time is continuous and does not stutter," he stated.

"Please take your seat. I will order Officer Taylor to shoot the next person who disrupts this meeting. We're upset, that's understandable. But, if you don't compose yourselves I will ask you to leave the room. We understand time does not *stutter* as you quaintly put it, but *something* happened. We must work through root causes and identify the least-disruptive course of action. First of all, can anyone think of a paper or study that might shed light on the data?"

The NIST staff exchanged troubled looks, but no one spoke.

Elmo continued. "A wavefront of unknown origin propagated through the earth's state vector. Surely someone has a theory."

Dr. Pefley whispered something inaudible.

"Speak up, Leo," Elmo said.

"It's the end of the world as we know it. God is displeased. His celestial finger stirs our temporal teacup."

"Metaphysics is unhelpful, Dr. Pefley. The collective intelligence quotient in this room is stratospheric and that's the best we can do? God is displeased? Anyone?"

The doctors looked at each other warily. In stark contrast to the earlier uproar, the silence was undisturbed.

AK-149

While waiting in an endless, serpentine security line at Atlanta's Hartsfield-Jackson Airport, AK-149 listened to a young woman murmur into a cell phone. Every few minutes, the line switched back and they approached each other again. She wore a scarf over her hair and her body was encased in a long dress. He tried to decipher the mysteries of her figure against light pouring through a window.

Was she thin and attractive or matronly and homely?

Her modest clothing made it impossible to tell.

At his side, she made a stern face while jabbering quietly into the handset. She wasn't loud like other cell phone users and Trent was annoyed that he couldn't grasp the nature of her call.

Buried deep in his carry-on bag, Trent had a foil-wrapped sample of marijuana extract used to train drug-sniffing DEA dogs. Carefully, using a tissue to keep the scent off his fingers, he unwrapped the sample and dropped it in the woman's purse. He almost reached the

X-ray machines when, on patrol, the excited drug dog pawed at her bag. Two ATF officers detained the woman.

Startled, she dropped the phone and protested loudly.

"I am a U.S. citizen. Take your hands off me. I demand a call to my lawyer."

Reaching, she nearly retrieved the phone, but Trent, with his back turned to the scene, was pressed backwards by the milling crowd. He stepped back and crushed it. This was unintentional; the gods of chaos work in mysterious ways.

CHAPTER FOUR

Mike Thomas

MIKE RECEIVED AN automated email reminder for his biannual performance review with Madison. He sighed and set aside the aluminum heat sinks he was inspecting. The drawings were in order and the dimensions were correct, but something about the blotchy finish troubled him.

Perhaps the sulfuric acid bath used in the anodizing process was not heated to a high-enough temperature?

In the old days, he could call the plating shop across town and discuss the problem, but these heat sinks were manufactured in Guangzhou, China. Generally, the quality of Chinese manufacturing was good and using offshore suppliers saved a lot of money, but Asian shops would sometimes shave a few pennies from their cost by subsourcing to a less-experienced, back-alley operation. Then there were problems.

Stalling as long as possible, he hovered outside Madison's door while she chatted on the phone. Holding up a hand, she made sure he stayed out until she was done, and then gestured for him to enter. She wore a sheer, satiny blouse stretched so tight around the chest that the lace texture of her bra was readily visible, as were her protruding nipples. She reminded him of a Venus flytrap; an interesting flower with an attractive scent, but deadly to the careless bug.

"Hello, Mike, how are things going?"

"I'm working on heat sinks—"

"Yes, that's fine," Madison interrupted. "Time flies, eh? It's review time again. Did you bring your self-evaluation form this time?"

Mike nodded and handed over a few sheets of damp paper. She picked them up with a look of distaste. After a quick glance, she spread them across her desk.

"You don't think very highly of yourself."

"I try not to think about myself at all."

"You circled all twos. You're aware that ten, the best score, represents the category of *performs all tasks in an exemplary manner* and that two indicates *well below standard*? I think you marked off all twos to get the self-evaluation requirement taken care of with the least possible effort. What do you say to that?"

"It sounds exactly like something a *well below standard* employee would do. Maybe it's a self-fulfilling prophecy."

"Clearly you do not take this exercise seriously."

Mike sighed.

"Employee evaluation is a management job *you're* paid to do. I don't ask you to measure coating thickness on aluminum heat sinks. So, if you make me fill out a self-evaluation form, I will do it as quickly as possible and score myself with an undisputable grade that gets me out of your office and back to work."

"Mike, that's the longest string of words I've heard you say all at once. It makes me wonder how dumb you really are. I reviewed your job application and checked your credentials because I had a gut feeling you lied about your academic history. And I was right, wasn't I? You have a Bachelors of Science in Mechanical Engineering; that checks out. Good for you. However, I talked to your thesis advisor and he told me you earned dual Master's Degrees in Applied Mathematics and Statistics and are a dissertation away from a PhD. The Chairman of the Math Department said you were the best student he'd seen in a decade. That's called sand-bagging. You didn't mention any of this in your resume or your job application all those many years ago. Why not?"

"I wanted the job and didn't want to be rejected for being over-qualified."

"What are you making? Forty-three grand? With your aptitude and credentials, you could make more. A lot more. What gives?"

"I make *enough* money and people don't bother me as long as I do my job. Which, I believe I am *not* doing while sitting here."

"I see. Filling out your employment application in a misleading manner is a serious breach of company policy."

"There are no errors on my application."

"But the information is incomplete, isn't it?"

"I didn't put everything down, that's correct," Mike said.

"I need to think this through." She leaned across her desk. Mike made an effort to look into her eyes and take no notice of the faint blue veins adorning the tops of her plump breasts. "We made a lot of progress with this conversation."

Mike rubbed his forehead. "All right, tell me. What progress did we make?"

"We established there is more to you than meets the eye. You are a secretive man deserving greater scrutiny. Now, if you want to run back to your precious heater things, then go. But remember, I'm watching. When you make another mistake—and I'm certain you will—I will be there to protect the company's interest and do that which must be done. Now scoot."

She shooed him away with a dismissive wave of her hand.

AK-149

On the ground in Seattle, Trent breezed through baggage claim and examined the National Car rental selection. He picked out a gray Ford Explorer, the very definition of a nondescript vehicle in Seattle. It was perfectly plain and boring. After plugging the address for Pacific ElectroMed into the GPS, he allowed the engine to warm up. After a few phone calls, he discovered no one at Pacific ElectroMed knew a Dr. Charles Robert Perry. However, there was an engineering manager named Robert Perry. Close enough.

We're called the Agents of Karnage, not the Agents of being careful about exposing only the right people to chaos.

With drizzle seeping from a thick, gray sky, he pulled the Ford into the line at a Starbucks drive-through window and ordered a triple-shot mocha. He loved Seattle.

National Institute of Standards and Technology

Boulder, CO, USA

Elmo was tired. Far beyond the point where coffee could keep him awake, he sipped a long-cold cup from habit. He refereed an ongoing argument between Doctors Snow and Singh, but only to keep them from getting physical. An administrative assistant entered and handed him a hand-written note and a stack of computer print-outs. After taking a quick look, he grabbed the admin's sleeve.

"Are you sure about this?"

The admin shrugged and brushed off Elmo's hand.

"I have no fucking idea, I just pass the word from above," he said, before leaving.

Elmo paged through the listings.

"Ladies and gentlemen, could I have your attention for a moment?" He waited until they settled down. "The gap between the UTC and the electro-mech clocks is shrinking."

A barrage of questions assaulted him.

"That's not possible. Are they sure?"

"Is the gap closing at an exponential or a linear rate?"

"How quickly is the difference changing?"

"One question at a time, folks. The gap looks as if it is closing at a slow, but exponentially increasing rate."

"Will it approach mech time asymptotically or will it cross over?" Dr. Snow asked.

"Of course it's an asymptote, you moron," Dr. Singh said. "What do you think? Reference times will cross and diverge again?"

"What I think, so-called Doctor Singh, is that time may overshoot but will eventually settle into simultaneity."

"My credentials are sound. You wouldn't understand my dissertation if it was converted into kindergarten English. I'm sick of your insults to Pondicherry University, you bloody, racist son of a bitch. The universe is critically damped. That's the only transfer function that makes sense."

"Stop this nonsense or I'll have you hauled out in restraints," Elmo said. "Let's focus on the good news. There are two ways the time references can realign. If the references cross over and continue to diverge—well, I don't care to think about that. Let's watch the situation and see what we can come up with to explain the phenomena." He reread the note. "There is an additional data item in this report. The temporal anomaly emanated from Seattle."

"Microsoft does a lot of research there."

"No, you mentally-retarded Yankee egomaniac, the University of Washington and the Boeing Space Group each have high-energy physics labs, those would be more likely candidates for creating a temporal event."

Elmo clapped his hands to restore order.

"People, please. We'll answer the question by zeroing in on the precise location. For now, let's assemble a team and prepare to visit Seattle."

CHAPTER FIVE

Mike Thomas, CB and Polly Patterson

MIKE, WEARING EARBUDS stuffed deep into his ears, composed an eloquent receiving inspection report for a shipment of terminal posts while listening to talk radio on a Sirius-XM receiver. He was startled by a tap on the shoulder. After sweeping off the earbuds, he turned around.

"Hi, Mike, I'm sorry to bother you."

"Oh, hey there, Polly, that's no problem."

Polly was accompanied by CB Barthre.

"I have a magazine for you. It looks interesting." She read the title. "*Chaos, an Interdisciplinary Journal of Nonlinear Science.*"

"Yeah, thanks," Mike said. He tossed it on a pile. "Don't you usually leave mail in my mail slot?"

"Yes, and I am sorry to interrupt, but I have a question. What's the atomic number of Lithium?"

"Three," Mike said promptly, "it's a lightweight alkali metal in the same periodic table group as sodium and potassium. It—"

"Okay, Mike, that's enough." She held out her hand as CB fished a five-dollar bill from his pocket. "Easy money."

"What's going on?" Mike said.

"At lunch, we talked about who the biggest geek in the company is. We wagered and she suckered me."

"I didn't use the word geek, Mike. I only said you'd be the most likely to know about the periodic table of elements."

"I'm pleased to provide for your amusement," Mike said, scowling. "Now, if you don't mind, I have work to do," he said while pressing the earbuds back in his ears. He turned his back and pointedly ignored them.

"Mike, I didn't mean any offense…" Polly began, but trailed off as she realized he couldn't hear her. "Now we've upset him."

"Who cares? He's a blue-coat."

"You don't have to be such an ass. Take your money back, jerk."

"Okay," CB said, pleased. "You cheated anyway. You deliver the company mail so you'd naturally know who gets the weirdest magazines."

"Being educated is not cheating. By the way, here's your Sports Illustrated," she said, while pushing the magazine into his hands.

"Cool, look, the Trailblazers made an insert on the cover," CB said. "They'll make the playoffs for sure this year."

Lorenz Hartz

Scouting, Lorenz cruised the Pacific ElectroMed parking lot in his rented Escalade. The building was a squat three-story structure resting on a ridge overlooking a shallow valley. The farms in the valley were slowly being replaced by housing developments and office parks—the inevitable march of progress. Tall trees dripped on cars in the parking lot. He backed into a spot overlooking the building and noticed an open window on a sad-looking Ford Maverick. Braving the wind and rain, he got out of his truck and rolled up the window.

The Sovereign Union of Vagabonds was formed by Andrew Wyatt. At one time, Andrew was, on paper, the richest man in the world. In 1999, Andrew sold his sixty-two percent share of MiniTek to General Electric for eighteen billion dollars in cash and disappeared from the public eye. He founded and funded the SUVs. Andrew believed the world was on the brink of an industrial revolution based on free energy. The problem: oil companies figuratively killed this technology by literally killing scientists making scientific breakthroughs.

Lorenz graduated from Cambridge in 1975 with a four-year degree in physics. He didn't want to go to school for another four years to get credentials for a teaching position, so he was stuck; at the time, no applied research jobs were available. An entry-level job repairing satellite electronics evolved into a design position and a career designing solar power systems. On a whim, he answered an advertisement in the back of the IEEE

Spectrum Magazine for a Field Facilitator for a start-up NGO, the curiously-named SUV group. The paycheck wasn't much, but all expenses were paid and Lorenz liked the freedom of field work.

Sitting in his vehicle, Lorenz looked over the paper that had attracted his attention. *Studies in Multidimensional Spherical Algebraic Analysis, Particularly Sub-Quantum Chaotic Gravitational Chronotrons.* With a topic this complex, it was impossible to tell if the paper was absurd nonsense or pure genius. Conventional knowledge in physics was based on interpreting data and making assumptions, so there were always alternate ways of interpretation and imagining different models and theoretical constructs. Even with a Bachelors of Science degree (or perhaps *because* of this BS degree), Lorenz was unqualified to judge the merit of the paper. However, he knew the oil cartel killed scientists exploring space-resonant-wave theories.

If energy could be rectified from earth's movement through the fabric of space, then mankind's new age would begin. Unfortunately, free energy from space would kill the oil cartel's revenue. It might be inevitable, but they could delay progress and profit during that delay.

Sub-Quantum Chaotic Gravitational Chronotrons? Energy extracted from standing wave interference patterns?

Lorenz sighed. He was getting a nasty headache.

National Institute of Standards and Technology

Boulder, CO, USA

The room lights were off—a large display projected against the conference room wall. The display showed several digital readouts, but the main image was a large analog dial with a needle slowly moving toward center-zero. Several exhausted researchers were asleep, but Doctors Snow and Singh, only a meter apart, typed incendiary SMS messages to each other on their laptops and glared at each other with unrestrained hatred.

There was a clock on the projected display, but Elmo shot useless glances at his watch as if he didn't trust anything. He walked around the table and gently roused the slumbering doctors. The displayed needle touched zero, hesitated, and then passed to the opposite region of the dial. Elmo noticed he was not breathing and forced himself to inhale. The room was deathly quiet except for the Geiger-counter-like staccato clicking of Snow and Singh typing flames at each other.

The needle slowed to a stop and then eased back toward zero. Elmo pumped his fist in the air. Doctor Yamahatsu openly wept.

"Okay, folks, that does it. The danger to our space-time reference frame is over. Let's figure out what happened. This is Nobel Prize territory my friends, so good luck and happy hunting."

He hugged several staff members and patted Dr. Yamahatsu on the shoulder in what he hoped was a comforting manner.

Rob Perry and Charles 'CB' Barthre

CB knocked on Rob's office door. With energetic index fingers, Rob battered his keyboard. His hair, mussed, stood straight up in the air.

"What's the atomic number of Lithium?" CB asked.

"I don't know. What's an atomic number?"

"It's the number of protons in an atomic nucleus. Never mind, I found the author of the notebook."

"Who?"

"Mike Thomas in Receiving Inspection."

"Who?"

"The guy that sleeps in the broom closet. You know, the fat guy with the bad skin who wears the same shirt every day?"

"I know who you mean. It can't be him—he's an idiot."

"I made a note of magazines he gets. *The Victorian Electrochemical Society Journal* and *The Physics of Plasmas*."

"A lot of people get free trade magazines they don't read. Like me—look at this pile I need to recycle," he said, gesturing at a stack of technology publications.

"Well, he actually studies them. They are splayed open at his workspace and filled with yellow sticky notes."

"Did you grab a sample of his handwriting so we could compare it?"

"That's a good idea, I should have. I'll grab something from his bench after he goes home tonight. I'm sure this is the guy."

"I can't get over it. He's a dolt. Once, he came to work wearing mismatched shoes. I know his boss—I'll talk to her and see what she says. If we fire him, maybe Hartz will go away and we can forget this sorry episode."

"Okay, let's touch base in the morning."

"Dude, we work here, we touch base every morning."

"Right. See you then, then."

"Whatever," Rob replied.

CHAPTER SIX

Rob Perry and Madison Howard

ROB SPOTTED MADISON reading a paperback novel in a corner of the cafeteria. He picked up his lunch tray and walked over.

"Do you mind if I join you?"

"I prefer you don't," she replied, after flicking her eyes to him and then back to her novel. "If you need to see me, schedule a meeting during business hours."

Rob noticed the title of her book. Sue Grafton's 'X' novel.

"Is that the one where the dentist X-rays his patients to death?"

"No."

"What's next? Z is for Trampled by a Zebra?"

"You're not going away, are you?"

Rob dropped his tray on the table and slipped into the seat.

"I want to talk about your man. Mike Thomas."

"What about him? Want him? I could sign an in-company personnel transfer, no problem."

Rob pondered for a moment.

"No, I'm just wondering about him. Is he a good employee?"

"Despite a certain over-zealous, meticulous, pedantic attention to picayune detail, he's all right. Between you and me, I don't think he'll make it past the next RIF. We should be able to find someone with better interpersonal skills."

"Do you get the idea there's more to him than meets the eye?"

"Are you talking about his odor? He smells like a camel."

"No."

"Fine," Madison sighed. "I know he sleeps in the broom closet. I don't even know if he has a home. If that's the problem, I suppose it's my job to speak to him about it."

"No, I don't care about the broom closet. Do you think he's some kind of undiscovered genius?"

Madison laughed. "You mean socially? Culturally? No way."

"I mean intellectually. Like a mad scientist or something."

"I haven't thought about it. Why do you ask?"

Rob dipped a potato nugget into a blob of ketchup and popped it into his mouth.

"No reason. Just curious." He stood and threw his napkin onto his tray. "Make an appointment—maybe we can talk about it."

"Rob, I'm sorry. That remark didn't come out right. I value my quiet time at lunch."

Rob leaned over. "I said, make an appointment," he said, before turning away and walking toward the dish-bussing conveyor belt.

Lorenz Hartz and Rob Perry

Rob scratched his head and shuffled the order of the slides in his presentation. He couldn't decide. Should he get the bad news out early to get it over with or lead with good news? Upper management would be happy with his spending, he'd been denying requests for business travel and training, so his department was under-budget for expenses. However, they were months behind in testing the new implants and worse, the clinical trial data did not support their business case. None of this was fatal, but the proper spin was necessary. He'd sprinkle Dilbert cartoons into his presentation to create the right mood. His phone tinkled and he picked it up unconsciously.

"Perry here, how can I help you?"

"Hi Rob, this is Jenny. I have a visitor in the lobby for you."

"I'm not expecting anyone." He pulled up his calendar and verified. The afternoon was free of outside appointments. "Is it a salesperson? Tell him to make an appointment."

"I'm not sure, Rob. He says his name is Lorenz with a 'z.' He seems like a nice man—I don't think he's selling anything. Shall I sign him in and issue him a visitor's badge?"

"No, I'll come out to the lobby in a minute."

Rob saved his presentation and sat for a moment with his head buried in his hands. He called CB.

"The guy that called Hartz? He's here."

"What do you mean he's here?"

"Here. In the lobby. And he wants to talk to me. Come along. I don't know what to say to him."

"Me? No way! Don't go. Let's take an early lunch and grab a few beers. Maybe he'll take the hint and leave."

"Coward. I'll see if I can get rid of him."

"Let me know. Don't worry about me, I'll just be here shitting my pants."

Rob stood and tucked his shirt into his trousers. He patted his hair to make sure it was not standing up.

The lobby was airy and accented by reflections from chrome features. Light poured through floor-to-ceiling windows. Low-backed leather benches lined the walls so semi-private meetings could be held in the reception area. The company, sensitive to leaking proprietary information, limited employee exposure to visitors. After catching Rob's eye, Jenny nodded toward a figure standing by the windows looking over the parking lot.

Rob studied him. Lorenz, dressed in a long black coat with a closely-shaven head, looked like a monk. It appeared he'd lived a rough-and-tumble life. Disturbing scars ornamented his head. His age was indeterminate— Rob judged him to be somewhere between forty and seventy. Wearing heavy black boots, his eyes were sunk

71

deep into his skull. All-in-all, he presented a melodramatic figure, like a priest from an old vampire movie.

"I apologize for appearing without prior notice."

"I can only give you a few minutes," Rob said. "I have an important meeting…"

"I'll be as brief as possible. Can we sit for a minute? My old legs are not what they once were."

After sitting, they studied at each other. Rob broke the silence.

"I found your book on the web."

"That?" Lorenz sighed. "I'll make a confession. I did not write it. It was intended as a decoy. What do you call that sticky stuff? Flypaper? Yes, flypaper. It didn't work and I'd delete the listing, but you know how things are on the Internet. No matter how many times you delete something, it never dies, it just changes servers and pops up somewhere else. But, that's not pertinent to our business. Our time is short, so I'll jump to my speculation."

From his coat, he pulled a leather-bound notebook from an inside pocket. The notebook was stuffed with scraps of paper, hand-written lists, newspaper articles and receipts. He handed over a note. Rob glanced at the hand-written numbers.

"Dr. Charles Robert Perry," Lorenz continued, speaking quietly as if to himself. "Your name is Robert Perry and you have a friend working here, a Dr. Charles Barthre. The paper's author appears to be a concatenation of those names. Since the author is apparently nonexistent, this synthesis of names is an unlikely coincidence."

"What are these numbers?"

"Server IPv6 addresses and hard disk serial numbers. When the email trail was traced, it led to your friend, Dr. Barthre. Source addresses can be concealed by routing though off-shore anonymizers, but it appears Dr. Barthre did not take the trouble."

"He's here if you want me to go get him," Rob said, while standing and preparing to flee.

Lorenz chuckled. "No, that will not be necessary. As I understand the company's organizational chart, he works for you, so I'll talk to you and assume you'll make the proper translations and inform Dr. Barthre as necessary. Please sit for a moment while I make a leap of logic. From observing you for the few minutes we've chatted, I don't think you're the author of that paper. And, to spread the wings of speculation further, I also doubt Dr. Barthre is the author. In fact, I conclude the submission of the paper was an inane practical joke, perhaps alcohol-inspired. Am I in the vicinity of truth, Mr. Perry?"

"I'm busy and don't enjoy being jerked around. If there is a point to your rambling, then get to it so I can go back to work."

"Very well. As I suggested, did you study the sad murders of Doctors Wang and Harr-Abbasi?"

"Yes, but I don't know what they have to do with me."

"It took me a few minutes of research and insight to determine your unlikely role in the creation of Dr. Charles Robert Perry's paper. My adversaries are equally thorough and prescient and would unravel the deception—figure out you're not the real author—but that's inconsequential. My end goal is to locate and speak with the real author. If you know who that is, I urge you to share the information."

Rob scanned the lobby as if looking for rescue.

"Uh, come back tomorrow and we'll talk."

"I'm not sure you'll be alive tomorrow."

"Is that a threat? I don't like your tone. Tell me what's going on."

"There is inertia in power, Mr. Perry. Things set in motion tend to stay in motion. Those who have power try to keep it. Disruptive change is unwelcome in those circles. Give me a name and I'll take the matter from there."

"Tomorrow."

"Very well, Mr. Perry. Per your request, I shall return tomorrow. Until then, be well and watch your back."

"Whatever," Rob said as he walked back to his work area.

He found CB sitting in his guest chair.

"What's the deal, dude?"

"Hartz is an odd duck. He figured us out quickly. He wants to know who wrote that stupid paper."

"What did you tell him?"

"I couldn't think of anything else to say, so I told him to come back tomorrow."

"I have sick leave saved up. Maybe I'll take a day off."

"Like that will solve the problem, asshole. We need a plan."

"I peeked. That's a scary-looking guy. What was he wearing around his neck?"

"A silver chain thing. Medallion. A snake eating its tail surrounding an hourglass."

"That's what I thought. That guy is a SUV," CB said.

"He's a sport utility vehicle? What the hell are you talking about?"

"No, bozo. I mean a sovereign vagabond, something like that. I thought they were an urban legend."

"Never heard of them."

"Well, I'll surf around and send you some links. Things get weirder, don't they?"

"I have my meeting to prepare for and I'm getting a headache. You're not helping, so get out of here and let me get my stuff done."

CB stood and snapped off a salute. "Whatever you say, boss," he said.

Charles 'CB' Barthre

At his desk, CB put out his 'do not disturb' sign and settled in front of his computer. After adjusting his headphones, he popped the tab on a can of Mountain Dew. He Googled the phrase "Sovereign Union of Vagabonds" and scanned the search results. He clicked on the Wikipedia link.

Sovereign Union of Vagabonds
From Wikipedia, the free encyclopedia.

Certain contents of this article are disputed, see the article's feedback forum for more information.

The Sovereign Union of Vagabonds (SUV), a legendary fraternal organization created in 1999 by Andrew Wyatt, is similar to organizations such as the Freemasons or Illuminati. The existence of this group is unconfirmed and may be an Internet-enabled conspiratorial fabrication. Members claim to be free world citizens, protected by diplomatic status, who voluntarily adhere to existing national and international laws (including taxation). The basis of their sovereignty is the unconfirmed threat of high-energy neutron weapons (in dispute: other researchers believe the weapons are biological or chemical) which threaten cities around the world—to be activated under certain circumstances if SUV member is detained or harmed. The scope and purpose of this organization is unknown.

Feedback Forum: Sovereign Union of Vagabonds

Facts in Dispute Section

You morons never cease to amaze me. This is another b***s*** fake urban legend conspiracy like the Rockefeller-Mellon-Rothschild-Bilderberg collusion, Skull and Bones Society, the Trilateral Commission, the Rosecrusians and alligators in New York sewers. You dimwits probably still believe global warming is caused by Hummers, Alar on apples causes cancer or that AIDS is a real disease. You knuckleheads should join the Flat Earth Society. At least then, you superstitious anti-intellectual retards will be in one place where we can keep track of you.

   – LectorWasRight

It's interesting that Mr. Lector mentions people and organizations that are well-documented. For example, the Skull & Bones Society and the Trilateral Commission. Does he claim John Davison Rockefeller, Andrew and Richard Mellon, and the Lord Rothschild never existed? Does he claim the internationalist meetings started at the Hotel de Bilderberg in 1954 do not continue to this day? We can debate in polite terms and in a respectful manner the one-world government's lofty goals and the unholy duopoly of government and big business. We can theorize about their global aspirations in a reasoned manner without resorting to infantile mudslinging and ad hominem attacks. Please?

    – WhoisJohnGalt

CB goggled at the entries.

Wow.

He prairie-dogged the cubicle walls to make sure no managers were around, then hit the 'print' button. Twenty-six pages spewed out. He crammed them into his briefcase.

This is cool stuff.

The Lucky Seven Saloon was packed with revelers enjoying a hot pants contest sponsored by Miller Beer. CB admired prancing girls in tight shorts, panty hose and high heels before catching sight of Rob drinking beer at a corner table. After weaving through the crowd, he slapped the printouts on the table. Rob poured a glass for CB who took a swig before shrugging off his jacket.

"What's this shit?" Rob said.

His words were slurred—CB was jealous. Clearly, Rob rolled out of work early to get a head start on intoxication.

"There's a lot of stuff on the Internet about the SUVs. Look at this picture. Does this look like the medallion Hartz wore?"

Rob took the picture and held it out for better illumination in the dim bar lighting.

"Yes," he admitted, "that's it. This is getting out of

fucking hand. We have to get this off our backs. It's making me crazy with worry."

"Man, you are so over-reacting. This is the shit. Check it out," he said, sorting through the papers for the printout he was looking for.

Rob adjusted his glasses and read:

National borders and polito-economic asymmetries are obsolete. Humans crave liberty unless their spirit is killed by totalitarianism or bound by philosophical chains of serfdom. SUVs throw off all obligations to dictatorship, elected and non-elected. The goal of our New World Order is releasing humans from the foul grasp of servitude. We will use our individual power to fight the creeping darkness of religious bigotry and corporate slave labor. We will bear witness to injustice and defeat evil-doers with every weapon we can muster.

—Manifesto of the Sovereign Union of Vagabonds

"These guys are like superheroes. They wear black coats and cool necklaces. Look at this cartoon—they're breaking Big Brother's legs. I'm sick of upper management's boot endlessly stamping on my face."

Rob drained his glass, and then refilled it.

"Oh, shit," he whispered, "there he is."

"Who?" CB asked, craning his head to look.

"That guy. Hartz."

"It can't be…"

"Hello, gentlemen," Lorenz said while pulling a chair from an adjoining table. "I hope I'm not intruding." He looked at their pitcher of watery-yellow beer. "I've acquired a taste for your local microbrews. Please allow me to purchase a pitcher of something more tasty."

"We like our ice lager, thank you. What are you doing here? I told you to meet me tomorrow."

"I'm sorry, but patience is not one of my stronger virtues. What are you reading? Not random rubbish from the Internet, I hope." He thumbed through the papers. "Hokum," he said. "Utter nonsense." He extended his hand for a shake. "You must be Dr. Barthre. I'm pleased to meet you."

"Being an SUV must be really neat. How do I join up?" CB asked.

Lorenz grinned. In the bar lighting, his molars gleamed like tombstones.

"In the unlikely event that my first impression is inaccurate and you are found worthy, an invitation will be extended in a formal manner in the proper timeframe."

"I think that means: don't hold your breath," Rob commented.

"Does he always talk like he has a corncob stuck up his ass?"

"Corncob. That's an amusing image," Lorenz said. His pitcher of beer arrived—it had the color and consistency of frothy coffee. "Ah, nectar of the gods. Mother's milk. Liquid manna from heaven." He poured a glass, then sipped appreciatively. "Equally as good as Bavarian beer, I must say. Amazing what you Yanks do when you set your minds to it. Delicious. Now, I insist you disclose the true author of that paper. It's a matter of grave importance."

"It's Mike Thomas," CB blurted.

"I don't think you should have told," Rob said, while slugging his friend in the arm. Addressing Lorenz, he said, "Now, are we out of the spotlight?"

Lorenz pulled out his notebook and made an entry with a thin gold pen.

"Okay, this Mike Thomas. I assume he works for Pacific ElectroMed?" Rob nodded. "Then my business with you gentlemen is complete," he said. Standing and draining his glass, he looked with regret at the remainder of the pitcher. Tossing crumpled bills on the table, he said, "Enjoy the rest of this fine beer on me."

"Thanks, man," CB said, pouring a glass.

"Wait, I want to talk to you. What's going on?"

"Don't worry your pretty little head about it," Lorenz said, turning to leave. He stopped and raised an index finger to emphasize his point. "However, I advise caution as you go about your business in the next few days."

In an instant, he disappeared in the crowd.

"This beer tastes like crankcase oil," CB said. "But, it's free, so what the hell."

"You are the King of Moronton. I find it hard to believe you earned a doctorate."

"Well, I did." CB turned his attention to the high-heeled ladies strolling through the bar wearing damp beer company t-shirts. "These girls are smokin'. Maybe we should order a pitcher of *their* beer."

"It tastes like left-over dishwater."

"Who cares? The babes are killer. Make a sacrifice for the team."

Polly Patterson

Per routine, her cats, Clem and Penelope, waited in the front window and welcomed her home. Eerily, their eyes reflected yellow light from street lamps. On autopilot, she fed and watered them. The cat box emitted standing waves of stench, so she raked it out and flushed away the poop and clumped urine.

Feeling tense and unfulfilled, she tied on dancing shoes and looked over notations. On impulse, she got up and sorted through her closet. She put on her most professional working clothes. After turning to a fresh page in her workbook, she scribbled *Office Politics* as the working title. Pink Floyd seemed like the right choice for music, so she cued up *Animals* and began working. She decided on the title for the first section: *The Minuet of the Upwardly Mobile Middle Managers*. It began with chaotic figures moving in fits and starts and bouncing off one other. The collage built in her mind made her laugh out loud. Between fits of giggles, she scribbled diagrams and instructions.

It may not be high art, she thought, happier than she could remember being in months, *but it's fun.*

Charles 'CB' Barthre

It was nearly midnight when CB arrived at his condo complex. Shadows under landscaped bushes seemed deeper than usual. Startled, he jumped when a cat slipped from under a car and dashed around a corner of the building.

At his door he fumbled with the key and for no logical reason stood to the side while gently twisting the knob. There was a sharp crack and a flash before his eyes. He couldn't process what he saw. A projectile ricocheted off a wall-mounted fire extinguisher and embedded in the wall. A chest-level hole, a half-inch in diameter, was in the middle of his door.

Crouching, he peeked while slowly pushing the door open. A crossbow mechanism stood on a plastic tripod on a pile of books on his bookshelf. As his heart rate slowed to normal, he looked around for other signs of danger. Searching his condo—he found nothing.

With curiosity, he examined the crossbow. An interesting mechanical design—it appeared to use synthetic fibers for the drawstring and a proximity sensor for trigger. It was unmarked and unadorned except for a small emblem. He looked it over for a few minutes before thinking to call his friend. Quickly, he punched numbers into his cell phone.

"Rob, there was a booby trap on my door. I could have been killed."

"You're drunk, CB. Get some sleep."

"No, man, listen. A crossbow-thing shot a hole through my front door. Be careful."

"Okay, I'm home. I'll stand away from the door and push it open."

Over the phone, CB heard the half-dreaded, half-expected snap.

"Holy shit, that scared the hell out of me," Rob said in a shaky voice.

"I'm glad I caught you in time, my brother."

"I pissed my pants, CB."

"That's okay, man, I won't tell anyone." At the same time, he decided he would not mention he'd almost forgotten to call and warn his friend of the danger.

Oops, my bad.

CHAPTER SEVEN

Rob Perry and Mike Thomas

AFTER A SEARCH for intruders in the corners of his house, Rob took a shower and fell into bed clutching a golf club—a three iron. Every little noise woke him and the intermittent sleep was exhausting. At four o'clock, he gave up, got up and dragged himself to work. After slipping through the vacant corridors, he walked to the broom closet and threw open the door. Mike, covered by a fluffy, lime green, down jacket, jolted upright from his improvised bed. The place smelled like a muskrat nest. Rob threw the lab notebook at him.

"Geez, sorry, I was taking a catnap," Mike mumbled.

"Don't bullshit me, Thomas. You've been sleeping here for years. Everyone knows about it."

"Everyone? That's embarrassing."

"Is this your notebook?"

Mike rubbed his eyes, then leaned back against the wall. He held the notebook and looked at it myopically.

"Yeah, this is mine. I wondered where it wandered off to. I lose things all the time."

Rob dropped the crossbow mechanism on Mike's lap.

"Ever seen anything like this?"

Mike turned it over in his hands.

"Interesting. I don't like things with moving parts, so the intricate mechanical design and precision machining is wasted on me. To answer to your question, no, I have never seen anything like this."

"What about Multidimensional Spherical Algebraic Analysis of Chaotic Gravitational/Chronotron Plasmas?"

"Yes, I experiment in those areas during my off-company time. Basically, I see interesting resonant effects when dispersed magnetic ions are subjected to simultaneous high-potential kilovolt fields and high-intensity, coherent Tesla waves. Of course, magnetism is not an action-at-a-distance field effect—it's a manifestation of imbalance between standing waves in space, but I get results in low temperature alloys under temporal-gravitational modulation. In an Einsteinian thought experiment, space time warps or, perhaps, a spherical standing-wave ethereal fabric Michelson and Morley couldn't measure with the crude apparatus available to them way back then is…"

"Argh," Rob interrupted while pressing his hands to his temples, "I already have a headache. Shut up, shut up. Look dipshit, you'll probably get a visitor today, a troublemaker named Hartz. I want to be present when you meet him, do you understand?"

"Hartz? I don't know a Hartz. What are you talking

about?"

"I won't waste time explaining. Don't meet this guy without me. Am I getting through?"

"Well, I suppose, but I'll have to check it out with Madison. She approves all meetings with outsiders. Doesn't read my paperwork and signs everything to get rid of me, so I don't see a problem."

Ron grabbed the crossbow from Mike's hands. "You're getting my goat. Please answer questions with a simple yes or no."

Mike sat on his improvised bedding with a confused look.

"Well?" Rob insisted.

"I'm sorry, what was the question?"

"Jumping Jesus," Rob groaned. "You're impossible. There'll be no more game-playing around here. Mark my words."

"Okay," Mike shrugged. "I should wash up and get ready for work. It was nice chatting with you."

Rob threw up his hands, then turned and stomped off. Mike tidied up the broom closet and found his way to the bathroom to clean up with dispenser soap and paper towels.

Mike Thomas

Mike's breakfast routine included two boiled eggs, wheat toast and a large mug of grainy hot chocolate spewed from a machine. He sat in a corner and exchanged a smile with Polly when she came in for her morning latté, but otherwise paid no attention to his fellow workers as they strolled in and out of the cafeteria foraging for food and drink. Back at his desk, he filled out an online meeting request form and emailed it to Madison. The reply came to his inbox a few minutes later with an authorization code. A few minutes later he had an instant message from her.

I approved the meeting request before I read it. Who is this Hartz character?

Mike typed in his reply: *I don't know, Rob Perry says he'll come see me.*

Rob Perry? Why is he meddling in our department?

He wants to be present if Hartz shows up.

This is bad protocol. He shouldn't involve himself in my department's affairs. I will approve this meeting, but make sure I'm informed and in attendance.

Yes, boss, as you wish, no problem.

A few hours later, while reviewing a vendor response to a rejected-material form, Mike's phone buzzed.

"Thomas here."

"Hi, Mike, this is the receptionist. I have a Mr. Hartz here to see you. He doesn't have an appointment, but insisted I see if you're available. He's making a pest of himself with some of the other employees and I'll send him away if…"

"No, it's okay. I'm curious. The meeting was approved, so I'll come out and see him."

He called Madison's cell phone. "That Hartz person is here. I'll meet him in the lobby."

"No, I'll grab a conference room. Get him signed in as a visitor and take him to the Garden Court."

"Okay." He called the receptionist and asked her to sign Hartz in and give him a visitor's badge. Then he called Rob.

"Hi, Rob, Hartz is here. I'm taking him to the Garden Court. Madison will join us."

"Madison? Okay, whatever. I'll see you there."

Rob called CB—his voice mail message was terse.

"Garden Court, five minutes, Madison will be there too," he said, before hanging up.

The Meeting in the Garden Court

Mike strolled to the lobby and found Hartz sitting in the reception area reading a company newsletter. Mike looked at him curiously before walking over to shake his hand.

"You caused quite a stir around here," Mike commented.

"Are we chatting here in the lobby?"

"No, my boss reserved a meeting room. Follow me."

The Garden Court was a small conference room filled with potted plants. Through large windows, an expanse of trees framed a view of the Sammamish valley. By the time

Mike and Lorenz arrived after weaving through the serpentine corridors, the room was crowded. Mike was surprised. Rob Perry, CB Barthre and Madison Howard were seated and looking at the newcomers with open interest. Mike flopped in a chair and looked around the room with amusement. The silence was broken by CB throwing his crossbow onto the table.

"What can you tell me about this thing?" he asked with a complaining edge to his voice. "The damned thing almost killed me."

"Us," Rob corrected.

"One crossbow almost killed you both?" Mike inquired.

Lorenz rotated the mechanism slowly in his hands.

"Corpus Christi," he whispered.

"What?" Rob demanded.

"I thought it would be something like this," Lorenz said quietly. "This is the work of the A-Ks. See the emblem?"

"Who are the A-Ks and why are they trying to kill me?" Rob asked.

"They are playing around. If they truly want to kill, they use more certain methods. However, almost always, they do things indirectly to allow randomness to be a factor."

"I could have been dead meat."

"But you aren't."

"You didn't answer my question about the A-Ks."

"I don't like compound questions. Shall we focus?"

Madison butted into the conversation.

"Will someone explain what is going on? Can I excuse Mike? He has important work to attend to."

"No, let me converse with Mr. Thomas before you dismiss him. I will explain, but there's much ground to cover and it may not make sense without context. To begin with, A-K stands for Agents of Karnage. They are a treacherous group of nihilists and radicals for hire. They go by numbers and their leader is the amusingly-enumerated AK-47—named for the Russian automatic weapon. I recognize this crossbow as the work of AK-3, one of the very early members."

"Wait a frigging minute, I don't get what we're talking about," Madison interjected. "Start from the beginning. Who are you, what is your business with Mike, who are these Agents of Karnage, what is this crossbow contraption and is it true that someone tried to kill Rob and CB? None of this makes sense."

"Mike, would I be correct to presume you are permitted to leave the premises during your lunch break?"

"Sure, I guess," Mike replied.

"I believe the current time is within the usual bounds of the luncheon period. Would you permit me the honor of purchasing you a meal at one of your fine local dining establishments?"

"Company policy prohibits gratuities," Madison said shrilly.

"Then we shall split the ticket." Lorenz suggested.

"Sure, let's get out of here," Mike said.

"I'm coming," Madison said.

She stood and smoothed her skirt.

"No," Lorenz pointed a long, pale finger in her face, "you're not," he said.

With that, he and Mike left the room and headed for the lobby. Polly, standing with her mail cart, looked guilty, as if she'd been caught eavesdropping. She flashed a smile at Mike who returned a wave.

"Hey, Polly," he said.

"Hey, Mike," she replied.

In the Garden Court, Madison sat down and took deep breaths.

"This pisses me off. Okay. First of all, explain this ugly thing. It's some kind of weapon?"

CB picked it up and showed off the features.

"It's very interesting. The bow is made of tempered steel and the drawstring is a woven synthetic material. It is charged by connecting a crank to this bolt. I hooked it to a torque wrench and it takes an amazing amount of energy to load it. I couldn't do it, even with a three-foot breaker bar. Once I managed to get it charged, the bow barely deflects at all. Millimeters."

Madison tapped her painted fingernails impatiently on the tabletop.

"*It's a weapon* would have been a sufficient answer."

"My long-winded explanation has a point. I studied this thing all morning and it's fascinating. I calculated—it takes something like ten-thousand foot pounds of pressure to cock it. That's a huge amount of potential energy. The projectile shaft is made of carbon fiber and the tip is weighted with a depleted uranium pellet. I checked. It's slightly radioactive. U-238. The release mechanism is activated with a fuel cell driving a solenoid. It has a microcontroller so the triggering method can be programmed or it can be tripped remotely via radio frequency transmission. For instrumentation, it has a CMOS video camera, an IR heat sensor and a real time clock."

"Please get to your point."

"That *is* my point. It looks like a cheap plastic toy, but it's a technological wonder. For example, I think this thing would pass through a scanner at an airport with no problem."

"Bullshit, they have radiation detectors now."

"Wrap the ballistic weight in a little aluminum foil and it would go unnoticed. The pellet is the size of a pea."

"Okay, it's the eighteenth wonder of the world. Where did you find it?"

"They were set up at our houses. The one at my place shot through my front door. It would have hit me right here," he said, gesturing at the center of his chest.

"Mine malfunctioned." Rob said. "The bolt slammed into my bookcase."

"I don't think it was a malfunction. Did you hear Hartz? They like to screw around."

"Who's this rude Hartz guy?"

Rob took over the explanation. "He turned up asking about a physics paper. He says he's an SUV. Have you heard of them?" Madison shook her head. "Well, you can surf the web and learn about them, Sovereign Unified Vagabonds—"

"No," CB interrupted, "it's Union of Vagabonds."

"Okay, whatever."

"Tell me about this physics paper," Madison said. "What was it about?"

"We have no idea. We sent it out as a prank."

"Sent it where?"

"To physics journals we found online."

"I'm starting to get it. I'm afraid to ask who wrote the damned paper. It was Mike, right?"

Rob and CB nodded their heads vigorously.

"Okay, I need to digest this. I'm going back to my desk and surf the web. Let's get together after work and compare notes."

"Let's meet at the Lucky Seven," CB suggested.

"Bullshit," Madison replied. "Six o'clock at the Lavender Rose. In the meantime, I need to deal with Mike. I don't appreciate his insubordination. There must be a drone who can micrometer frickin' machine screws without creating havoc in my department. I don't care if he is an unknown genius—I will not tolerate usurpation of company policy and disruption of its normal operation."

With that, she left the room. Polly stood nearby reading company announcements on a cork board.

"Did I get mail today?"

"It's in your mailbox as usual," Polly said.

"Great, thanks," Madison said.

Lunch with Lorenz Hartz

Lorenz parked his Cadillac Escalade at an upscale eatery a few miles from the Pacific ElectroMed facility. They were early, so the hostess was able to seat them in a quiet corner per Lorenz's polite request. Mike ordered an iced tea.

"With your permission, might I enjoy a pint of your local microbrew?"

"I'm not your mother. Drink what you want," Mike replied, while scanning the menu. A steaming platter of fajitas was paraded by. "Hey, get me one of those," he said to the waitress.

"And make it two. A perfect choice," Lorenz said in an oily manner while grinning at the waitress. He turned his attention to Mike. "I suppose you're curious about why I went to considerable effort to track you down?"

"Not really," Mike replied, shrugging. "You'll tell me when you're ready and I'll find the story interesting or not. To be frank, I doubt it has relevance to my life or my work. Also, I don't give a damn about company policy. If you insist on picking up the lunch tab, that's fine with me."

Lorenz chuckled. "No problem, Mr. Thomas. I'll share an observation. Deficiencies in personal charm and common courtesy of manners are characteristic among intellects of your caliber."

"Whatever," Mike replied while trying to free debris from between his teeth with the edge of a sugar packet.

"Have you heard of a Doctor Wang or a Doctor Harr-Abbasi? No? How about Doctor Gell-Mann, Mead, or Jun

Ye?"

"I've read their papers. What about them?"

"How about Doctor Charles Robert Perry?"

"Nope."

"That final name was a jest. Your coworkers Mr. Perry and Dr. Barthre took the liberty of submitting your work to a several physics journals. The paper caused a bit of a stir in the field. Get it? Field? That was another little joke. I'm sorry. To get to my point, we are on the verge of society-shattering breakthroughs on the same scale as the industrial and information technology revolutions. History will name this rupture in the infrastructure, but the name will be something like the energy revolution. These are heady, breathtaking and exciting times to be alive. Do you follow me so far?"

"I guess, but I don't see what it has to do with me."

At this point, their lunch arrived and they busied themselves with rolling seared meat and vegetables into warm tortillas. Around a mouthful of green peppers and grilled chicken, Lorenz continued speaking.

"Perhaps I get ahead of myself. First of all," he said while brandishing a copy of the paper produced from inside his coat, "did you write this paper?"

Mike paged through it, then tossed it back.

"Other than a few stupid errors in the equations, I recognize it," he said.

"Would you take a look at equation 3-22? Is there anything that attracts your attention?"

Sighing, Mike reached over and picked up the paper. He turned to the proper page and studied the equation.

"Yeah, the square of p under the radical should be a cube and the parentheses are not mated properly. It makes the equation indeterminate in that form. Are you always so tedious?"

"My girlfriends accuse me thus, but overall, I don't think so. I apologize, but I needed to be sure. Let me explain the current geopolitical terrain and macro economics."

Lorenz paused to take a deep draught of beer.

"We have balance between big oil companies, governments and manufacturers—a symbiotic relationship between OPEC, petroleum companies like Exxon-Mobile-Chevron-Texaco, leadership of western nations and the big-four automobile manufacturers, among others. We're talking about trillions of dollars of international trade. Fortunes built on the backs of consumers for the benefit of an elite few. One day, this interrelationship will fracture, but there are those who will do anything, and I emphasize that word *anything,* to keep the current system running a while longer. If a clever physicist, such as yourself, comes up with a cheap, alternate source of energy, that's disruption the masters of infrastructure find unacceptable. Do you follow my train of thought?"

"Sure. But I don't see how I trouble these mysterious powers-that-be."

"Then you aren't seeing—how do you say it? The big picture?"

"All right, Mr. Hartz. All I care about is being left alone to do my work. Can you help me?"

"Yes, of course. You need protection, that's all."

"Protection from the Agents of Karnage?"

A shadow fell over Lorenz's mood. He pushed his plate away and finished the last of his pint of beer. He belched quietly. "Excuse me," he whispered. "Yes, the Agents of Karnage. Those motherfuckers. Did I say that right? Motherfuckers?"

"You'll protect me from these A-Ks?"

"No one can be fully protected from the A-Ks. They are resourceful and relentless. Do you know of the SUVs?" he said, lifting his medallion from under his shirt and holding it out for Mike's inspection.

"Cool. I'd buy one if I saw it on sale at JC Penney's. But, to answer your question, unless you're talking about a Chevy Tahoe, I don't know anything about SUVs."

"I won't waste your time by delving into ancient history, but essentially, we are protected. If we keep a low profile, governments leave us unmolested. Unfortunately, the A-Ks will blow up the planet. They're insane."

Mike wiped his mouth with his napkin and tossed it onto his empty plate as the waitress swooped by to clear it away.

"I appreciate your offer of protection."

"Ah, protection. I don't want to oversell our power. Generally, all we're able to do is bear witness to injustice."

"Bear witness? What good does that do when a thug thumps me upside the head?"

"You're right. The end result can be less than satisfying."

"I should get back to work."

"I suggest an alternate plan for the afternoon. I'll call your boss and leave a message that you're ill and will be using sick leave for the rest of the day. Then, we can order more of this delicious ale and continue our conversation."

Mike looked around the dining room as if seeking inspiration.

"If you talk about sports or television programs, I will open my veins with a fork and save the A-Ks the trouble."

Lorenz raised his hand and hailed a waitress. "Please bring us another pitcher of this exquisite ale, my dear." Turning back to Mike, he continued. "You could contribute to our cause if you're willing."

When the pitcher arrived, Mike grabbed it and poured a pint. After taking a deep swig, he put his glass down and wiped foam from his lips.

"Let's hear your proposal."

"It hovers in the back of my mind that you might make us a weapon."

Mike spent a moment focusing on CO_2 bubbles rising in his beer. Then he shrugged and said "Okay."

"Splendid," Lorenz said enthusiastically. In toast, he tapped his glass against Mike's and drained it. "I forget myself."

He fished around in his coat pocket, and pulled out a black jewelry box and slid it across the table. Mike opened it and examined the medallion inside.

"Am I supposed to wear this?"

"Yes. Press the center for a few seconds and a rescue team will come."

Mike slipped it around his neck and under his t-shirt.

"Can I call you guys if I lock my keys in my car?"

"No."

"So, we're good? I make you a weapon and you guys cover my ass?"

A troubled look flitted across Lorenz's face.

"In full disclosure, we'll do everything we can to protect you, but the A-Ks resources are great and, of course, it's always easier to destroy than build or protect. That's a sad reality of life." Lorenz sat up in his seat and made an obvious effort to cheer up. "However, for now, we have good beer in front of us and an American Express card that will cover our lunch. Life is good. How about a nice piece of cheesecake to finish off the meal?"

Mike pondered the matter.

"Sounds good," he said.

"There is one more thing. I'd love to observe a demonstration of your experiment."

"Sure. No problem. I'll sneak you in the lab over the weekend. Your timing is good, I'm going to try something new."

CHAPTER EIGHT

Rob Perry and Madison Howard

ON HER COMPUTER screen, Madison read through an article about the Agents of Karnage when Rob, carrying a piece of paper, ambled by.

"You're not fooling anyone," Madison called out to him. "If you insist on passing every ten minutes, you might as well come in and sit down so we can talk this out. Can you believe that twit Thomas called in sick for the afternoon? He's already on my shit list—this might be it for him. I'll happily fire his fat ass. He should keep pushing my buttons if he doesn't believe it."

At that instant, an old man hobbled by. An eccentric historical figure at Pacific ElectroMed, his bald head was covered with flecks of skin cancer and he wore a pale-yellow jumpsuit with bright-white basketball shoes. Using a walking stick as a cane, he moved slowly. Frail, it looked as if he might keel over and die at any instant.

After turning his head toward Madison's doorway, he said, "Excuse me, madam. In my heyday, women didn't use such colorful language. Do you mind if I pull your door closed to spare affront to innocents in the hallway?"

"Sure, go ahead, sir," Madison said. Once the door was closed, she asked: "Who the goddam hell is that fossil?"

"I think he came with the building when we took it over," Rob replied. "Maybe he's one of the old custodians? He's always been here, so who cares who he is?" Changing the subject, he brandished the paper he carried. "Did you see this article about the A-Ks?" He began reading. "A shadowy group of mass murderers, arsonists, saboteurs, animal rights activists and practical jokers. Their mission statement says they intend to light the world's fuse and blow up the whole freaking thing. They took credit for killing Japanese Premier Yakomenta and sinking that luxury cruise ship in the Mediterranean. Remember? Two-hundred and twenty-three people died. They used a laser to etch a four-hundred meter high image of their symbol into the Rock of Gibraltar. One of their suicide bombers vaporized Mount Rushmore, remember that? Then they killed a thousand kids in Mexico City with a fuel-air vapor bomb."

"I thought the Koranic Zionist Jihad took credit for the Mexico thing?"

"I'm reading a blog, I don't know all the facts. Do you mind if I finish?" He found his place in the article. "The A-Ks do occasional contract work. Murders and assassinations. Pope Pious IV said: 'I have seen the face of Satan in the works of the Agents of Karnage.' Do you know what this means? I'll tell you. It means the international terrorist group, the Agents of Karnage, tried to kill me, but failed. I'm invincible."

"That's stupid. Besides, Hartz said they weren't trying and almost got you anyway. That's another way to look at it."

"How would that guy know? He has a long way to go before he proves himself—maybe he's just a crank in a black coat."

"How dumb are you?"

Rob deflated. "Look—there's been contention between us, but I really like you."

Madison stared at him for a long minute while he fidgeted in his chair.

"We may lose control of our destinies in this company," she said. "We could form our own conspiracy to look out for each other. Working together, maybe we can come out on top."

Rob brightened. "Yes, that's what I was trying to say. I'd love to be on top of our situation."

Madison, unconsciously chewing her bottom lip, got up and slowly walked to him.

"I suppose you'd like to see *benefits* attached to our coalition?"

Rob licked his thin lips. "Well, sure, but I'm patient. I can wait a couple of weeks for things to happen at the right time."

Madison laughed. It was a throaty chuckle causing jiggling under her silky blouse. She ran a painted fingernail over his flushing cheek and leaned in to give him a soft kiss on his neck.

"Well, Mr. Patience, we shall see what we shall see." Then, standing, she pointed. "Now, get out so I can finish my research and see if I can find a way out of these troubles."

"Can I see you after work?"

"Go," she said.

An hour later, Madison, deeply concentrating on her video screen, looked up when Todd, one of her employees, poked his head in her office. Todd was a pimply intern who packed boxes in the shipping area.

"Hey Maddy, what's with Mike? Is he taking the day off?"

"Don't call me Maddy. Mike called in sick."

"That's funny, he didn't look sick when I saw him drinking beer at lunch. In fact, he seemed to be getting pretty lit up."

Madison mulled this over. "Does your digital camera include a time-date stamp?" Todd nodded. "Then go back there and grab pictures of him drinking on company time. If I fire his sorry butt, would you like to take his job?"

"Sure I would."

"Get me those pictures and get back here as quickly as you can, dear."

At the *dear*, Todd flushed a deep crimson.

"You can count on me."

Madison leaned back in her chair and began mentally composing the termination memo.

This should be a slam dunk.

Mike Thomas and AK-149

Mike lost track of the number of pitchers of beer they consumed—the total was at least three by his recollection. During their lunch, Lorenz excused himself and made a call on his cell phone. Once the tab had been signed, Mike got up and was surprised at how looped he was—he could hardly stand. After enjoying a long, satisfying piss, he met Lorenz in the restaurant reception area. There, Lorenz talked to a young woman who looked like a college student. She wore a black pantsuit which covered her figure thoroughly—it was impossible to tell if she was slender or heavy.

Her face was nearly expressionless, but she conveyed disapproval at their inebriated state. She took the Escalade keys and climbed in the driver's seat while the men poured themselves in the back.

She drove directly to Mike's house. He was impressed, she knew the side-street shortcuts that avoided the worst of the traffic snarls. Mike got out of the car and walked around to thank her.

"Thanks for the lift," he said.

Her response was a gesture with her index finger—a curt directive to go in the house. Lorenz lowered his window to talk to Mike.

"See you on Saturday? What time?"

"Ten o'clock should be safe. Some folks work overtime, but the lab should be clear."

"Ten it is," Lorenz replied.

The Escalade rolled away smoothly.

Mike stumbled at the steps in his walkway, but found his way to his front door. It was never locked. He went in, cleared off a stack of magazines from his easy chair, and plopped down with a feeling of great satisfaction. At that moment, he noticed a man across the room sitting on a kitchen chair. Most of the man's body was concealed by shadow, but light spilling from the adjoining room illuminated his hands; he cleaned and trimmed his fingernails with a small black knife.

"Hey, who are you?" Mike said.

"Call me Trent. You will be judged by the company you keep. What tall tales did Hartz spin? Did he present you with the magic medallion of safety and regale you with epic stories that illustrate the power and the glory of the Sovereign Union of Vaudevillians?"

Mike sat up straight and perched on the front of his plush chair.

"Something like that."

"The SUVs are a sad joke. Pathetic posers."

"I suppose you'll kill me now."

The man laughed and scooted his chair into the light so Mike could see him more clearly. The young man was dressed neatly in a long-sleeved, open-collar shirt and khaki slacks. His hair was brushed back into a ponytail and he was younger than Mike first thought, perhaps in his mid-twenties. When he grinned, Mike noticed his teeth were straight and white like an A-list movie star.

"No, no, no. That's not how we do things. First we offer you a great job. If you refuse and we don't see any other way to slow you down, then we might kill you.

We're a long way from that, so don't let the thought trouble you." He folded his black knife and put it away, then leaned forward. "What kind of trash talk did Hartz spew about the A-Ks?"

"He didn't say much, but if this was an old western film, you guys would wear black hats."

The young man laughed out loud. "If only things were that simple. White hats, black hats, good guys, bad guys, virtue and evil, love and hate. You're too much of a student of physics to buy into the artificial simplicity of such models. A-Ks believe in beauty. The beauty of the flickering flame as it converts candle wax into plasma. Does that image resonate with you?"

"Not really," Mike replied.

"Okay, how can I put this? We're not nihilists. We believe in a universal spirit that seeks balance and equilibrium. Why do gas molecules disperse until they are evenly distributed? Why do hot and cold mix into warmth? There is beauty in decay. The pattern and coherence we admire, from the loveliness of a woman to a rose, the awesome spectacle of sunrise, a magnificent painting or the joy of a baby's smile? All are temporary and artificial.

"Everything dies and dissolves into disorder. The only question is when. Suns collapse into black holes. Our civilization collapses on itself when the inevitable Ice Age occurs, or when we're struck by an asteroid or during a decade-long winter caused by a massive volcano eruption. Famine, pestilence, death. In a few billion years, the sun will expand and burn the earth to a crisp. Long before that, the delicate balance that supports our existence will evaporate, dissipate and cease. Do you understand?"

"No. We have to go down fighting," Mike said.

"I'm sorry you feel that way, but it's irrelevant. Regardless of how you struggle, the universe wins. Why not relax and embrace the joy of acceptance? Here's what I want you to do. Imagine the most perfect job, one that frees you to do research with the help of clever people, a job that includes a budget for equipment and supplies that will boggle your mind. Imagine a huge paycheck, and then double it. Once you have your mind around all that, maybe we can negotiate a deal you'd be insane to reject."

The young man stood and weaved his way through the magazine maze until he stood before Mike. He offered a business card.

"Think it over for a couple of days; then we'll get together and chat."

He walked toward the front door, opened it, then turned.

"I will leave something for your amusement." He put a hand in his pocket and removed a small object. After looking at it for a moment, he tossed it to Mike who surprised himself by easily plucking it out of the air.

"Catch you later," the young man said before pulling the door closed firmly behind him.

CHAPTER NINE

Mike Thomas

WHILE SITTING IN his living room, Mike watched shadows shift as the afternoon waned. He thought about recent events and tried to digest and process the information. His mind was sodden with alcohol, so it was hard for him to string coherent thoughts together. His mind bounced from topic to topic like free electrons in the outer shell of a highly-conductive metal like gold or silver.

No, that's silly.

He didn't accept the theory of elemental electron particles orbiting like tiny solar systems. Electrons were standing waves in Space Resonance Theory.

He twisted the switch on his lamp to create a cone of light around his chair and picked up the object the A-K left behind. It was a small cube, two centimeters on a side. A convex activator protruded from one side with a dome-like lens structure on top. A rich brick-red in color, it was made from rosewood polished into a mirror-like finish. After placing it on a stack of magazines littering his coffee table, he activated the switch. It whistled for a few seconds as if charging up, and then a holographic three-dimensional image projected from the top. It was the A-K symbol, rotating on its axis and enveloped by lapping flames. Mike had seen holographs like this created by laser-light interference patterns.

Idly, he ran his finger through the image. Light beams, made of photons, have no mass, so his finger might get warm, but should pass through the projection as if it were smoke. However, this projection was physical. Shocked, Mike jerked violently in his chair. The cube and its projection tipped over and eerily moved on the magazine as the image rotated.

Holy crap. That's awesome.

He up-righted the cube and pressed on the projection with the palm of his hand to compress it. It resisted as if made of hard rubber and created an uncomfortable heat on his palm. Then, the image went black. After a loud ripping sound, the thing disappeared leaving a perfect conical hole about an inch deep in the stack of magazines. With a pencil, he explored the apex of the hole and worked out a black, highly-dense pellet.

If they were trying to impress me with their technical capability——it worked.

Yes, I'm impressed.

Madison Howard, Friday Afternoon

"Perfect," Madison thought as she reviewed the termination letter.

It referred to warning letters in Mike's file and included time-stamped photographs of Mike drinking beer on company time; uncontestable evidence of violation of company policy. Todd had the presence of mind to retrieve the discarded customer copy of the credit card receipt that documented the pitchers of beer and proved Mr. Lorenz Hartz paid the entire tab, three-hundred and twenty dollars, including the substantial tip. Her document requested executive management approval to terminate Mike, for cause, immediately.

After quickly reviewing the spelling and grammar one last time, she sat for a minute with her index finger on the mouse button that would send the email to the Human Resources Department. The delicious power was intoxicating. Finally, she pressed the button to send the message on its way and bathed in the glow of contentment of a job well done.

Rob poked his head in her office doorway and watched for a moment. With bright eyes, her cheeks were flushed and she looked aroused. She radiated angelic flawlessness.

"Madison."

"Yes, Rob?"

The honeyed tone of her voice stroked something deep. If he was a cat, he'd purr.

"I have tickets to the theater. I'd be honored if you'd join me."

"Which show?"

"Phantom of the Opera. The only way I could get them was from Craig's List; they cost me a week's paycheck."

"I'd be delighted." She scribbled her address on a sticky note. "What time will you stop by and pick me up?"

"Six-ish?"

"See you then."

It was only through extreme effort that Rob prevented himself from skipping down the hallway as he headed back to his office.

Madison and Rob Go Out on a Date

Running his electric shaver over his neck for the third time, he finally felt like his skin was smooth enough.

Cultured, sophisticated women don't like scruffy men with rough cheeks.

After patting aftershave lotion on his face, he looked over his teeth for stray vegetable matter.

Going all out, he pulled the plastic off his best suit and examined his collection of neckties to find one that presented the desired trendy image of metrosexual style and muted elegance. Engineering work in the 21st century was casual, so his formal wardrobe was limited. He carefully trimmed and buffed his fingernails to prevent a hangnail from ruining the evening by catching on her nylons or scratching her soft skin. He worried over the choice between boxers and briefs until hedging his bet and putting on a boxer-brief combination.

Unsure which medication worked best, he swallowed pieces of all three erectile dysfunction aids: Levitra, Cialis and Viagra. He didn't generally have trouble achieving erection and satisfying his girlfriends, but he did not want to disappoint a modern woman like Madison. She was the demanding type that might hold a grudge. The pressure would be on and he would make sure he was up to the job.

After calling credit card companies, he totaled available balances to avoid the embarrassment of a declined transaction. His shoes were clean and polished, his toenails were trimmed, and he wore a new belt and socks without holes or thin spots. He vacuumed his car, made sure his jacket pocket held a supply of lubricated, ribbed condoms and rechecked for errant nose hairs. He was ready for the date.

A few minutes early, he parked in front of Madison's apartment building. Unconsciously, he almost called on his cell phone to tell her to come out before he realized she would not appreciate that. He gathered the bouquet (sixty dollars at the florist's shop) and bounded up the stairs to her unit. He did a final inspection, head to toe. He couldn't think of anything he missed, so he pressed the doorbell.

After a minute, about the time he thought it worth the risk of an additional press of the doorbell, she appeared. She'd spent time primping. Her hair was pulled back in a vertical roll and held in place with a rhinestone-flecked pin. She wore a flowing, silky dress that hugged her sleek figure. The flag-like fabric wafted around her knees.

Rob counted. She'd left the top three buttons of the dress undone. This was a good omen. For him to admire, she exposed a full inch of luscious swelling above her black, lacy bra. The sexy bra, in itself, was a good sign. He felt his penis swell, but his shorts were tight and his package was arranged—he was unworried about an untoward display of male excitement.

Her eyes were carefully decorated with mixed shades of electric blue and her lashes were darkened and curled exotically. She looked like a movie star or an actress who sold corn chips on TV; an immaculate vision of youthful perfection. She wore black pumps with two-inch heels and glittering bracelets on both ankles under her nylons. Her earrings fell nearly to her shoulders—strings of diamonds set in gold. The closest Rob had been to a woman this beautifully turned-out was when he splurged on a one-thousand-dollar-per-hour hooker in Las Vegas while working a medical equipment trade show. She'd been nice, but he was too drunk to fully appreciate the experience. This thought cemented Rob's resolve to limit drinking this evening to maximize the sensory input.

"Turn around for me," Madison demanded.

Rob handed her the flowers, then, as gracefully as he could manage, spun on his axis until he faced her again.

"I approve," she said, after immersing her nose in the flowers. "We have ourselves a date." After dropping the flowers on her breakfast bar, she held out her hand and allowed Rob to lead her to the car and get her seated. When he climbed behind the wheel, she said "To avoid wrinkling my dress, I'm not going to wear a seatbelt, so you'd better drive safely."

"No problem, Madison," he said. "You can count on me."

While driving across the Evergreen Point floating bridge, he kept both hands on the wheel and maintained a safe following distance. Cars darted into the space between cars, but he gritted his teeth and held onto his composure. She wouldn't be impressed if he cursed and screamed at the other drivers. After pulling up to the valet parking area in front of the restaurant, he collected his ticket. The valet drivers looked like they were about twelve, but Rob pretended not to care. The car was several years old and had a ding in the driver's side rear quarter panel, so he wasn't anal-retentive about it anymore.

The restaurant was small and trendy; it had been selected as the best French restaurant in Seattle for two years running by a notoriously fussy Seattle Times food critic. The meal would cost nearly a car payment if Madison liked good wine, but Rob was determined not to think about that. It turned out that she *did* like fine wine and the Merlot she picked, when decanted, was a perfect match for the tint of her fingernail paint. This symmetry charged the blood pounding in his ears to an additional degree.

He had to concentrate on breathing, or black frames appeared in his peripheral vision and he risked passing out. Slow, deep and easy respiration was a mantra echoing in his head. It wouldn't do to fall face-first into his *Escargots Sautés Bourguignon*. He wasn't sure what Roast Challans Duck, *Foie Gras en Croute* and *Puy Lentils en Sauce Rouennaise* were exactly, but that's what they ordered. They sipped wine while waiting for the meal to appear.

"Have I mentioned how stunning you are tonight?" Rob asked.

"Yes, but you can sprinkle it in the conversation a few more times because I'm not tired of hearing it. I'm glad we have this time to chat. We can work on our plans for climbing the corporate ladder. I have trouble with the software testers. It would be better to transfer them to Wyle's group. Then I could cover part of marketing, which has higher visibility with the upper echelon. If you have inter-group problems, maybe we can gerrymander the org chart for you."

"I'd like to get to know you better. Where were you born and raised?"

"Boise, Idaho, mainly. What's your budget increase for next year? I asked for eleven percent and they only approved six. That seems a little light. Where did your numbers come out compared to last year?"

"I got over seven percent, but that includes additional funding for a pain management electrode project the marketeers dreamed up. Where did you go to college?"

"Whitman in Spokane. My performance review was good except I got marked down in the *meets schedule commitments* category. Was that just me or is a company-wide continuous-improvement program going on?"

"I don't remember. Generally, I came out all right. I don't study my performance appraisal very closely. Do you have brothers and sisters?"

"Two older brothers and a younger step-sister. Our stock market cap took a hit around mid-year, probably due to problems at another division. I heard rumors about product recalls or something. What do you think about the situation?"

"Went right by me. Have you ever been married?"

"Once for a few months. It didn't work out, so I had it annulled. Have you looked into the Spanish Theory of Value management training sessions? It's the hottest thing at the Harvard Business School right now. I'm told there will be a huge feature in the Wall Street Journal next month."

"Sorry, I'm not familiar with that one. Do you have nieces or nephews?"

"Yes, two of each at last count. Maybe one or two more coming; I don't know." She reached her hand across the table and ran a fingernail across the back of his hand. "You know, I feel really comfortable communicating with you. We're going to make a great team, you and I. Do you feel the synergy?"

Rob made his first *faux pas* of the night when slipping up and saying in a crass tone, "Yeah, baby, I'm feeling your *synergy* tonight."

"Excuse me?" Madison said.

"I'm sorry, that didn't come out right. Yes, I feel an intimate soul-connection with you. We'll make waves at the company once we engage our efforts and look out for each other. Have I mentioned how stunning and lovely you are tonight?"

"You mentioned it, but that was a sweet variation on the theme, thank you."

At this point, their plates of stuffed duck with string beans in cream sauce were presented and Rob took the opportunity to order another bottle of wine. The smile she rewarded him with was ego-fulfilling and pleasing. Apparently, neither were fond of baked duck, so they only nibbled around the edges, but the wine was good and flowed in compensating volume. The meal was successfully consummated. They shared a dessert of Iced Banana Parfait with Butterscotch Sauce. When a drop of syrup fell on his finger, she pulled it over, locked eyes with him, and lapped it off. He thought his erection would explode from his pants, but a careful review of the breathtaking bill tempered the situation.

He dropped a ten-dollar tip on the 'free' valet parking attendant to get his car back and assisted Madison in being seated. He noticed she was less careful—her dress hitched up to expose a sleek expanse of firm thigh. Rob felt as if his body was a swollen sexual organ on the edge of a juicy explosion. Madison knew the effect she had on him; she wore a Mona Lisa smile, similar to a starving shark when the ocean-borne scent of a mackerel drifts by.

Rob turned on the satellite radio tuned to a mellow chick-music station. He adjusted the sound so they could still talk, but loud enough so it would fill the empty spaces between their words.

"If you had a choice of any vacation in the world, where would you go?" Rob asked.

"I haven't had many vacations, I'm too busy. I went to Branson once with a girlfriend. We saw Glen Campbell and Roy Clark; that was nice. Have you used the new Business Objects report that displays our top-selling products on a daily basis? The trends are interesting."

"I need to do that."

They arrived at the theater and passed the car to a new set of pre-puberty valet attendants. Rob escorted Madison to the entry where ticket-takers, in crisp white tuxedos, scanned passes. In the lobby, both took the opportunity to freshen up. Rob had trouble pissing with a half-erect penis, but after agonizing patience, managed to drain his bladder. He splashed water on his face and tipped the bathroom attendant. The smallest bill in his wallet was five bucks, so that's what he left.

"Thank you very kindly, sir," the attendant said gratefully.

Five bucks for handing me a towel, you're damned right you'll kiss my ass.

He didn't say anything. After nodding at the attendant, he made sure his zipper was pulled up fully and walked out. They found their seats a minute before the curtains were raised. The Phantom of the Opera sets were spectacular and the performances were great, but Rob had seen the movie, so, except for the flying chandelier, the ending came as no surprise. Afterward, he suggested a nightcap at the martini bar down the street and Madison gave him a stellar smile and took his arm as they strolled down Fifth Avenue. The streets were wet and the air was misty, but the rain had stopped so the stroll was pleasant. Rob could not believe how his luck held up so far.

They sipped sour apple martinis at twenty bucks a pop. It was too loud to hold a conversation so they smiled at each other and held eye contact over the wide rims of their glasses. After the second drink, Madison slipped off a shoe and gently caressed Rob's foot. Skirting disaster, Rob almost offered a tapped-out credit card to pay for the drinks, but recovered smoothly by offering one that could cover the bill.

They laughed at bums sleeping in doorways as they walked back to pick up the car. Rob was in a good mood. The last valet on duty yawned and complained about how late they were, so Rob laid a twenty on him to shut him up. It worked like a miracle and the driver was all toothy smile and *have a pleasant night sir and madam* after that, so the mood remained magical. Rob was tipsy, but felt enough in control to drive. He didn't say anything when he noticed a new scrape on the driver's side door.

Damned kamikaze valets, what did he expect? They drove like maniacs and parked the cars like matches in a book. Scrapes were bound to happen.

Rob, concentrating intently on the task of driving, moderated his speed while watching for crazy drivers. It was late on a Friday night, so plenty of drunks were on the road, but he gave them lots of room. Soon, they pulled into the parking lot of Madison's apartment complex.

He came around to open her door and took her hand to help her out. Her eyes were bright and she was unsteady on her high heels. Rob had never been so sure of a score in his life. He had the condoms and the girl. He felt overripe, like a hothouse tomato screaming to be plucked from the vine.

"I'll escort you to your door," he said.

She linked her arm through his as they climbed the stairs. She slipped her key in the door and turned to face him.

"I had a lovely evening. Thank you so much," she said.

The first warning bells of the evening clamored in Rob's head.

"I have time, maybe I could come in for a goodnight snifter of brandy."

"That would not be a good idea. I hope you didn't get the wrong idea. I never sleep with a guy on a first date. Never."

Rob's head felt like it would burst into flames.

"No, of course not," he said calmly. "We should get to know each other first."

"I agree completely; thank you for understanding," she said. She gave him a small kiss on the corner of his mouth. "I'll see you at work on Monday."

"Until then," he replied.

He waited until she was inside. After the deadbolt slammed into place, he walked back to his car. Once seated, he lost control and beat his hands against the steering wheel until the edges of his fists were swollen and purple. He didn't notice Madison watching through her curtains. It was several minutes before Rob calmed and felt safe to drive. His penis had not received the rejection message and was inflamed with painful swelling.

Just you and me tonight, big fella.

He rammed the car into gear and pointed it toward home.

Not the first time and certainly not the last.

He calculated the financial carnage the evening wreaked on his credit cards.

Catastrophe.

Stopping at a 7-Eleven, he bought a quart of beer, three hotdogs (the French food did not stick to his ribs) and a copy of the latest Maxim magazine. It ate his last twenty dollar bill—he'd started the evening with three hundred in cash. He wanted to kick his car door or break something expensive, but reined in the urges and sat behind the steering wheel listening to Tool on his CD player while sipping beer. The Asian clerk waved him away because the cops came down hard if he let drivers sit in their cars and drink.

Yeah, I get it. I'm not welcome here either.

Rob started the car and drove home.

Back at Madison's apartment, she shrugged off her pretty dress and hung it up. After peeling off panty hose and brushing her teeth, she realized the evening left her stimulated and yearning. A gentle, but insistent throbbing heat radiated from her genitals. She took a quick shower and checked to make sure her doors and windows were locked and the shades were pulled. She flopped into bed. In her nightstand, under an emergency supply of sanitary napkins, she kept a large, purple, vibrating dildo affectionately named Mr. Angelo.

Come to me, my sweet Mr. Angelo.

She oiled him up with aromatic lubricant and prepared him for active duty.

CHAPTER TEN

Mike Thomas and Lorenz Hartz

LORENZ EASED THE Escalade to a stop in front of Mike's old house. After waiting a few minutes, he tapped the horn and was rewarded by a flick of a bedroom curtain. Five minutes later, Mike stumbled down the walkway buttoning a flannel shirt over his bulbous, hairy belly. Though the temperature was forty degrees and the sky drizzled rain, Mike wore sweat pants and cheap plastic flip-flop sandals.

"Sorry man, I slept in. I was up late thinking about turning my experiment into a weapon. You picked the wrong guy. I play around for fun. I never thought anything useful could come from my work. My messing around is not based on natural physics, I revisit assumptions like the wave-particle quantum duality experiments that reflect electron beams off various metals. Observing interference patterns, I dream up lab experiments using more accurate equipment than they had way back when to see if new interpretations can be resolved…"

"Good morning to you too, Mike. Shall we go through the McDonalds drive-through and get some breakfast?"

"Yeah, I'm starving—that would be great. I suppose what I'm trying to say is, I'm not sure my work is practical."

"It's too early in the morning for deep thoughts."

"Okay."

They ordered at the drive-through speaker and Mike tore into the bags of food; he couldn't remember eating anything since the big lunch the prior day. When they reached Pacific ElectroMed, Mike badged open the door and signed Lorenz into the visitor's logbook, meticulously filling all the requested information and handing Lorenz a visitor's badge to clip on his black coat.

"I want to grab stuff out of my office," Mike said. "Then we'll head down to the lab."

They walked down the deserted corridor and wove through the cubicle maze. In Mike's office, Polly was engrossed in one of his magazines. Her tiny feet, encased in blue walking shoes, were planted on his desk as she leaned comfortably back in his chair. She was dressed casually in blue jeans and a pink Gap t-shirt. Braless, her shirt stretched across her chest like shrink wrap.

"Polly, what are you doing?" Mike said.

"Uh, looking through your papers. Are you earlier than usual?"

"Yeah, I guess. I'm showing Lorenz an experiment. Want to come along and check it out?"

Lorenz rolled his eyes and smiled.

"Oh, sorry, Polly. I should introduce you to my friend. This is Lorenz Hartz."

Polly stood and offered her hand. "I'm pleased to meet you, Mr. Hartz. You've caused turbulence in the hallways of our little company."

"That's a charming way of putting it. Might I ask about your role in the company?"

"I administer document control and deliver the company mail. Sometimes I command a copy machine."

"I see," Lorenz mused.

"Let's not dilly-dally. Hand me that stack of lab books, will you, Polly?"

"Sure," she said.

They paraded to the lab where they watched Mike gather equipment from various workbenches and storage lockers. Some of the equipment looked expensive and professionally-manufactured, but some was home-made and assembled from scraps; electronic kludges crudely soldered together. It took nearly an hour before everything was arranged to Mike's satisfaction. He kept track of things by scribbling in a lab book.

"Today, I'm trying something different. After dispersing hexavalent Cesium, I'll synthesize element 115 by triggering a Bismuth reaction with fused calcium and Americium nuclei."

"Wait," Polly said. "You're synthesizing element 115?"

"Sure, I've been doing that for a couple of years. The secret is to create a resonant microwave plasma chamber in a near vacuum." Pointing his index finger at Lorenz, he said "I'm using the last of my hexavalent Cesium. Is that something you can get? I need a few grams to hold me for a couple of months."

Lorenz made a notation. "I can get it, no problem, but why don't you synthesize that too?"

"Are you stupid? We'd get a tricadmium dinitride ionization that would flash over and create a fusion-reaction[3] plasma. The point temperatures would reach eleven-hundred degrees Celsius in short order."

"Pardon me, but couldn't something like that be turned into a weapon?"

While chewing on a fingernail, Mike mused. "I suppose I could make a light sabre. The beam would be a cool color—near ultraviolet. I'll see what I can do. I watched the original Star Wars movie forty-five times when I was a kid. Now, pay attention. This could be interesting. I'll bring up the voltage slowly. Oh, I almost forgot, we should wear eye and hearing protection. Polly, would you grab the welding shields? Thank you."

They hovered over Mike's glass bulb as he adjusted knobs and flipped switches. The metallic smell of ozone filled the air as a high pitched squeal—similar to the characteristic *screaming* emitted when a bar of pure cadmium is flexed—rattled the fillings in their teeth. This went on for almost a minute before quantum flash-over

---

[3] Some of the chemistry and physics in this novel are marginally plausible, but this particular reaction is completely fabricated and used for dramatic purposes only. In other words, it's bullshit.

triggered and the glass bulb disappeared with a loud pop. Startled, Mike fell backwards. Lorenz caught him before he sprawled on the floor.

"What happened?" Polly said.

"I'm not sure," Mike replied. He flipped up his welder's mask and leaned over the bench. A perfectly round impression was eaten into the surface. He ran his hand over it; it was glassy and smooth and covered with a fine black powder. "This residue is dense. It might be radioactive or toxic, so we'd better be careful." Then he noticed the front panel of the Gallium-Heisenbach X-ray Diffractometer had a perfectly spherical hole in it.

"Oh, shit, I've damaged this gear. I'm fucked."

"Maybe the SUVs can kick in and buy a new one."

"Sure, if you have a couple of million dollars sitting around."

"I guess you're right, you're fucked." Lorenz made a sour face. "Please forgive the crude vulgarity, my dear," he said, addressing Polly. She shrugged. He continued, "Would you speculate about what happened?"

"I need to work through the equations. I have a tickle of an idea, but I might be wrong, so I'd rather not comment right now. We need to get out of here before we get caught. Take me home."

Lorenz shrugged. "Sure, Mike, let's go."

Over his shoulder, Mike called out to Polly. "See you on Monday?"

"Yes, see you then," she replied.

After Lorenz and Mike were gone, she spent a few minutes examining the equipment and workbench. The hole was about the size of a baseball. Hearing voices from outside the lab, she walked quickly to the opposite exit. She didn't want to be anywhere near the lab when the damage was discovered.

National Institute of Standards and Technology

Boulder, CO, USA

Elmo sat behind his desk and looked up as Doctors Snow and Singh entered. Tired from the long work week, he was unhappy to be working on Saturday, but there was no option. He could tell by their somber looks—the news was not good.

"Good afternoon, gentlemen."

"Doctor," they mumbled in greeting. They looked at each other. Doctor Snow spoke.

"It happened again. 2:37 local time."

"What was the magnitude of the slip?" Elmo asked.

"It was worse this time. Zero point two-eight-nine-seven-two seconds give or take a few microseconds. We're recording this one as a four-point-seven on the temporal-seismic Bohr-Snow-Singh scale."

Feeling like the world was lined up against him, Elmo leaned back in his chair and rubbed his eyes.

"Gentlemen, I know this is discouraging, but we will uncover the cause of the temporal upsets—the reason will be rational and understandable. Let's not give in to despair. Can I count on you?"

Both nodded stiffly. None of the scientists at NIST were getting much sleep.

"Do we have a more-accurate source vector?"

Again, they nodded.

"Very well. Thank you for bringing this information to me personally. We'll keep working until the answer unveils its secrets to us like the slow undressing of a fresh virgin in a sheik's harem."

Dr. Singh's face twisted with disapproval. "Excuse me, Dr. Bohr, but I don't appreciate graphic sexual imagery. It's inappropriate."

"I acknowledge your discomfort and I apologize," Elmo said. "Go back to work, okay?"

"Yes, sir," they said before leaving his office.

CHAPTER ELEVEN

Polly Patterson and Lorenz Hartz

AFTER DROPPING OFF Mike, Lorenz drove back and lurked in the Pacific ElectroMed parking lot. Settling in to wait, he opened a paperback novel, a poorly-written and moronic book about a nonsensical conspiracy in the Catholic Church. After reading a few minutes, he tossed it aside and pulled out one of his favorites.

He tried not to let people see him reading them, but he was addicted to the Star Trek series of novels. There were at least thirty—counting the Original Series, Voyager, New Frontier, The Next Generation and Deep Space Nine versions. His rationalization was that he needed something light and easy to pick up and put down because there were many interruptions to his day.

How could I handle anything long and complex?

Mainly, he hid the habit so no explanation would be necessary.

After a couple of hours of reading and listening to rain battering the Escalade's sunroof, he saw Polly come from the building carrying a heavy box. He started the car and rolled up beside her.

"Can I give you a lift to your car?"

Wet, she readily agreed. After heaving the box in his back seat, she climbed in the front.

"Thanks, it's a mess out there. I was waiting for the rain to ease. Sometimes it seems as if the Seattle rain will never stop and we'll be forced to evolve gills and fins."

"Why don't we get dinner and chat? I know a place that has a gas log fireplace. It will be warm and cozy."

Polly mulled it over. "Sure," she said.

Lorenz was pleased.

Women can hardly resist radiant heat on a bitterly cold day.

At the restaurant, Lorenz gave the hostess a business card with a twenty-dollar bill folded behind it and they were promptly seated near the fireplace. They ordered coffee and brandy. Polly asked for a dollop of whipping cream. The waitress took their coats. In a lapse of discipline, Lorenz gaped lewdly; Polly's damp t-shirt did nothing to conceal pert nipples. She had a slender neck and a sprinkle of freckles across her nose. All in all, the packaging could have more meat for Lorenz's taste, but her figure was pleasing and worthy.

I hope she cannot read my mind.

"Your full name is Pollyanna Elaine Patterson, twenty-eight years old. You were born in Rexville, Washington. You graduated in the class of 2002 from Central Washington University with a four-year degree in English Literature. You are unmarried, you've worked at Pacific ElectroMed for five years, you're a home-owner, and are lapsed from the Latter Day Saints. Identifying marks are an appendectomy scar and a burn on your lower left leg. I didn't get where the burn came from."

"A boyfriend's motorcycle. Exhaust pipe."

"Are you impressed I know this much? Anything to add?"

"I went to CWU, but didn't graduate. You mixed my record with my sister Peregrina; she earned the degree. Otherwise, your information is right. Impressed? Not really. You spent an hour surfing a subscription-only Internet database. No big deal."

"Okay, you got an abortion in Portland. Pregnant by the motorcycle boyfriend? How many people know about that?"

"Again, that was Peregrina. I was there—I drove her to the clinic."

"Do you feel guilty about the baby?"

She stared at him for a minute, and then took a sip of her drink. After licking whipped cream off her upper lip, she spoke.

"Yes, during long, dark sleepless nights I feel the gravitational tug of guilt on my soul. I tried to talk Peri out of it, but her mind was made up. Is there a point to your probing?"

"I was prepared to dislike you, but I suppose that's impossible."

"Everyone has enemies, Mr. Hartz. So, yes, it's possible to hate me. Are we getting to business or will you keep jabbing at me until I bleed?"

Lorenz drained his coffee and held the cup above his

head until the waitress took it. At her cocked-eyebrow inquiry, he nodded and held up two fingers to order another round.

"I don't understand your interest in Mike. He's too introverted to notice, but you're reading his notes and loitering. Are you spying for the A-Ks?"

"No. To anticipate your next question, I'm not working for anyone but myself and my employers at Pacific ElectroMed. My day job is clerical; there are no secret treaties or hidden agendas. Now, ask me why I'm interested in Mike—why I follow him home sometimes, why I watch him wander the halls, and why I sneak around and read papers I can't understand and his email if he leaves his PC unsecured."

"Okay, consider the compound question proffered."

"I'll give you the short answer first. It's because he's cute."

"Interesting, but implausible. What's the longer answer?"

Polly sighed and slumped in her seat. She stirred her coffee with an index finger, and then stuck her wet finger in her mouth.

"What did your research say about my father?"

"I didn't dig that deeply."

"He died when I was seven—murdered. He was a geneticist, a biochemist, a natural philosopher, a nerd and my best friend. Does that stimulate your Freudian fantasies?"

Lorenz was uncomfortable. It was as if the room was a sauna with the thermostat welded on high. He pointed at a random entry on the menu while Polly ordered a salmon filet with almond slivers and steamed saffron rice. He opened his mouth to speak a couple of times, but changed his mind before saying anything.

"Are you the kind of woman who can hold her tongue and let a man think?"

She nodded. They ate dinner while silence stretched. They listened to inane conversations at adjoining tables and exchanged a few words with the waitress. Outside, the rain relented—it was misty, but no longer pouring. After dinner, Lorenz drove Polly to her car and helped her move the heavy box from the Escalade into her trunk. There were no more words; they shook hands and went their separate ways.

Lorenz Hartz

Lorenz did not want more coffee, but stopped at Starbucks and ordered a large cup of drip. He settled into an overstuffed chair, booted his laptop, logged onto the SUV network, and triggered a series of deep searches. He quickly verified everything Polly said and cursed himself for not picking up the details without her help. Before an hour passed, Lorenz was certain that the A-Ks were involved with Polly's father's death twenty-one years earlier.

Freak Accident Claims Life at Carnival

ZBS News – North American Herald-Star

A tragic Ferris wheel accident ended the life of University of Washington Professor Roland Patterson early on Saturday. A support strut fractured and pierced Dr. Patterson's chest. He was pronounced dead on the scene by EMTs. Dr. Patterson was accompanied by his daughter, who was uninjured. Professor Patterson was best known for a book called Quantum Resonance—Interference and Cognition with coauthors Melvin Rastin and Dr. Heinrich Ottoplatz. In an unrelated, but equally-tragic accident, Dr. Rastin was killed while climbing Mount Rainier last week. Mr. Patterson leaves behind a wife, Claire, and twin daughters Pollyanna and Peregrina.

Unconsciously, Lorenz sipped cold coffee and stared into space while the Starbucks crowd ebbed and flowed around him. He closed his laptop. Without thinking, he found himself at Polly's house. He walked to her door and pressed the doorbell. It took her almost ten minutes to appear. During that time, he looked around the neighborhood and tried to shake feelings of dread. When she appeared, wiping her forehead with a fluffy towel and breathing deeply from exertion, he made a noble effort not to stare at her lithe body encased in nearly-transparent, silvery-sheer tights. Lorenz handed her a jewelry box. She opened it and pulled out a SUV medallion on a silver chain.

She did not speak, but asked questions with pretty eyes.

"For what it's worth, I'm taking you into the protection of the Sovereign Union of Vagabonds. Press the red jewel in the center of the medallion and help will come as quickly as it can be dispatched. We're on a small budget and spread thin, but we'll risk our lives to help you. That's the end of the speech; you can talk if you wish."

"What is the likelihood of our story having a happy ending?"

"The odds are poor," Lorenz admitted, "but we'll die trying. I'm sorry for my skeptical attitude during lunch."

"That's okay, I understand how things look. I could have said more earlier and avoided some of the misunderstanding. What about Mike? Do you think his work has value?"

"I'm no expert in these matters, but indications are that he's onto something. We haven't talked about my mission, but we're the good guys. We want to fan the fires of liberty and prosperity. I suppose that sounds dumb when I come right out and say it like that, but there you are. Life and freedom and children and nature and trees and flowers. Motherhood, apple pie and patriotism, all that good stuff. I'm sorry, perhaps I drank too many Irish coffees. Could I come in and rest a bit?"

"I don't think that would be a good idea, but I thank you for the lovely medallion."

"Right, you're right, I understand. Until we meet again."

While gently closing the door, she smiled with guileless, loving purity, or perhaps, he was deluded by the influence of alcohol. He tried to remember how many drinks he'd consumed, but could not grasp the number.

The sound of door locks being engaged broke his drift. He walked back to his car and pointed it toward his hotel.

Sleep, that's what I need, a dozen hours of uninterrupted sleep and then, perhaps, things will make more sense.

Mike Thomas

On Sunday morning, someone who would not go away pounded on his front door.

"Leave me alone. I'm taking a day off," he shouted.

Finally, wearing baggy boxer shorts and one furry slipper, he opened the front door, and walked back to collapse in his chair.

Am I coming down with a terrible disease?

His head was fuzzy and he couldn't tell if the room was too hot or too cold. It was one or the other. The A-K entered behind him and pulled the door closed.

"Hello, Mike," he said.

"Feel my head. Am I running a fever?" Mike said.

"I'm not touching you. You're not sick, you're hung over from drinking all afternoon with that lout Lorenz."

"Oh. I don't remember your name."

"Call me Trent or AK-149, whichever you're more comfortable with. You need to haul some of this crap out of here. This place is a fire hazard," he said as he cleared a chair by gathering a heap of periodicals and stacking them on top of another tall pile in a corner.

"You just put *New England Journal of Medicine* on top of *Nature*."

"We are called the Agents of Karnage, not the agents

of tidy and everything in its place."

"Asshole."

"Last month I was called a feral shit-eating mutant donkey-fucker, so you'll excuse me if I'm unimpressed with *asshole*. Let's get to the point, shall we?"

"Okay, Trent, let's get to the point. What point?" Mike massaged his temples. "Maybe I have radiation sickness."

"You don't have radiation sickness or you'd be bleeding out your bung hole and eye sockets. The point is you need to align yourself with the drunken-bozo SUVs or the golden A-Ks."

"I suppose—if I pick the SUVs, you'll kill me."

Trent laughed heartily. "Is that what you think? Well, you may be right. We *are* under contract to rein you in or neutralize you. On the other hand, we're trying to increase worldwide chaos and you are doing a great job regardless of whether you're aligned with us or them." He held out his hands like he was trying to find the balance of two weights. "What to do, what to do?"

"Do you have aspirin or cough syrup?"

"No."

"I made up my mind. I'm siding with the SUVs. They're more my style."

Trent made a point of looking Mike over from head (with oily hair standing on end) to foot (with one dirty slipper). "That doesn't say much for their style then, does it? I'll feel your forehead if you'll change your mind."

"No, I have a thermometer around here somewhere. I'll take my own damn temperature. Maybe I ate bad fish."

"You smell like bad fish, but that doesn't mean you ate any. All right, Mike, that's that."

"I guess."

"See you around."

Trent got up and weaved toward the front door.

"And Mike, what you're doing in that lab gives the clock-watchers at NIST and Switzerland a lot of heartburn. Keep it up, we like it."

"Cesium clocks are being perturbed, that's interesting. Once I feel better, I'll think about that. Graviton-Temporal shock waves, I see that coming from my experiments. I wonder if it causes a permanent offset or if things get out of alignment temporarily but eventually re-achieve synchronization?"

"I don't know. You can ask them yourself when they track you down, bind you in chains and put you in a Homeland Security torture chamber. They are unhappy with you. The clock-watchers are notorious for having no sense of humor. Until later," Trent said as he let himself out.

CHAPTER TWELVE

Mike Thomas

ON MONDAY MORNING, Mike still felt under the weather, so he slept in before dragging himself to work at nine o'clock. After logging onto the company network, he read through his email. He was startled by a cane slapping against his cubicle wall. Turning, he saw the old man wearing his typical washed-out yellow jumpsuit. Because he looked like a street bum or nursing home escapee, no one paid any attention to him—he was nearly invisible.

The corporate nervous system that recognized important people skipped over this old coot. However, this grumpy old man was Preston Stanwood, former CEO, but now a minor shareholder of the corporate conglomerate that devoured the company. Sliding stock prices eroded his net worth, but he was still good for a couple of billion and held a seat on the board of directors.

"Dagnab it, Mike, you've done it this time. What did you do to the Gallium-Heisenbach X-ray Diffractometer?"

"Uh," Mike said.

"Don't hornswoggle me. For years, you've been messing around in that lab, we have it recorded on security video. Do you know what that'll cost to fix? And what it'll cost in schedule slides by having it out of service for a few months? If you're trying to kill me, why don't you just stab me in the heart with a letter opener and save me grief?"

"Sorry, boss. It was an accident."

"I suppose you expect me to cover for you again? Smooth things over? Pull some strings? One day, Mr. Thomas, my kindness and generosity will expire, tap out and run dry. Do you understand?"

"Yes, I understand. Thanks."

"You're welcome." The old man got his cane under his center of gravity and turned to leave, then turned again. "The company is not paying the bill this time, there's no room in the capital equipment budget."

"That's fine, I understand."

"Very well. Have a good day."

Madison Howard and Preston Stanwood

Rob poked his head into Madison's office. He was still upset about the way their date turned out (more precisely, didn't turn out), but had so much invested—he wanted to see the matter through to the end.

"Hey, Maddy."

She hated the nickname, but decided to cut him slack. *Not much, just a little.*

"Good morning. Thank you again for a lovely

evening; it was great fun."

"Yeah, I had fun too. Maybe you'll join me again on Friday?"

"I should be able to, but let's wait until later in the week before I make a solid commitment."

Her: *There's no sense in giving him too much comfort.*

Him: *She's jerking me around so I won't get too comfortable.*

"No problem, I'll check with you later. Here comes that old fart in the yellow jumpsuit. Did you figure out who he is?"

"Who cares?"

"Crap, I gotta run," Rob said. He waved and dashed off for a ten o'clock staff meeting. Madison intently studied her computer screen. The old man cleared his throat and got her attention.

"Miss Howard, is it?"

"Sure, can I help you?" The old man threw a pile of papers on her desk, then slowly lowered himself into her guest chair. "I'm wrapped around the axle this morning," she said, "but I can give you a few minutes. What is this about?"

"I'll tell you a tale about a young engineer who worked for me many years ago. Modern managers aren't excited about ancient history, but I hope you'll indulge me for a minute or two. In the annals of company lore, long before this company was melded with the multinational corporation that now owns it, there was a young man named Mike Thomas. I was busy building the business and didn't supervise him carefully.

"He spent his personal time working on a hare-brained scheme for applying electro-cranial stimulation to pain management. Many lived in horrible agony and the precocious young Michael helped them. In doing so, he put this company on the map, which led to a lot of profit for me, then to a corporate buy-out and a lot of money for other people too. Now, things are different and Mike, for personal reasons, works in obscurity in our Receiving Inspection department. Few remember or recognize his vital contribution to this company unless old equipment comes in for repair or someone orders the classic product, but I'm still alive and I still have pull around here. *I* remember."

Nervous, Madison nearly squirted in her panties.

Is this old man who she feared he might be?

"So, Miss Howard, if you ever again submit termination paperwork against Mike, mark my words, I will cross out *his* name and replace it with *your* name. Are we in concurrence, concordance, oh hell, what's the right word? Consensus. My mind doesn't work like it used to, but there it is. Have we achieved consensus on this topic, you and I?"

Numbly, Madison nodded.

"Good," he said while struggling to his feet. "Because it seems I have to urinate every five minutes, and I have to go now. Have a good day, Miss."

With that, he hobbled down the hallway toward the restroom.

Madison dialed the extension for the HR department. With a shaky voice, she said: "Hey Tim, does Preston

Stanwood still come around here?"

"Sure, you see him hanging around. I don't think he has anything else to do. Some people don't like him, but I've never had any problem with him. He's the old guy in the yellow jump suit—you can't miss him."

"Thanks," Madison said before cradling the phone.

She couldn't believe her internal warning system left her so blind.

Do I have other blind spots?

Her MBA classes didn't cover workplace situations like this. Corporate executives were supposed to wear fancy suits and expensive ties, not WalMart jump suits. She felt frozen, as if made of stone. The phone buzzed and computer tones announced incoming email, but she could not move. She felt herself getting smaller and more helpless, like a child.

Shaking the spell, she pulled a pair of scissors from her desk drawer and cut a shape from a sheet of legal paper. Old guilt surfaced, but it was guilt mixed with cruel pleasure, a mix that could not be explained, only experienced. When she was a child of eight—hidden behind her locked bedroom door—she made a similar paper doll decorated with orange flowers matching the print dress of her hated teacher, Mrs. Blandon. She used lemon yellow to make curlicues of wiry hair and brick red to color in lurid lips. Black shoes and horrid legs covered with twisty purple veins completed the picture.

Slowly and ritually, she used snub-nosed scissors to decapitate the figure; then placed it between the pages of her English workbook. A week later, Mrs. Blandon slipped on a patch of ice and hit her head. Something in her skull swelled, then ruptured. After a few days of lingering in a hospital bed, Mrs. Blandon died and the cute Mr. Lewis took over second-grade English. Life was better because Mr. Lewis liked flirty little girls in patent leather shoes, white stockings and blue jumpers. Her grades improved immediately.

Madison realized she'd cut out the outline of a man— a bent-over, shriveled and dissipated old man. Using a coarse black Sharpie pen, she drew a cane and used a yellow highlighting pen to emulate the florid jump suit. She drew in a red heart and, as if hypnotized, unconsciously stabbed the figure into her corkboard with a pushpin piercing the crudely-drawn heart. This released something in her; she grabbed the phone the next time it blatted.

"Good afternoon, this is Madison, how may I help you?" she said professionally.

AK-149 Emails his RAK Report

To: RAK Accounting Department
From: Agent AK-149
Subject: RAK Report for Friday

If you'll permit a personal note, I'm particularly proud of this one. I accept your comments regarding the quality trend of my Random Acts of Karnage over the last month and I understand— merely breaking expensive things does not reach a proper level of elegance. I am making an effort to do better, as I believe this report will indicate.

First of all, I like the ovulation gloves. The idea that we can touch a woman and read the state of her fertility has delicious potential for fanning the flames of chaos. Bravo to comrade AK-21 for devising this innovation.

I was at a café enjoying a large stack of blueberry pancakes. A group of noisy construction workers seated at the booth behind me swigged coffee, harassed the waitress and recovered from a late-night drinking session—eating breakfast to fuel energy to lay pavement or build bridges or whatever it is that people of their ilk do. It was tedious to overhear their exploits in selecting winning football teams, drinking huge quantities of mass-produced beer and exploring the charms of bar girls. They seemed particularly proud of one cretin who seduced and violated an overweight young lady in a pickup truck after the bar closed.

When I walked to the restroom facilities, I noticed a pretty girl seated at the counter enjoying an English muffin and a cup of caffeine-free raspberry tea. She studied a psychology textbook— clearly she was a student at the local community college. On instinctual impulse, I touched her arm as I slipped by and checked when I reached the restroom. Sure enough, she was in the fertile region of her monthly cycle and not using birth control. It was a simple matter to stop and exchange a few words with her, then slip a few drops of triazolobenzodiazepine hypnotic (as cleverly devised by AK-276) into her tea. For obvious reasons, she accepted my assistance in paying her bill and navigating the parking lot. I used her keyfob to locate her car and got her comfortably arranged in the back seat.

Then, on another trip to the restroom, while following one of the annoying young men, I struck up a conversation. He was completely unsavory—bleary-eyed, unshaven, and still inebriated from the festivities of the night before. Also, dumb as an ox, if I may be permitted the crude observation. Here is my recollection of our conversation:

Me: Excuse me, I couldn't help overhearing, you guys had a wild party last night.

Him: You're fucking-A goddam right.

Me: Did you notice the pretty lady sitting at the counter? She noticed you.

Him: What the fuck are you talking about?

Me: I'm just saying, the young lady told me that she saw you with your friends and felt an instant chemistry. She mentioned she'd be delighted to get to know you better.

Him: No shit? How can I find her? Did you get a number?

Me: I can do better than that. She's outside in a blue Honda Accord and hopes you'll visit her right away.

Him: If you're fucking with me, I'll come back and rip out your fucking kidneys and I'm not fucking kidding.

Me: [Editorial note, he may have slipped a fourth instance of the word 'fucking' into that sentence, but I'm not sure.] Go see for yourself.

I will leave the rest of the story to your imagination, though I will mention—when I finished my pancakes and walked to my car, the windows on the Honda were steamed up and there was noticeable rhythmic action going on.

This Random Act of Karnage will have repercussions extending far into the future. I will make every effort to make sure the future quality of my work achieves or exceeds the high standards of the Agents of Karnage. I received your message and I appreciate your guidance.

   —Until tomorrow, best regards from AK-149

Mike Thomas

The day was not going well for Mike. He generally ignored his coworkers, but the research team was angry with him for the damage in the lab. He passed his makeshift broom-closet bedroom—someone posted a professionally-drafted sign, *Mike's Roach Motel* in blue neon lettering with a red neon *No Vacancy* emblem completing the image. Awash in bad temper, he almost tore it down, but left it up as a reminder of how malicious and spiteful his well-dressed coworkers could be.

A video clip, cribbed from the security video system hard disk recorder, shuttled electronically around the world on YouTube. It was viewed by giggling schoolchildren in Kiev, Islamabad and Manila before appearing in his email inbox for him to see for himself. The image quality was surprisingly good—the pan and tilt camera focused tightly on his work area. Lorenz and Polly's facial expressions were captured in crisp detail.

The most interesting fragment was the instant when the plasma flash-over occurred. By stopping the frames and sequencing them one-by-one, it was apparent something solid appeared and moved quickly before bursting in the air like a soap bubble. There was comedy when Mike and his friends jumped back in stunned surprise. The clowns who ripped the video dubbed in squeaky voices with Japanese accents.

"EE-EE-EE, Doctor Hashimoto-san, you have created a huge artificial fart and, by the spirit of my forefathers, it really, really stinks."

"Behold the wonder of my stench! Soon, I will mass-produce and unleash my noxious gasses on the world."

Very goddamned funny, Mike thought bitterly. *Someone will send this to the Fox network and I'll be as famous as that silly Star Wars kid[4]. Perhaps I should end my life now to avoid the endless, humiliating spectacle.*

After a few miserable minutes, he remembered—he genuinely did not give a flying fuck what other people think. Dealing with unsubtle hallway mockery was more tolerable after rediscovering this fact.

He edited the video into a repeating sequence so he could study the formation and deconstruction of the

---

[4] Rotund teenager, Ghyslian Raza from Quebec, was an international spectacle when video clips of his goofy mock battle using the handle of a golf ball retriever as a lightsaber, filmed in November of 2002, spread around the world in many millions of downloads. Ghyslian could have leveraged this fame into financial success by exploiting genuine hero status among gawky teenagers around the world, but chose to be ashamed, embarrassed and litigious against the people that released the video. Carrot Top would kill for this kind of worldwide exposure; this kid got it for free. The world can be an odd place.

plasma bubble. Sitting at his lab bench inspecting beryllium-copper inserts under a lighted magnifier, his mind drifted. Between inserts, he watched the video loop and imagined metaphysics that would explain the strange phenomena. It's hard to discard particle notions and embrace entangled quantum states. Everything is waves and packets of waves. Matter is a standing-wave resonance in space.

He was close to touching the mind of God when a wad of paper, following a least-energy arc through the air, bounced off his head. He stood and looked over the cubicle partitions, but found no evidence of the assailant. He uncrumpled the paper and studied the crude scrawl.

Fuck you, Geekwad, it said with eloquent brevity.

Mike flattened it, and with a pushpin, stabbed it into his corkboard between printed emails from Jack Kilby and Milo Wolff. There, it would provide an eternal reminder of how cruel of his fellow man could be.

Plus, it would remind him how to spell *geekwad* in case he ever forgot.

CHAPTER THIRTEEN

Preston Stanwood

PRESTON SETTLED INTO his reclining leather chair and unfurled the latest issue of Fortune magazine. He realized he was hungry.

"Babe, do we have any food in the house? Leftover meatloaf or something?"

His wife, Sonia, walked down the long hallway from her media room.

"I'm sorry, what did you say?"

"I forgot to eat lunch—now I'm dying. Do we have any leftovers?"

"I can find you something that isn't too green or fuzzy. We have roast beef—I could make you a sandwich. Would you like a beer or a glass of wine with it?"

"A cold beer would be great, thank you."

Preston pressed buttons on his chair's remote control and activated heating pads, lumbar massage and high-intensity reading light. He read an article on tricky new tax breaks for off-shore investment accounts.

Sonia brought him a tray and set it beside his chair. A trophy wife, she was acquired after his first wife passed away. Tanned, blond and slender, she claimed to be thirty-five, but Preston noticed her age did not change over the several years they'd been married. As long as she cheerfully brought him sandwiches and beer he did not mention the conundrum. At seventy-nine, he had no basis for commenting on anyone else's age.

"I think we should do Christmas in Paris this year," she said.

"I'm sorry, what did you say?"

She spoke louder this time. "I've been thinking we should do Christmas in Paris."

"Sure, whatever you want," he responded, "but if you want to freeze your buns off, we could go to Victoria instead."

"Paris would be lovely."

"Whatever you want."

She kissed him on the cheek. "You're too good to me."

"I know," he replied, while nuzzling her neck.

She walked back toward her computer room. "Call me if you want anything else."

"Hmmm," he said, while chewing the sandwich and adjusting the magazine to catch the light so he could read it. Unconsciously, he took too large a bite of beef and began choking. After a few seconds, he got scared and smashed the reading lamp with the meal tray. Sonia came running.

"You can't breath?" she said, near panic. He nodded vigorously. "All right, I'll try the Heimlich, get ready."

He leaned over and she got behind him with her arms wrapped around his abdomen.

"Here goes," she said.

Lifting vigorously, she expelled the meat. Unfortunately, his old bones were brittle and she fractured several ribs. Within three minutes he was dead from internal bleeding. By the time the paramedics arrived six minutes later (the upscale neighborhood had excellent EMT coverage), his body was cooling. Sonia, hysterical, required sedation before she would stop crying and pulling at her hair.

"He was a good man," she mumbled as they helped her to the couch and wrapped her in a quilt.

Madison Howard

When Madison heard the news—announced over the company's public address system—about the sad passing of the company's founder, she looked around to make sure there were no witnesses before tearing down the paper voodoo doll. She wadded it up and hid it under a latté cup and other trash as if it was smoking-gun evidence of a crime.

She was not sorry, the old man was evil. The modern world was for the young, not for old farts overstaying their welcome. She was not superstitious, but her paper figures seemed to have mysterious power.

Opening her desk drawer, she pulled out her *Mike*

Thomas file.

I'll see your ass terminated if it's the last thing I do on this earth.

She stuffed the papers in a transmittal envelope and dropped them in the company mailbox.

Sayanara, Mike Thomas.

Rob Perry and Charles 'CB' Barthre

Rob scanned his email while partially listening to CB's epic story.

"I told the little punks my toy crossbow would blast a ball farther than their slugger. You should have seen this kid, a hundred-eighty pounds or I'm a monkey's grandpa. And they're like *no way* and I'm like, *yeah-way, big time, slimers.* These kids desperately needed a lesson in humility.

"Gather your money and line up your hitter, it's time for batting school. The kid blasts one out. *Not bad* I say, *but step back and let papa show you how it's done.* I set the thing up and let her loose. Bam! The ball streaks over the outfield fence like a rocket and you shoulda seen the looks on their pimply faces. Magic, baby, magic. And I'm rolling out of there with their money. It was sweet."

Rob swiveled in his chair and leaned over his desk toward CB.

"You're a mechanical engineer, right?"

"Yeah, PhD. Why do you ask? You know that."

"I want you to think for a minute. Doesn't it strike you odd that this crossbow thing can hold and release so much energy? Every force creates an opposite and equal force, right?"

"I ain't thought about it. I'll look into it and get back to you."

He reached the desk and grabbed Rob's crossbow.

"No you don't," Rob complained, "you're not taking that. Are you off your meds?"

"No."

"Well, get your doctor to change the cocktail. And listen, about Friday, I know we're supposed to go to the Trailblazers game, but I may have a date with Madison."

"Might have a date? Ooh, Madison, she's already snipped off your balls. Where does she keep them? In a bedside drawer with tampons and yeast infection cream?"

"That's a cheap shot, man."

"You're the one bailing on a friend because you *might* have a date with a slick bitch who doesn't even open the cupboard and share the sugar."

"Get out of here, I'm tired of your guff. Don't forget Lorenz's warning. We may still be in danger."

"Sure, boss, see ya," CB called over his shoulder, while waving the crossbow.

Charles 'CB' Barthre

CB stopped at a grocery store and bought a twelve-pack of Coors beer and frozen pizzas on sale three-for-five dollars. He planned a feast. After pulling up to his apartment complex, he cracked open a beer while listening to the end of Led Zeppelin's *Black Dog* on a classic rock radio station.

He never got tired of the golden age of rock. After this song, the playlist served up *Walk This Way* by Aerosmith. CB drank beer and beat the time signature on his steering wheel.

After the tune, a block of commercials started, so CB gathered the groceries and walked to his front door. He idly thought about the crossbow and the ominous warnings, so he dropped the plastic grocery sack, kneeled, and reached out to insert the key in the lock. Staying as far away as possible, he turned the knob and pushed open the door a few inches. There was a loud crack and the door was pierced by yellow tendrils. They looked like tree roots—three inches in diameter where they blasted through his door.

His neighbor poked his head out. "Keep it down, will ya?" he said. He looked at the hallway mess incuriously. "Maintenance is going to be pissed if you don't clean up this shit."

CB touched one of the tubes. Like extruded foam, it was grainy and stiff. He pushed harder and broke off a piece. While examining the fragment, he was startled by a voice from behind.

"Use vinegar and the stuff will dissolve. It's an easy clean-up."

"I don't have vinegar."

"Use pickle juice, same thing."

CB turned. "I've seen you hanging around."

The young man held out his hand to shake.

"I'm Agent AK-149, but you can call me Trent if you prefer."

"Why are you trying to kill me?" CB said.

"I'm not trying to kill you. If that's what I wanted, it would be easy."

"I could have been killed by this stuff," CB complained, gesturing.

"Sure, but you weren't. I'm having a little fun by shifting the odds against you, that's all. We're called the Agents of Karnage, not the Agents of Killing Insignificant Morons, Losers and Bozos. I wouldn't kill you directly unless the company had a contract and it's hard to imagine anyone bothering. I'll help you clean up, then we'll chat."

As Trent said, when wiped with paper towels soaked with pickle juice, the foam dissolved and cleaned up nicely. Still, yellow stains remained and, of course, there were eight large holes in the door.

"Who's going to pay to fix this stuff?"

"Not me." Trent shrugged. "Let's get those pizzas in the oven, I'm hungry."

CB examined the mechanism that created the foam.

"We call it the 'squid', because the foam spews like tentacles," Trent said. "It uses a butane fuel cartridge."

"I can't believe you almost killed me and now you want me to give you pizza."

"The world can be a funny place, eh? Throw me a beer, will ya?"

After the pizzas were consumed and the discarded beer cans created an impressive pile, Trent leaned forward and spoke seriously.

"I see some of myself in you, CB. If you survive a few more random acts of murderous violence, maybe I'll put in a good word for you with headquarters. We're always looking for good men and if we can't find them, we settle for lucky men like you."

"What's the job pay?"

"Pay? That's funny. We get expenses and a few bucks here and there, but basically it's a part-time, volunteer position."

"I don't get it? Why bother?"

"You're a veritable comedian. Why? Why do people do a lot of things? Pardon my offense if you're a religious man, but why do people believe in a Supreme Being when there isn't a single bit of scientific evidence to support the idea? Why do people spend time and money following sports or buying lottery tickets? Astrology? Fashion? Fords are better than Chevys? Ashlee Simpson? Reality TV shows? People believe and invest their time in a lot of things that don't stand up to objective analysis and cold exposure to logic and reason. I didn't invent the system. Why are you asking me?"

"What could I do to convince you to stop skewing the odds against me?"

"That's easy. Convince me you have special significance."

"I'm a guy who likes sports, beer and chicks. I don't have any special significance."

"Then what difference does it make if you live or die?"

"It makes a big difference to me."

"You're insignificant, so it doesn't matter what's important to you."

CB put his head in his hands. "This is a nightmare. I

don't see how this works out for me at all."

"That's the situation for most of the people in the world. You're in great company."

"Why are you here, besides glomming pizza and beer?"

"I stopped by to pick up the crossbow. Those things are expensive. You broke one and I have to explain it to the bosses back east. I want the other one before you break it, too."

"If I hand it over, will you leave me alone?"

AK-149 considered the matter.

"No," he said.

"Well, then, you can't have it. Screw off."

"I already have it. You left it in your car, so I helped myself." He stood. "How about another beer for the road?"

"Go ahead, take them all, I don't care," CB said.

"That's the spirit," AK-149 responded, smiling, while taking a beer and leaving the apartment.

Caller X

In a junk yard a year earlier, Caller X found an AN-AAQ Navigation Pod scavenged from a decommissioned Nellis F-16 fighter jet. He mounted it in a plastic utility shed and powered it up. The green lights illuminated, it powered up. With a slapdash cable, he hooked it to a laptop's serial port. Now, the screen flashed and the speaker honked. There was no doubt—low-flying aircraft were headed his way. Three bogies approached at two-hundred knots. With regret, he took a sip from a hot cup of Brazilian coffee. There would be no time to finish it.

After flipping circuit breakers, he took a last look at his lair. It was madness to get attached to anything, but he'd miss the compound. Around back, with a pack thrown around his shoulders, he climbed a wooden ladder and followed a narrow track along the ridge behind his trailer. From the east, there was no way he could be seen. Panting, he reached the top of the escarpment.

With field glasses, he looked over the compound as three black helicopters swooped and dropped to the ground in a formation surrounding his compound. Three figures dressed in black and bearing automatic weapons jumped from each helicopter and scattered. Within seconds, they opened fire. After the first volley, bundles were tossed at each building. Explosions ripped the air and the ground shook. Cascades of gravel dislodged from the cliff and Caller X moved back in case the face collapsed.

The raid was well-planned. The helicopters were several hundred yards from the compound, right where he predicted they'd be.

Let's see how you like this.

After backing farther from the face of the precipice, he lifted the protective shield and pressed the red button on a Rothenbueler military-surplus remote-controlled detonator. He was a quarter-mile away. Nonetheless, the roar temporarily deafened him and left teeth loose in his jaw. Several hundred cubic yards of rubble dropped down the cliff and covered part of his Airstream. Two of the helicopters were completely gone; the last was on its side—burning. A disoriented pilot staggered and limped in a tight circle before collapsing. Caller X adjusted the scope on his Barrett Arms XM-109 .50-caliber sniper rifle, but decided the pilot was not worth a five-dollar bullet.

He knew a fourth helicopter would come from the west, but he was ready. It took longer than expected, but soon, hugging the desert, it appeared. Caller X locked on it with an infrared targeting system and fired a surface-to-air missile. The chopper veered sharply, but could not evade the missile. Soon, the chopper was another burning heap on the ground. Caller X threw canvas aside and started his sky car, a souped-up Moller M400 Volantor. A standard Moller 400 could cruise at 322 knots, but this modified one was faster. After the vertical take-off maneuver, he headed west at 410 knots, roaring thirty feet above the desert.

CHAPTER FOURTEEN

Mike Thomas

MIKE NEVER BOTHERED to think about practical applications of his research, so he was intrigued by the idea something useful might come of it. The question was, what sort of weapon could he create? Making a plasma blade had promise and the intellectual resonance of implementing a Star Wars lightsabre was amusing.

However, it was impractical. The handle would get hot and the emission would be a wide swath of energy instead of the truncated, tubular beam of the movies. Still, he downloaded the Star Wars films and watched the battle scenes over and over to stir inspiration. He fell asleep in front of his monitor while the sixth film played. His dreamy subconscious was unleashed and he came up with the idea of an anti-proton bubble gun.

He woke at three A.M. with the idea fully-formed. He was sure it could be made portable enough for a man to wield; he ran out of the house and jumped in his car. The lab had the necessary parts and he couldn't wait to try out the idea. The fact that he was partially dressed, wearing only unlaced basketball shoes, stained boxer shorts and a wife-beater t-shirt, did not enter his mind.

After arriving at Pacific ElectroMed, he gathered equipment. He started with a short piece of stainless steel coupled with a hydrogen fuel cell for power and soon had an ugly, crude mechanism to try. The secret parts were buried in an evacuated glass bulb filled with a dispersion of the last of his stash of hexavalent Cesium combined with a wireless LAN antenna and the backlight high voltage power supply stolen from a laptop computer. In the end, it looked like random junk soldered together.

He took a deep breath, made a superstitious cross over his chest and pressed the button. Three-inch plasma bubbles, iridescent like butterfly wings, burbled from his *gun*. They drifted a few feet and dissolved into solid objects before blinking out of existence with subsonic shock waves and audible snaps. He examined the holes in the walls. They were perfectly smooth and the inside surfaces were coated with a fine, black powder. He watched one of the bubbles pass into a fire extinguisher. Soon, steaming drifts of CO_2 were sprayed all around the room.

He took a minute to celebrate.

I did it.

He'd created anti-proton bubbles and was dizzy with the potential. Unfortunately, one of the bubbles hit an eight-foot fluorescent tube and he was showered with shards of broken glass. Bleeding, he recognized the spectacle created for the security cameras, so he walked over, aimed his weapon, and dematerialized them, one-by-one. He'd never felt so fulfilled and satisfied.

Within a few hours, the security video, captured prior to destroying the cameras, was on the Internet. A crazed-looking man, dressed in dirty shorts and laughing hysterically strode around a laboratory firing a high-energy anti-matter bubble gun. The video was a hit after being linked to the Drudge Report where it single-handedly resulted in a 2.4% increase in worldwide Internet traffic. By the end of the day, fake versions of the ungainly weapon, hastily assembled in China, were available on eBay with an average sales price of one-hundred dollars.

Mike was totally oblivious. Bone-tired, he went home to catch up on his sleep.

Mike Thomas and Scientists from the NIST

There was a loud banging on the door, but Mike assumed he was dreaming. The door slammed open. Three men in dark suits congregated around his bed. Mike sat up and rubbed his eyes.

"What are you doing in my bedroom?" he asked.

"Are you Michael Wilson Thomas?"

"What do you want?"

Adding to the crowd, Lorenz and AK-149 forced themselves into the bedroom.

"Mr. Thomas is under the protection of the Sovereign Union of Vagabonds," Lorenz shouted.

AK-149 watched with silent amusement.

"I'm sorry, who are you?" Elmo Bohr asked.

"My name is Lorenz Hartz and I'm a member of the Sovereign Union of Vagabonds. Mr. Thomas is under our protection. Please leave immediately."

"I'm here on official government business," Elmo said. "I've never heard of your organization."

"Have you heard of the International Brotherhood of Free Citizens?"

"No."

"The World Wide Web of Anarchists and Libertrarians?"

"No," Elmo said, growing more exasperated. One of his aides whispered in his ear. "Shit, are you guys like the Organization of Unassociated Free Thinkers?"

Lorenz twisted his face into a sour expression. "Yes, like them, except…"

One of the suits accompanying Elmo tapped him on the shoulder.

"Boss, we got a call. If he's under the protection of the SUVs; we have to leave him alone."

"Who called?"

"It was the Secretary of Defense, sir. Authenticated on the encrypted line. It was really him."

"All right," Elmo said, "I get it. Can I ask your client to cease and desist perturbations of the temporal-space continuum?"

"Go ahead," Lorenz said, gesturing.

Elmo turned to Mike who had reached inside his shorts for a vigorous scratching.

"You heard me. What about knocking it off?"

"Hmmm, I don't think so," Mike said, "but I appreciate you fellows stopping by." He waved his hand as if to shoo them away. Soon, it was just Lorenz, Mike and AK-149 in the room.

"Nice how the mention of the SUV name strikes terror in the hearts of bureaucrats," AK-149 said.

"Like everyone has heard of the stupid Agents of Karnage, besides, it worked in the end. I didn't see you jumping in to assist."

"Assisting is not really one of the things A-Ks do. Hey, is this the weapon?" AK-149 spotted something on a chair buried under soiled clothing. He hauled it out. "This *is* it."

"How do you know about the bubble gun? I just invented it," Mike said.

"It's all over the Internet. Let me try it." AK-149 pointed and pressed the trigger-switch. "What's wrong? Is it busted?"

"Put it down. You have to turn it on and let it warm up first."

"How do I turn it on?"

"Give it over," Mike said. "You'll hurt yourself."

Petulant, AK-149 surrendered the weapon. "I could wreak a lot of carnage with a cool weapon like that."

"I believe he made it to assist the SUVs," Lorenz said with his hand out.

Mike handed it to Lorenz.

"Get me more hexavalent Cesium and I'll make more." He waggled his finger at AK-149. "And don't try to steal my design. You'll never get the standing wave bias right without my help."

AK-149 shrugged his shoulders and tried to look innocent. "Steal? Not the Agents of Karnage."

"I'd like to dematerialize you right now, but I guess that would be improper." To Mike, Lorenz said: "Show me how to work this thing."

Mike gave a short lecture. Lorenz kept his body between AK-149 and the weapon. "How long will it run? Will the charge run out?"

"Of course the charge runs out—it's not perpetual motion. If you use it a couple of times a day, we'll have to recharge it with a fresh fuel cell and more hexavalent Cesium in a few years. Maybe a decade; I'm not exactly sure. Now, if you don't mind, I'd like to get some sleep. Thanks."

Mike stuffed earplugs in his ears and pulled on a sleep mask. Soon, he snored like a diesel truck.

Lorenz and AK-149 exchanged a look.

"Nerds," AK-149 said with bitter irony in his voice.

Polly Patterson

Polly, dripping with sweat, made notations on her rehearsal tablet and listened to her stereo at high volume when she became aware of her ringing doorbell. This puzzled her—she rarely had visitors. She peeked through the window and opened the door when she recognized the young man from next door.

"Hey, sorry to bother you. My name is Roland Olson," he said.

"What's on your mind?"

The young man peeked inside the house.

"You were listening to Pink Floyd. Animals."

"Yes?"

"That's my favorite."

"Okay."

"I want to talk to you about something. Can I come in?"

Polly considered. Worn out, she was done rehearsing for the day.

"Okay," she said, standing aside to allow him to enter.

The living room was outfitted with mirrors and a suspended hardwood surface for dancing. Roland looked around with wonder.

"You're a dancer?"

"Yes."

"That's the rumor around the neighborhood. Do you have a video recording of your work I could look at?"

"What's the point?"

"Right," he said, making no effort to explain.

After a few moments of thought, Polly sighed. Her work was complicated. To most people, dance meant Saturday Night Fever or the Macarena. Sighing, she pointed the remote at her TV and selected a performance from a menu on the hard disk. In order to get rid of him, she picked the weirdest thing she could think of.

"This one is called Midnight Rendezvous. The girls in pink are supposed to be fairies and the boys in black are supposed to be trolls. It's a playful exploration of Victorian courtship rituals."

The video quality was marginal. With an all-black

stage background, pinpoint spotlights created pools of light on the stage. It became clear—all the dancers were played by Polly and overlaid with crude video processing. The soundtrack was performed by a string quartet, Roland did not recognize the piece. It segued between aggressive and percussive discord and sweet singing strings. Achingly beautiful. For a minute, he tried to hide it, but eventually let tears flow freely. The performance lasted ten minutes before fading out.

"My God, that was the most beautiful thing I've ever seen," he said. Polly handed him a box of tissues. He pulled out a clump and blotted his eyes. "Thank you for showing it to me."

"You really liked it?"

"Like it? I'll never be the same. It was astounding and incredible. Am I correct in noting Twyla Tharp's influence?"

"I studied her videos for years."

"Breathtaking, that's all I can say."

"I appreciate your kind words, but perhaps it's time you explain why you're here."

"Sure. My band signed a contract with Geffen records and we're planning our first video."

"No, thank you."

"You can't say no, you haven't heard the idea yet. Are you worried about budget? Our lawyer negotiated a great deal. We have funding, don't worry about that. We can pay."

"No. I work by myself and do things my own way."

"You don't understand. We'll let you do your thing,

believe me."

"I think David Geffen is a soulless corporate suit."

"He just approved the contract; he has nothing to say about our work. I told you, we have a great lawyer. The band is the hottest thing out of Seattle since Alice in Chains. We have the power to do this right."

"No, thank you."

"You can't say no until you hear the song."

"I already said no," Polly said.

Roland walked to her CD player, slipped in a disc and hit the *play* button. The music started with backwards guitar and twinkly sitar-like chords, then settled into a hammering beat. She counted out the rhythm; it was two cycles of 5/4 followed by a cycle of 6/4, then repeated. This was lucky for Roland, because she'd already decided that if the song was in 4/4 she'd throw him out on his ass.

You're the real thing, a boy wonder
A king of thieves, a viscous fluid thunder

The guitar player was slick and slippery and she loved the keyboard doubling of some of the fast melody lines mixed with sampled construction noises and machinery sounds. The music was dense and complex, like a heavy metal string quartet.

"I like the drumming. It's slinky, but has a lot of power."

"Thanks. I'm the drummer."

"Well, you're very good. I appreciate the offer, but I still don't want to do this."

"We'll give you a budget and complete creative control. Give us five minutes of four-year-olds tap dancing and that's what we'll use. It'll be your deal to run as you please."

She sighed. "I suppose it would be dumb to turn this down."

"You'll be famous, bigger than big. Geffen signed us because we sold 125,000 downloads on the Internet."

"I don't want to be famous. I want people to leave me alone so I can do my work."

"You can quit your job. I see you getting in your car in the morning when you could be working on your dancing."

"Give me a day to think it over. I'm not going to make a snap decision on something this vital."

"Thank you. I won't ask for more. I'll get a contract started just in case. For the record, I think you should say yes."

"We'll see. For now, please let me get back to work."

Roland walked toward the CD player.

"Leave the disc," she said.

Roland smiled. "Gotcha," he said.

He waved and walked to the door to let himself out.

"What do you guys call yourselves?"

"Nabokov's Hammer," he replied with a broad smile.

By the time the door closed, and before she was consciously aware of making the decision, she'd turned to a new page in her notebook and started preliminary sketches and diagrams.

CHAPTER FIFTEEN

Mike Thomas

SLOWLY, MIKE EMERGED from an uncomfortable sleep and the last dream tendrils evaporated. Lingering images included disjointed chase scenes, the embarrassment of appearing nude in public and an endless, terrifying fall from a high cliff, all typical subconscious madness. Lying in bed, he watched dust dancing in light beams streaming through a gap in his curtains. Slowly it occurred to him: it's Monday morning and he should get up and go to work.

I drift through the events of my life. Maybe no plan is a bad plan. Things are out of control. A week ago, I did my job, played in the lab at night and nobody bothered me. Now I star in mocking videos streaming around the world, strange people invade my bedroom, I may get fired and my life is, reportedly, in danger. How did this happen? How do I get off this carnival ride?

I should calm down and think. I'm under the questionable protection of the Sovereign Union of Vagabonds. What good is that? I could make more bubble guns, but would that help? I'm blind in a storm and I don't know which way to go. I'll die if I don't move, but I don't know which way to go.

His belly grumbled. Looking around the room he spotted an apple on his nightstand. It was soft and shriveled, but might be edible. If he could break free of his paralyzed muscles, he could reach out, grab the apple and eat it. Then, the rest of the day might follow in sequence and he'd get through. But his arm would not move. After a moment of panic, he realized he'd slept on the arm and, tingling, it was asleep. Slowly, he flexed his fingers and stretched.

The apple was grainy and had large brown spots, but he ate it anyway, then discarded the core on the floor. The apple did not help; now he was thirsty—parched—and desperately craving a cool glass of water. A glass rested on the nightstand, but it was empty and bore a film of dust on the bottom. If he was going to drink, he would have to get up. And, once he was up, he might as well go to work. Gradually, this became the plan. After a long draught of tap water while standing in his kitchen, he pulled on clothing and headed to work.

It's ten o'clock and I'm late, but who cares? The world is hell-bound. What difference will it make if I'm tardy?

Madison Howard and Harris Stanwood

Madison made her fourth call to the receiving inspection area and listened to the reply to her query.

"No, Madison, Mike is not in yet. Do you want me to call him at home?"

She made eye contact with Harris Stanwood, who walked in and plopped into her visitor's chair.

"No, that won't be necessary," she said into the receiver before placing it in its cradle. "Hello, Harris. I'm sorry to hear about your father—he was a great man."

"Mostly he was a pain in the ass and an embarrassment. Half the people around here didn't even know who he was. I need to quit this company. I started working here when I was eight. As a kid, Pop made me carry out trash and scrub bathrooms. But why should I move to another company because of an accident of birth? I'm tired of struggling with everything."

"How are things going in marketing? Can you give me a hint about new product requirements coming down the line?"

"We do endless focus-group studies. We may have to buy a startup company to get innovative new products. It's depressing. We used to be able to invent things. But, that's not why I'm here. My dad was protective of Mike Thomas and I understand he reports to you."

"Don't start. Mike is on his way out. Do you know what it will cost to repair the damage he caused in the lab? To replace the equipment he ruined? He didn't even bother to show up for work today. Don't tell me you'll stick your neck out to protect him."

Harris scratched his bald head. "I never saw the fascination. Whatever Mike did to get this company started happened a long time ago. Ancient history, water under the bridge. However, I told Dad I'd watch out for him, so here I am. Consider Mike a protected species. Hands off."

"Excuse me a moment," Madison said. She fluffed her hair and pulled an atomizer from her desk drawer. She stretched her neck and sprayed a shot behind each ear. Leaning back in her chair, she adjusted her stockings, which caused the long length of her firm thighs and calves to be prominently displayed. She flapped the lapels of her blouse so the tops of her freckled breasts stroboscopically appeared and disappeared.

"It is just me, or is it warm in here?"

"Son of a bitch," Harris complained bitterly. "Does everyone know about my divorce?"

"Afraid so. Sorry."

Harris shifted uncomfortably in his chair.

"Knock it off. You win. It's not fair, the power a beautiful woman holds over a man. I told my father I'd do what I could to look out for Mike."

"You did what you could, but it didn't work. Not your fault. Listen, if you want him on *your* budget, I'll transfer him. Say the word."

Harris considered.

"We're having trouble maintaining the current head count. Wait until Dad's body cools in his grave?"

"No," Madison said, "I don't think so."

Wearily, Harris got up. Madison stroked her legs with slim fingers bearing crimson-painted fingernails.

"I don't suppose you'd go out with me on Friday night?" he asked.

"Go away," Madison said, pointing down the hallway.

Rob, hovering nearby, pretended to read a memo posted on a bulletin board. When Harris was safely away, he poked his head in Madison's office.

"What did Harris want?"

"He tried to save Mike's job."

"Did it work?"

"No. Mike is toast." She swiveled to get her legs off the desk and Rob got an accidental view up her skirt.

"About Friday, has your schedule settled so I can confirm reservations for our date?"

"Not yet. Give me a couple more days."

"Sure, Maddy," Rob said with a pained look on his face. "Let me know as soon as you can."

"I will. The instant I can commit, I will. Now beat it, I'm busy."

Agent AK-149 Sends an email

To: AK-18, Supervisor of Field Operations
From: Agent AK-149
Subject: Notes on Mike Thomas

First, I hope you'll reconsider rejecting coffee shop entries on my expense report. Everyone uses Starbucks as a remote office. The $268 I spent since I arrived should not be considered unusual. Business is transacted this way in Seattle. I urge you to reinstate those reimbursements. Thank you.

In the matter of Mike Thomas, I have great respect for his ability to initiate chaos. Please note the attached Internet hyperlinks. In particular, the most recent video that shows the anti-proton bubble gun in action. I have seen this gun and I believe, no matter how easy it is to fake such a thing and how bogus the video looks, that the events depicted are real. Mike's potential for advancing the randomness of the universe is boundless. I understand the needs of our clients and that we require funding to continue operations, but we must maintain balance. What benefit comes from acting against our philosophy for money?

I ask management to consider my comments and review the decision to randomize Mike Thomas. In the meantime, I'll be waiting for instructions.

To: AK-149, Field Agent
From: Agent AK-18, Supervisor of Field Operations
Re: Subject: Notes on Mike Thomas

Tomorrow, at the executive roundtable session, we will discuss your comments about Mike Thomas. Hold off on randomizing him until we review our contractual options. Remember, we often compromise and take counter-intuitive steps in the greater cause of global chaos.

PS: Your Starbucks charges are still denied. In addition, we're concerned about miscellaneous and entertainment expenses. Please provide justification or these expenses will also be declined.

Mike Thomas and Madison Howard

Rubbing grainy deposits from the corners of his eyes, Mike walked, heavy-footed, down the hallway toward the company cafeteria. He bought a large coffee and two bagels, and then walked toward his work area, sipping and nibbling. While passing a computer screen, he glimpsed his image cavorting on a security video loop—partially dressed with hair standing on end. After pressing the computer reset button, the image disappeared. The computer's owner, a cubicle troll, wouldn't meet his eye.

Someone waved over the cubicle partitions. Mike sighed when he saw it was Madison. It was clear, if he took evasive action, she would just head him off at the junction of corridors, so he acknowledged her with a listless wave and walked toward her office. He could muster energy to inspect incoming mechanical parts, but not to deal with the petty corporate trivia Madison represented. There was a bright, glittery gleam in her eye Mike had not seen before. In fact, she glowed in shades of pink (skin, lipstick, nail polish and blouse) and auburn (hair, skirt and eyes).

For the first time, it occurred to Mike that a woman might spend time coordinating clothing and makeup. It seemed like an incredible waste of time. He did a quick calculation and estimated that 295,000 acres of corn could be cultivated with the hourly effort women applied to their hair and makeup, but gave up on the calculation when he realized he'd have to adjust for added productivity from farmers who worked harder to please well-groomed women. He sighed.

If only life could be as simple as temporal-gravitron antiproton four-dimensional mathematics and space-time system modeling approximations...

He abandoned that train of thought to focus on the

here-and-now of Madison's office.

"Good morning, Mike. Did you have problems getting to work this morning? You're later than usual. A flat tire? Medical emergency? A convergence of events beyond your control?"

"I'm sorry, Madison. I was up late and couldn't drag myself out of bed."

"Indeed, you *were* up late last night. I've seen the videos. Very amusing. I want you to know some folks are impressed with your magic show, but I'm not one of them."

"Okay."

"What I really want to talk about is the sad passing of our beloved founder, Stanwood."

"Yeah, he was a decent old guy. Thanks for reminding me. I should attend his funeral. His wife used to bake for me, but she's been deceased for many years. Nice lady. Nothing against the current wife, I don't know her."

"I didn't call you over to talk about the funeral or his family. Stanwood protected your job, but now he can't meddle in my group's operation. The wheels of corporate karma will roll freely, if you'll forgive the weak metaphor."

"I'm not sure I follow your point."

"My point is, I sent in the paperwork to finalize your termination. All that remains is formality. You're fired. A security guard will escort you to your desk and watch while you collect your personal belongings. Don't try to walk out with any company property. You'll be asked to come back for an exit interview. Otherwise, that's it, you're finished. Your final paycheck will be direct-deposited into your bank account. Do you have questions or comments?"

Mike slumped in his chair, stunned. He reached into his back pocket and pulled out a ragged checkbook. "I suppose I should settle up, then." He scribbled a check to Pacific ElectroMed and handed it over. She had to look twice at the amount.

$67,350.

"What's this for?"

"I rounded it off, but that's close to the right amount. This will cover supplies I ordered on the company account, mainly hexavalent Cesium."

"I knew it had to be you, but I couldn't prove it. You're lucky I don't file formal legal charges. Perhaps I will. Besides, this doesn't begin to cover the cost of the Gallium-Heisenbach X-ray Diffractometer you destroyed."

"That money needs to come from another account. I don't keep that kind of money in checking. Don't worry about it, I'll take care of it. In fact, I don't have anything at my desk that I care about, so why don't I just leave now? I'll stop and say goodbye to Polly and a few other folks on my way out."

"Please hand over your badge and card keys."

"Sure." Mike produced the items and Madison slid them across her desk until they fell in her desk drawer. Mike got up. "This is farewell then."

He strode away.

"Wait. You're not going anywhere without an escort." She scrambled to keep up with him. "Wait until I find a security guard."

"What are you going to do? Fire me?"

Mike walked out. Teetering on high heels, she trailed along behind him. He walked by Polly's desk, but it was vacant. He exchanged hugs with a few older folks scattered around the building. None seemed surprised he'd been fired. Madison did not know most of them, though she'd seen them lurking in the hallways. She wouldn't have guessed he had so many friends, but there were damp eyes, heartfelt hugs and futile promises to stay in touch. Finally, Mike threaded though the crowd toward the front door. He turned to face Madison.

"Take care."

"You too," she replied, and that was it.

Mike walked out the front door.

Madison tried to enjoy her grand victory, but it seemed empty and sad. She walked back to her office.

Outside, Mike saw Lorenz wave from his Escalade.

"We need to talk," Lorenz said.

"Okay," Mike replied.

Inside, Madison collapsed behind her desk and stared vacantly at her computer screen. When she looked up, Harris Stanwood hovered over her.

"I heard about Mike," he said.

"Yes, it's final. Now I need to get a requisition in place to hire someone else."

"You shouldn't have done it. It turns out Dad talked to the Board of Directors and they are working on an employment contract for him. It was Dad's final wish."

"I don't think so. Mike's gone and he won't be coming back." In a flash of inspiration, she blurted out: "Besides, I didn't fire him, he resigned. There was nothing I could do to talk him out of it."

"Crap on a cupcake. I don't believe you."

"Are you threatening me? I'll slap you with a sexual harassment lawsuit faster than an ex-wife can find a lottery winner. Now, get out of here, I have paperwork to catch up on." She realized she was screeching like a harpy.

Not attractive or professional.

She wasn't sure where the defiance came from. The Board of Directors could flick her aside like a bug. Could she sell the lie that Mike resigned? *Maybe.* In her heart, she knew keeping Mike on the payroll was not the way to run a modern company in the 21st century. There must be some way this would work out for her.

There simply had to be.

House Resolution 57A7C

House Resolution 57A7C. Declaring certain temporal-gravitational activities to be prohibited. Whereas perturbations in the temporal gravitational continuum disturb worldwide clock references, this resolution will prohibit temporal particle fusion experiments and other related activities unless approved and issued a permit by the National Institute of Science and Technology.

Enforcement.

(1)   The NIST, with the assistance of the attorney general, may sue in courts of competent jurisdiction to enjoin any threatened or continuing violations of any permits or conditions thereof without the necessity of a prior revocation of the permit;

(2)   The department may enter any premises in which an temporal gravitational perturbations are created or in which records are required to be kept under terms or conditions of a permit, and otherwise be able to investigate, inspect, or monitor any suspected violations of temporal-gravitational quality standards or limitations, or of permits or terms or conditions thereof;

(3)   The department may assess or, with the assistance of the attorney general, sue to recover in court, such civil fines, penalties, and other civil relief as may be appropriate for the violation by any person of (a) any temporal-gravitational perturbation standards and limitations or temporal quality standards, (b) any permit or term or condition thereof, (c) any filing requirements, (d) any duty to permit or carry out inspection, entry, or

(4)   monitoring activities, or (e) any rules, regulations, or orders issued by the department.

(4)   The department may request the prosecuting attorney to seek criminal sanctions for the violation by such persons of (a) any temporal standards and limitations, (b) any permit or term or condition thereof, (c) any filing requirements.

(5)   The department, with the assistance of the prosecuting attorney, may seek criminal sanctions against any person who knowingly makes any false statement, representation, or certification in any form or any notice or report required by the terms and conditions of any issued permit or knowingly renders inaccurate any monitoring device or method required to be maintained by the department.

Elmo shook hands with his congressional representative.

"Thanks for taking time to see me," he said.

"Always a pleasure."

"Can you give me an honest assessment of the House Resolution's prospect?"

The congressman sighed, "Not good, I'm afraid. Most people can't understand what you propose or the nature of the public hazard related the creation of temporal-gravitational fluxions. It would be better if there was real property damage you could point to."

"It screws up the GPS system."

"So you say, but only a few inches for a short time. Does this create a serious problem? The congressman from Hawaii claims he found a constitutional right to create fluxions and the congressman from Wyoming wants the right protected for religious reasons. If we could explain it more clearly, maybe we could get more votes, but the way things stand, there is no hope. I'm sorry."

"Crap," Elmo said. "We'll allow citizens to create temporal-gravitational time-space disruptions as much as they please? This is insane. We're flirting with epochal disaster."

"I'm really sorry. Bring us a bill to protect kangaroo rats or butterflies, we understand those things and can work with proposals like that, but this thing? We don't know what to do with it."

"So, that's it? There's nothing else we can do?"

"Sorry."

"I understand. Thanks for trying. If the cosmic fabric rips asunder and the earth decomposes into individual atoms flying apart faster than the speed of gravity, don't come crying to me."

With that, Elmo gathered his papers and walked out of the office.

CHAPTER SIXTEEN

Agent AK-149 Embraces Chaos

WHILE SITTING AT the breakfast bar of the Village Green restaurant, Trent—Agent AK-149—read a folded newspaper and lustily consumed a pancake drenched in butter and syrup when he was interrupted by a tap on the shoulder. He turned to find two bulked-up men dressed in construction clothing, heavy leather boots and plaster-streaked overalls. It was not yet eight o'clock in the morning, but these men wore dark glasses.

"Can I assist you gentlemen in some manner?" Trent asked.

"We'd like to have a word with you outside," the slightly larger of the two men said.

Warning bells rang in his head, but he didn't see an option. They could drag him out and Trent did not want to use his weapons in public unless absolutely necessary. Better to get these guys out of sight, neutralize them, and then dispose of their bodies. One of the men tossed bills on the counter as if they were not coming back. They walked out single-file. Following, Trent noticed the man's haircut was incongruously fresh and precise and his hands were pink and manicured. He was not a working-class laborer.

Outside, a white van idled. The sliding door rumbled open and it took two seconds for them to hoist him in like a sack of dog food. After his hands were painfully tied behind his back, duct tape was slapped over his eyes and mouth. Trent thought about the error of his ways as they cut off his clothes, took his watch and jewelry, and left him completely naked, and worse, helpless. He had weapons, but they were hidden in his coat.

Fundamental to our training is varying our routine. If I have one thing to blame, it's blueberry pancakes. The restaurant laid out dispensers of real maple syrup, used fresh blueberries in the pancakes and served them with genuine, dairy-churned butter. They were so good that I came back for more over and over. A big mistake. In addition, I found too many of my clients there.

He wracked his brain to think of which victim led to his downfall. There were many.

In particular, he remembered a girl walking through the parking lot toward a private Christian school housed in the strip mall. She carried a metal lunch box with a ham and cheese sandwich. The crusts were carefully trimmed off. The sandwich was delicious. The ultimate fate of the little girl in the hands of the middle-eastern men he sold her to, must have been unpleasant. Perhaps these were her father and uncles? There were many civilians with reason to be upset with him.

After driving for nearly an hour—rising in altitude

and getting further from the busy suburbs, the van pulled off the highway and immediately yawed and slewed on rough roads for a few minutes. When they stopped, Trent, naked, was thrown from the van into cold mud and slush. They dragged him through underbrush and held him down with his bare ass sticking over a splintery stump.

"Who are you avenging?" Trent asked.

"Do you remember selling marijuana cigarettes to a young man behind the Sunset Bowling Alley?"

I remember the kid.

He had jet-black hair, fake tattoos and a skateboard covered in macabre decals. The weed had been sprayed with a chemical causing a permanent psychosis. The kid was probably screaming in a padded room somewhere. This was one of his more delicious Random Acts of Karnage.

"There is a cure, a remedy," Trent said hopefully.

Maybe there's a way out of this.

"No there isn't, asshole. We had a dozen doctors look at him."

Then again, maybe not.

Trent experienced a shock to his left leg at the same time he heard a loud 'thock', the sound of an axe embedded in a stump. He did not like the resonance of the word *stump* as it echoed through his mind. He felt nothing. There was another 'thock', then he was released. However, he still couldn't move. Then they did something cruel, they pulled the tape off his eyes.

A small clearing in the middle of a thick evergreen forest. Wisps of misty clouds clung to the tops of tall trees. He saw patches of white snow contrasted with a bright cascade of gushing blood where his feet had been. He tried to scream, but the tape on his mouth allowed only muffled grunts. Then, inevitable, brutal pain washed through his body. He did not know embracing chaos could be so horrible and harsh.

It took an eternal minute for the loss of blood and the cold to sap his consciousness. One of the men suggested he should "Rot in hell, bastard," before his eyes and ears failed.

He sensed the van reversing and leaving him alone with the pitiless, throbbing universe. His last thought was the hope that the A-Ks were right and death was empty and black with no heaven or purgatory where souls were punished for unreconciled sins. No eternal hell. It was funny, but he seemed to be praying for vast emptiness and wondering if this prayer would be answered and, if so, by whom.

Lorenz Hartz and Mike Thomas

Lorenz pulled the Escalade to a stop in front of a small house in a lower-middle-class neighborhood between Bellevue and Renton. Wind whipped at the large vehicle; it rocked on its springs.

"I have a problem. I just got fired," Mike said. "What will I do?"

"There's a bigger problem. That agent? Trent? AK-149? He was found dead up on Snoqualmie Pass."

"What happened to him?"

"It doesn't matter. The problem is that his replacement is already in town."

"What happened to him?"

Lorenz signed. "You can't take a hint? Very well, he bled to death after his feet were chopped off."

"Oh, that's harsh. Is that how underground groups do their work? Is there a Secret Fraternal Order of Foot Choppers?"

"No. We suspect this was revenge for one of his Random Acts of Karnage. Perhaps a victim's family tracked him down? We may never know. Murders like this are common and are rarely solved if the murderers use common sense about leaving evidence behind. The cops are lazy and too busy writing profitable traffic tickets to spend time or effort on a case like this. Unless his family is rich or famous or the media stirs up a manure-storm, it will fade into history like margarine melting into toast."

"Margarine melting into toast? Isn't that a little florid?"

"Sorry, I didn't eat breakfast this morning. The bottom line is this: AK-149 is history and now we need to worry about his boss, AK-18. You probably think the A-Ks are cute and harmless, but that's dead wrong. They can be dangerous."

"AK-149 could have killed me many times."

"That's not the way they work. Almost always, they do things indirectly. They set up situations where the odds stack against you. However, sometimes they accept a contract and kill for money. We think a contract like that has been placed on you."

"Why would anyone want to kill me?"

"You still don't get it, do you? Your work threatens the established order. Over the last decade, there have been discoveries that promise clean energy in vast amounts. Cold fusion or whatever you want to call it. Power companies, oil companies, automobile companies and world governments all profit from the current petroleum-based economy. They don't want cheap, decentralized power sources. Hundreds of physicists have either been killed or quietly stopped working on breakthrough technologies. That's why we believe a contract has been placed on your head. The A-Ks have a cult-like religious belief that they are on this earth to increase chaos, so we don't know if they've decided there is more chaos by allowing your work to progress or if they should earn the contract paycheck."

"I'm starting to get it. Trent was a goof-off, but this AK-18 is a different breed."

"Exactly."

"Will you be able to protect me?"

"I will place my body between you and a bullet if I can. But that's all I can offer. It's not much and, frankly, the odds are poor. If you have a better plan, I suggest you execute it. Run and hide. Stop your research. Maybe you should publish a retraction and tell the world your ideas were wrong."

"I don't like those suggestions. What's *your* plan? Where are we and why are we here?"

"This house," Lorenz said, gesturing, "is Polly's place."

"Polly Patterson? What does she have to do with anything?"

"She is also under my protection. I can protect you better if I keep you together."

"Oh. Is Polly okay with the idea?"

"I haven't asked her yet. Let's see what she says."

"Oh," Mike said.

As they walked up the sidewalk, music became more audible. Windows shook in their frames. Lorenz pressed the doorbell. The curtains flicked and the music stopped. Polly pressed her face into a three-inch opening as the door strained against its security chain.

"I'm in the middle of something, guys. Come back later."

"Let us in, Polly," Mike said. "We need to talk."

She mulled over the idea, then resigned herself to the idea of opening the door.

"Very well," she said.

She wore a sheer body stocking soaked through with perspiration. It was hard not to stare; the damp fabric was more revealing than nudity. She wiped her forehead with a towel and drank deeply from a plastic water bottle.

"You weren't at work today," Mike mentioned.

"I called in sick."

"Ah," Mike said, looking around the living room and noting its functional dance-studio austerity.

"Please excuse us for barging in. There are events we need to discuss…"

"Let me do this," Mike interrupted. "We're going to get killed directly or indirectly and Lorenz says he can protect us better if we stick together. So, we're moving in."

Polly stood up and paced. "First of all, any danger to you has nothing to do with me. Yes, I find you attractive and cute, but that doesn't mean I'll open my house to you. I'm working on a dance project and I need time and solitude to get it done. I will not allow anything to interfere with my life's work. I agreed to this project and there is a deadline for the video shoot. I have to finish instructions for twelve dancers, set up cues and design sets, create backdrops and define stage lighting. Rehearsals start with principal dancers tomorrow. Meddling and distraction will not be tolerated. I want you to leave immediately."

"Wasn't that a nice speech?" Mike asked Lorenz. Then he addressed Polly. "I'll order pizza. Do you have any beer? How many beds does this place have? What are the sleeping arrangements? And, which way to the toilet, I need to crap out a loaf."

Flustered, Polly stared at Mike's back as he wandered down the hallway looking for the bathroom. "Keep it down while I'm working, do you read me?"

She turned the stereo back on and, with her eyes closed, waved her hand in the air to recapture the beat. When finished with the bathroom, Mike wandered through the kitchen and found cold cans of Diet Pepsi in the refrigerator. He flopped on the couch with Lorenz and watched as Polly, pointedly ignoring them, stopped and started the music, made notes and practiced vignettes until she was satisfied. Lorenz and Mike sipped their drinks and watched the scene with wide eyes.

Agent AK-18 Arrives in Seattle

AK-18, whose real name was Arthur—Artie—Pike, did not carry much in his wallet; no driver's license or personal pictures. The only form of identification he carried was a U.S. passport tucked in an inside jacket pocket. His wallet held a trust-fund debit card and several hundred dollars in cash. Aside from Pedro, everything about him was shiny and sterile, although, tucked deep under a flap in his wallet, he'd irrationally saved a newspaper clipping.

Freak Accident Kills Eleven

ZBS News – North American Herald-Star

Two Sunday school buses collided near Grand Mesa on Highway 65. Eleven were killed in the fiery crash. From the police report, the Saint Mary's Church bus from Lowell Parish was traveling downhill when it hit a patch of black ice. The bus hit the Lutheran Children's Outreach bus and both rolled down a 250 foot grade. Several children were thrown clear of the crash and survived. "There was no way the Saint Mary's bus could stop," said Burt Zinn of the Whitewater Volunteer Fire Department. "I'll never forget the sight; there were little kids scattered everywhere."

Across the bottom of the clipping, Artie had written in block letters:

IF GOD EXISTS, I LOVE HIS SENSE OF HUMOR

Artie was a small man, about five-feet-four-inches, though he appeared taller due to lifts in his ornate, custom-made Gila boots. He wore a bulky black overcoat, which contained a special pocket for Pedro, his Mexican Ringtail Cat. Pedro traveled with him everywhere. His anal musk organs were surgically removed, so he did not stink. A quiet animal, the loudest sound it made was a cat-like hissing when upset. Artie never had trouble carrying Pedro around; the jacket-nest was waterproofed and lined with cotton padding to absorb urine. During the day, the nocturnal animal happily shredded cotton and slept most of the time.

Warily scanning the milling airport crowds, Artie strolled through Sea-Tac until he found the baggage claim area. A man, dressed professionally in a black suit, held up a sign that said: Pike. Artie followed him to a black Lincoln Towncar that idled at the curb. The driver smoothly opened the door and Artie slid inside. Per his request, a cold bottle of Diet Dr. Pepper and a New York Times, with all the advertising inserts removed, waited. Artie unfurled the paper and scanned headlines while waiting for the driver to locate and load his luggage. Soon, they headed for downtown Seattle where his suite at the M Hotel awaited.

Artie liked the M because of its central Seattle location. The beds were as comfortable as the imported Italian mattresses he slept on at home. The noisy bar and the dark hallways didn't bother him. It didn't take long to get known as a big tipper, so room service was snappy and the food was hot and the beer cold when his orders showed up at his door.

He was tense from the flight and recent events, so he palmed the concierge a c-note and asked him to send someone up for a complete massage with a happy ending. He never got tired of hearing the words: 'Yes, sir.'

After changing into the hotel bathrobe, he finished a blood-rare, room-service steak topped with grilled onions. Pedro hyperactively ran around the room; his little claws clicked on the tiles like grains of rice on a tin roof. Artie tossed slivers of steak and cantaloupe which Pedro acrobatically grabbed from the air.

The girl showed up at ten o'clock; perfect, slender and wearing a slinky satin dress that showed off jiggly tits and thong panties. In particular, Artie noted, her dental work was stunning, someone had spent forty or fifty grand on bright whitecaps. They quickly negotiated a rate that insured he wouldn't have to listen to her bitch about messing up her hair or makeup. Like most people, she was surprised to see a little skunk running around, but quickly accepted the explanation that he couldn't spray. She petted his soft fur and made baby talk to him. Artie tossed off his bathrobe and told her to skin down. She was a good sport and didn't complain when Pedro licked her and nosed around her private parts.

In the bathroom, the shower stall was so immense it echoed. Artie ran the water steaming hot and stepped in. The girl washed him thoroughly until his skin turned red, tingling on the near side of pain. She left off soaping up his groin for last, per his suggestion. Just for laughs, he dropped the soap to see if she'd slip and crack her skull, but she had a dancer's grace and was uninjured by this silly random act of chaos.

After, he was ready to sleep, but stayed awake long enough for her to blow him while Pedro nuzzled her neck and licked her ear. Her technique was serviceable, though uncreative. Artie was dead-tired, so he didn't complain. She wanted to stay and blow-dry her hair, but he told her to beat it. He gave her another hundred bucks to erase the pouty look on her face. Soon, she was gone. Like a little prince, Pedro made a nest of shredded toilet paper and one of the M's expensive pillows and quietly slept beside him on the king-sized bed.

Madison Howard in an Executive Staff Meeting

With thumbs working vigorously, Madison created an instant message for Rob.

'Meeting Garden Court 11:00. B there. W/Eli.'

He replied: 'Conflict. Sorry.'

Madison's hands clenched into claws. She barely resisted scratching deep, bloody welts in her face. Slowly, she regained composure. Taking a deep, cleansing breath, she typed:

'B there or date = cancelled.'

Sensing a bargaining position, Rob wanted to ask about her attitude toward having sex on a second date, but he refrained. Only a smooth man would get sex with Madison. A cultured and patient man. Unless...unless he could slip something into her drink that would make her pliable and responsive to his advances. He'd surf the Internet and see what he could find. He cursed himself for not thinking of this strategy earlier. It seemed to work well for CB.

He responded: 'we = there'

Madison hid in a ladies room stall until she was a few minutes late. When she arrived, the room was nearly full. She tossed her schedule book on the table and greeted everyone briskly and politely. She scanned the room to gauge her odds. The room was stacked four-to-two in her favor, with Rob, software manager Eli Trivedi and her friend and former college roommate Brenda Swensen from the legal department on her side. Harris Stanwood was present, but he should, at worst, be neutral. She exchanged firm handshakes with the company President, Emmett Friaf and one of the Directors, Boris Plotnik.

Once they were seated, Emmett spoke first.

"I don't recall inviting everyone. This was intended to be a meeting between Madison, Boris and I."

You'd like that, wouldn't you? Two-to-one odds against me. Kangaroo court. Massacre. Witch hunt.

"I'm sorry if I misunderstood. You were a little sketchy on details, but I believe the meeting topic is the termination of Mike Thomas, so I invited the responsible management team."

This was the crux; the meeting's balancing point. Rob squirmed uncomfortably, but Madison glared at him until he settled down. He stared out the window into the trees. Brenda was cool under pressure and quick on the uptake.

"Could we get started? I have a web conference with the legal team in Houston at noon. A wrongful death case took a turn for the worse and could impact next quarter's revenue and stock price."

Thank you Brenda. These assholes only care about things that affect their golden parachutes, the value of their stock options and their year-end bonuses.

Emmett and Boris exchanged a long glance. They might be self-centered and ineffectual modern corporate executives, but they were not stupid.

"Very well," Boris said. "We're also on a tight schedule, so let's boil this down. We want you to call Mike Thomas, apologize, and offer him his job back. This request is not optional. Let us know when this is done. Sooner is better than later. Thank you for coming on such short notice."

He stood in a crude attempt to bring the meeting to an end.

"With all due respect, Mr. Plotnik," Madison said while pulling a stack of paperwork from a hanging folder. Boris sighed and sat back down. Madison continued calmly. "I kept track of Mike's schedule for the last year.

199

He violated the corporate core hour requirement twenty-three times. He was reported for sleeping in the Corridor E building maintenance closet six times, which is a violation of company policy. He came to work in an intoxicated state. He improperly filled out a lab notebook and left it unsecured. I have documented this in detail and submitted reports and eye witness validation to the HR group."

"That's very impressive, Madison, but…"

"Please allow me to finish, sir. We have security video recordings that show unauthorized use of company equipment and damage to facilities and in particular the destruction of our Gallium-Heisenbach X-Ray Diffractometer." She emphasized her points by tapping her painted fingernails on the table. "He ordered expensive chemicals and rare earth materials with company purchase requisitions. As an aside, if I might ask, what is hexavalent Cesium, how is it different from regular Cesium, and why does it cost seventeen-thousand-dollars a gram? Please don't answer, I'm being rhetorical. He cost us almost two million dollars this year. I have all the backup data. The point is, I followed company bylaws and personnel procedures to the letter. This man is a loose cannon, a danger to company operations and perhaps to the public at large. He violates company policy with reckless disregard and disrupts the important day-to-day activities that make this company profitable."

"Is it possible she doesn't know?" Emmett asked.

Boris shrugged. "Did you know Mike paid all that money back?"

"That's impossible. We're talking about millions of dollars."

"He has a trust account. After he invented the pain-management electrodes, he was granted company stock that split eleven times and was fully-vested when United Diversified Technology acquired us. He's among our largest stock-holders. Are you really so ignorant?"

Madison's mind froze. On the outside, she was calm, but inside, she visualized her career crashing in flames.

The damn loser was rich and powerful?

Inconceivable.

"Excuse me, but I didn't see anything in the company policy handbook that provides special treatment for stock holders and secret millionaires. I fired him and I'll scream bloody murder to the ethics board, the industry press and in-person at the stock-holder's meeting if the termination is reversed."

There it was.

In the silence, she scanned the faces around the table. Expressions varied from Rob's sheer terror, Harris Stanwood's evident desire to be anywhere else and Emmett's look of amused indifference.

"It may not be my place, but I agree with Madison on this," Rob said. He tried to mask it, but nervousness and hesitation were evident in his voice.

"Of course, Madison's right; it's a waste of executive management time and effort to even question the decision," Brenda said.

A fragment of an old maxim drifted through her mind.

Be bold and mighty forces will come to your aid.

In her head, these words echoed like a sad epitaph.

"We agree, Madison. We'll withdraw our objection to your decision. Good work," Emmett said. "Let's adjourn," he suggested to Boris. Boris looked puzzled, but shrugged his shoulders.

"As you wish," Boris said, while rising. He shook hands around the table. "It's been most interesting," he said.

"Madison, please stay behind for a minute," Emmett suggested.

She sat back down and smoothed her skirt. After everyone else filed out, Emmett got up and closed the conference room door.

"That was quite a performance," he said.

"Thank you," she replied.

"While sitting here, a thought crossed my mind. My wife is taking our daughter to Italy for a couple of weeks before she heads off to college. Florence and Venice if my memory serves. During that time, I have the use of the company's Citation biz jet. Stop me if I presume too much, but I wonder if you might join me for a long weekend someplace exotic and private, like Sandals Royal Bahamian Spa Resort, for example."

"Are you talking about a once-only on-the-quiet getaway? A weekend of unfettered intimacy, and then we're done? A top-secret one-off tryst?"

"Yes, that's precisely my thinking."

"How many Viagras are we talking about?"

"I hadn't thought about it. I'd take a bottle, I guess."

"Bullshit. I'll allow you everything you can manage on two hundred-milligram pills."

"I understand." He considered the offer. "Let's say four."

"Three," Madison said firmly.

Emmett looked into her eyes.

"Very well. I agree. If I might make an observation—I predict you'll enjoy a long and successful career."

Sure, until my skin gets flabby, my tits sag and old perverts turn their sights toward a younger, fresher generation.

"As a down payment, might I touch you briefly in an intimate manner?"

Madison stood and gathered her papers.

"Not a chance," she said flatly. "No freebies."

She turned, opened the door and walked out, leaving Emmett to stare out the window with a wry smile flitting across his face.

CHAPTER SEVENTEEN

The Sanctuary

IN THE KITCHEN—on the back corner of a shelf—Lorenz found a bag of popcorn kernels hidden behind antique cans of chicken noodle soup. He used an iron skillet to pop the corn before garnishing it with salt and a drizzle of melted butter. He poured the popcorn into a bowl and flopped on the couch. Angrily unselfconscious, Polly ran snippets of music repeatedly while making notes on her tablet. It was impossible not to notice the curves and surfaces of her sleek form; her damp leotard seemed vacuum-formed. She writhed and gyrated as if flaunting youthful vigor and slim femininity. Lorenz pinched Mike's arm to get his attention.

"Ouch. What?" Mike said.

"We're in trouble. I believe the A-Ks will accept the contract to kill us."

"You're the bodyguard. What do you expect me to do about it?"

"We need weapons."

"I built you a bubble gun."

Lorenz looked sheepish and embarrassed.

"It's an interesting weapon, but not an effective one. Besides, I shipped it to Shanghai to be analyzed and redesigned for volume manufacturing."

"That's frigging great. Now what am I supposed to do?"

"I took liberties, I bought a case of optical remotes that could be used to trigger booby traps. We could build a defensive perimeter."

"I don't have the right supplies or equipment."

Lorenz had a proud glint in his eyes. He pulled a small metal vial from his coat pocket.

"I imagine you'll need hexavalent Cesium…" he said.

"Hey, where'd you get that? You should be careful, it's radioactive."

"I know."

"What about lab facilities? I can't build weapons out of hexavalent Cesium, popcorn and diet soda," Mike said, while gesturing with a greasy handful of popcorn and his can of pop.

"Maybe I presume too much, but I'll bet you still have a badge or two that will get you into Pacific ElectroMed. Lost badges?" He waved a keycard. "Like this one I found in your car…"

"Might work," Mike said, deep in thought. "I have an idea, something interesting to try."

Polly, breathing deeply from exertion, flopped on the couch and grabbed a handful of popcorn. "What are you brainiacs whispering about? Some grand plan to save our collective asses, I hope."

"Mike is going back to the lab to build weapons," Lorenz said.

"Polly, about your dancing…"

"Your uneducated opinion means nothing."

"I want to pay you a compliment. I had no idea you were so talented and graceful."

"Good or bad, your ignorant opinion still means nothing, so shut up."

"I just want to say…"

"I said, shut the hell up. I don't comment on the props for your scientific magic show and you don't comment about my kinetic body designs. Uneducated commentary is background noise and a waste of my time."

"Okay," Mike replied. "I get it."

"I'm going to rinse off in the shower and then jump in the hot tub," Polly said, while wiping her forehead and tousling her hair with a towel. "You guys can join me or not, but rinse off the stink first. I don't want my water smelling like rancid nerd."

"I don't have a swim suit," Mike commented.

Polly unlaced her shoes, pulled them off and arced them into a corner. She stood and peeled off her tights. Mike and Lorenz, shocked, sat frozen with hands clutching clumps of popcorn on approach to their mouths.

"If we're going to live together, we might as well get over irrational modesty. I don't have a problem with nudity, do you?"

She turned and walked toward the bathroom with the

firm muscles of her buttocks clenching and releasing under her creamy skin.

"Holy shit," Mike said, stunned.

"Ain't she something?" Lorenz said.

"I get the shower first," Mike said before cramming his mouth with popcorn.

Peeking through the sunroom doorway, Mike watched Polly relax in the hot tub with her head tilted back and her eyes closed. The greenhouse-glass windows were steamed up and the hot water burbled.

With her eyes closed, she said, "Watch your step; there's condensation. If you're not careful, you'll fall and break your ass."

Walking gingerly, Mike dropped the towel at the last possible instant and tried to slip in the water before she looked, but her eyes popped open. She examined him openly.

"I can stand to lose a few pounds," he said.

"I like a man with meat on his bones. Mom always said a big man is easy. If you get angry and out of hand, I'll make you a batch of spaghetti and calm you down."

"I like pasta."

"What a surprise. I thought you earned that belly with tofu and carrot sticks. Now shut up and let me enjoy the music."

Mike leaned back and tried to be casual while watching the tops of her breasts intermittently emerge from the foamy water. When Lorenz joined them, Mike scooted over and his hip accidentally brushed Polly's. She unconsciously pushed him away.

"She likes meaty men," Mike whispered.

"I heard," Lorenz replied.

"Shhh...," she hissed. "No beer if you can't keep quiet." She flopped out an arm and opened a small cooler. With eyes closed, she pulled out long-necked beers and distributed them. "If you don't like dark beer, then buy your own. I don't want to hear any bitching."

After a long soak, their skin turned pale and wrinkly. Polly heaved herself out and sat on the edge.

"I'm tired—I'm going to bed."

She idly toweled her hair while Mike and Lorenz admired her trim form. Her skin turned pink as she briskly dried off. She had an appendectomy scar on her lower abdomen. Otherwise, there was no visible flaw to her figure.

"I suppose you guys would like brandy and a cigar— don't sit there gawking—I don't smoke but I inherited a box of cigars from my father. They are in the humidor. All I ask is, open the damned window to air it out in here, otherwise this place will smell like a whorehouse ashtray. And, light a match if you stink up the bathroom again. That's all for now. Goodnight."

After she left, Lorenz opened the seal on the humidor.

"Very nice," he said. "Dominicans—almost as good as Cubans. You want?"

Mike nodded. "Sure, why not? Pop the window open while you're up, will ya?"

"Absolutely," Lorenz replied. "Lady's house, lady's rules," he said while striking a kitchen match and getting his cigar burning properly.

Madison and Rob Go Out on Their Second Big Date

Rob spent the afternoon calling credit card companies and calculating his total available credit. Two cards could not be used at all, but three were still active and, in total, he had a one-hundred-and-thirteen dollar budget.

As a piece of good news, payday was the day before and his paycheck was direct-deposited in his bank account. Unfortunately, there were automatic transactions paying his mortgage and car payments that left him two-hundred and seventy-eight dollars, including the cash in his wallet, to live on until the end of the month. He owed CB fifty dollars from the previous weekend's bar tab and needed at least forty dollars for groceries and beer. His Chevron gas card was still good, so he could drive his car to work. The challenge? How to knock Madison's socks off with a total date budget of two-hundred and ninety-one dollars. He walked the corridor and gestured for CB to follow him to the cafeteria for Friday afternoon's company-provided free sodas.

"CB, about that fifty bucks I owe, can I catch you next payday?"

"No way, man, I need to pay my bills. You said you'd pay up."

Sighing, Rob nodded and pulled the bills out of his wallet. The transaction left him with eighteen dollars in cash.

"What do you use to soften up the high school girls you date?"

"Club drugs? I use Super K, Cat Valium, Ketamine. I get it from an online veterinary site. The brand name is Ketalar."

"Score me some."

"That stuff is expensive and I have to keep some for myself. It's Friday night, man."

"Come on, brother. I need help with my date with Madison."

"The Frost Queen? You're right, you need something strong to slice off any of that. Tell me everything on Monday, okay?" He looked around to make sure no one was watching and slipped Rob a twist of plastic wrap holding a pinch of white powder.

"Sure. How do I use it?"

"Put it in her drink and stir it in. It will dissolve quickly. It works fast, so don't screw around. The moment she drops off, get busy—she'll be agreeable. Guaranteed, you'll score nook. She deserves it for holding everyone off. Did you know she used to date Marvin in the legal department? Six months invested and he couldn't get in her bloomers."

"Thanks, you're a real friend."

"No secrets on Monday, that's all I ask."

"You got it," Rob replied. "Thanks a lot."

Madison sipped her martini. Dressed more casually this time, she wore a cashmere sweater and tan slacks and her blonde hair was pulled back in a ponytail. Her makeup was sparse; just a hint of color on her lips and around her eyes. They had drinks and sushi at the bar (budget: $128 including $5 for the valet parking) then were going to the Tom Hanks movie everyone raved about—something absurd about Leonardo Da Vinci and the Vatican. She seemed pleased about the day's events and touched his arm when she laughed at his little jokes. He overflowed with desire—and imagined semen seeping from his pores.

Leaving her glass half full, she went to the restroom. Rob tapped in the Ketalar and stirred it with her swizzle stick. The bartender was onto him, or he imagined a malevolent and disapproving stare. He needed to urinate—he'd better take care of it—he passed her on his way to the restroom. He tried to kiss her cheek, but she deflected the gesture. When he got back, he drained his drink.

"We'd better get rolling," he said.

She looked surprised. "Don't we have plenty of time?"

"I want to make sure we get good seats."

"Okay," she said, while gathering her jacket.

Rob helped her slide in her arms.

He had the valet's tip ready in his front pocket. Madison leaned against him heavily. He felt good about getting her out of the bar. Very good. Ecstatic, as if he was floating.

The martinis must have been extra strong.

He drove a few blocks before realizing the need to pull over. He found a parking place and angled in. He was very sleepy. Madison—talking to herself—slumped against the passenger side door. Fading fast, Rob rested his forehead against the steering wheel and drifted into unconsciousness.

The radio oozed soft rock when Rob woke up. His head pounded with a massive headache. It hurt bad, he touched his ears to see if he was bleeding. In the vanity mirror, through bloodshot eyes, he could see the texture of the steering wheel imprinted on his forehead. The car was still running, but the gas gauge pointed much closer to empty. He looked at Madison curled against the door. Nestled in her jacket, her hair was tousled and she snored in a raspy, annoying manner. He grabbed the lapels of her coat and shook her.

"What the hell happened?" he asked while rubbing his temples.

"Uhnn," Madison responded. "Where are we?"

"I don't know." He wiped the foggy windows and peered out. "Still in Seattle, I guess. I only had two martinis."

"Halcion."

"What?"

"I put Halcion in your drink."

"What the hell is that?"

"Sleeping pill."

"Why the hell did you do that?"

"I wanted to slow you down because I wasn't going to have sex with you. I thought you'd take it better and not get so upset. I did this before and it worked fine. Once, I *told* the guy we had sex and he believed me."

"You bitch. I can't believe you dosed me up."

"What about you, asshole? I feel like I'm floating. What did you slip me?"

"Vitamin K."

"Shit on a stick; you're not supposed to mix that with alcohol. Aren't we a pair? What time is it?"

"Five."

"Can you drive?"

"I think so. My head is killing me. Do you have aspirin or something?"

"I have some Codeine 222's and some Haldol."

"Give me some of your 222's."

"How many?"

"Three." He moved papers around in the back seat and found a partial bottle of Gatorade. He washed the pills down with a swig of the warm drink. "We need to stop this nonsense before we kill each other. Just tell me when you'll have sex with me."

"Fine," she said, gesturing for the bottle. "If I still like you after we get to know each other better, I'll let you have your way with me on our sixth date."

"Come on, this is the new millennium. Fifth date."

She pondered the matter. "Okay, fifth." She held out her hand to shake on the deal.

"You'd better not turn psycho after we have sex," he grumbled.

"You'd better not start taking me for granted with cheap dates and not calling the next day. I still expect to be treated like a lady. Would you take me home now, please?"

"Yes." He put the car in gear and, after pressing on his

palms on his forehead to ease his headache, shakily drove out of the parking space.

Mike Thomas

Lorenz is not a night person. At two A.M., it took me several minutes to wake him. Wrapped like a mummy, he slept in a sleeping bag on an air mattress in an empty bedroom. I was excited about going back to the Pacific Electro-Med lab one last time. My subconscious worked overtime; I had several ideas I wanted to try. Interestingly, the most promising was inspired by Polly's dancing—I wanted to see what happened when orthogonal standing microwaves were combined with laser light pulses in an inert Argon atmosphere with my dispersed hexavalent Cesium powder. If my mental models were right, there would be greater stability in the temporal-gravitational plasma bubbles. Would they self-sustain? I was curious.

Lorenz was right about the security badges, Mike had lost many and tossed them in the glove box of his car after they turned up later. Perhaps some had not been disabled; he didn't know how often they purged the access files.

However, this was irrelevant, because he carried a forgotten Board of Directors pass in his wallet. He never used it, but remembered Mr. Simpson saying it would grant entry to any keylock in the building. He could even use the executive restroom and dining room if he liked, but he never wanted to sell out like that. Inside, he felt like a working stiff and didn't want to arrogantly put himself above his coworkers. He never thought about his trust fund—what was it worth? If he remembered the orders of magnitude correctly, he owned something like 14×10^6 dollar's worth of company stock.

Lorenz dropped him by the back service entry and set a time of 7:30 to meet again. He badged in and was soon in the lab. The brand new Gallium-Heisenbach X-ray Diffractometer was beautiful. Uncrated, it conveniently rested on a roll-around cart. The shiny instrument, elegantly miniaturized, had additional features, like an infrared plasma probe. It was not dented and corroded like the old one.

What a pleasure.

He enjoyed blissful hours, but soon it was time to clean up and put everything back. At the last minute, he realized he'd paid for the old Diffractometer, which sat in a forlorn heap in a corner, so he helped himself to the ion emitters and high-voltage fluxion manipulators.

He walked by his old workbench. A roll of electromagnetic shielding, covered in red *urgent* labels, sat on the line-down shelf. Production was line-down because this filter material was uninspected.

How long would they let this sit around?

For an instant he wondered why he hadn't been paged before remembering he'd been fired. His pager probably sat in Madison's desk drawer beeping and flashing an angry red light. He pulled the source control drawings off the server and borrowed his neighbor's micrometer. It took ten minutes—he performed the inspection and made sure the shielding got on the outbound materials cart. The line would be good-to-go when the morning shift clocked in. Silly, but it felt good to get it taken care of.

He gathered his new invention and carried it out. On the way out, he exchanged a greeting with the security guard.

Was he aware I'd been fired? Or, did my Board of Directors credentials give me corporate immunity?

It didn't matter. The bored guard offered to help carry one of the bulky boxes.

Outside in the visitor's parking area, Lorenz dozed. He'd reclined the seat all the way back and sat with the engine running and the heater going. They piled the gear in the cargo compartment and climbed in. Lorenz rubbed his eyes.

"Do any good in there?" he asked.

"Oh, yeah," Mike replied. "I'll show you when we get back to Polly's."

AK-18 Enjoys Breakfast

Artie waited until he could be seated by a window so he could watch the traffic climb the 6th Avenue hill. Though he was one of the A-K executive managers and was not required to perform daily Random Acts of Karnage, sometimes he could not resist.

Surreptitiously, he'd sprayed NoTract on the pavement before the stop light. NoTract was a water soluble lubricant, perhaps the slickest substance known. If applied to a fork, for example, the fork could not be picked up. While Artie peered over the top of his newspaper, most of the traffic slipped a little, but got by the patch where the lubricant had spread.

However, after a few minutes, he watched an Acura MDX SUV, stopped at the light, slip backwards and smash the headlights of a shiny new Ford GT sports car. Artie was no judge of these things, but it looked as if the GT driver threw his Starbucks grande, triple shot, Toffee Nut Cappuccino with legs at the lady driving the SUV. He sighed with satisfaction as the yuppie-scum Microsoft millionaire took a blow in the head from the MDX-soccer-mom's home-made weapon, which looked like a cue ball in a sweat sock—a very effective sap.

A passerby stopped to help and slipped, earning a nasty forehead gash on the MDX's rear-view mirror. All-in-all, the cause of chaos was off to a good start this morning. Artie smiled, slipped a morsel of Honeydew melon inside his jacket to Pedro, and finished browsing his newspaper.

CHAPTER EIGHTEEN

The Sanctuary

WHEN LORENZ AND Mike arrived at Polly's house, they found her drinking a cup of coffee, nibbling a rice cake and reading the newspaper. Dressed casually in faded blue jeans and sneakers, she ignored them as they hauled in supplies from the grocery store—including important staples like bacon and imported beer.

"Polly? Want a donut?" Mike asked.

"Only on my birthday," she sniffed in reply.

The doorbell chimed and Lorenz peered through the curtains. "It's some long-haired kid," he said.

"That's Roland from next door. You can let him in."

Roland was thin and wore his hair in a bleached mullet, a style inexplicably in fashion again.

"Who are these people?" he asked.

"They're my friends," Polly replied.

The casual way she said 'friends' made Mike's heart stutter.

"Hey, guys," Roland said.

"Hey," Lorenz and Mike replied back.

"I hear the music so I know you've been working. Can I get a sample?"

Polly shrugged. "Okay," she said. She took off her sneakers, laced up her ballet shoes and cued the music. She handed the remote to Roland. "When the song gets to the bridge, restart it from the beginning. You'll have to imagine the movements overlaid, but I'll show you all three parts."

She stood in the middle of the room with her arms outstretched.

"Ready? Go," she commanded.

In the gentle introduction, Polly flitted like a dragonfly. When the hammering beat kicked in, she scampered and jumped. The overall effect was intoxicating; they could imagine the three parts interlocking and interacting.

Hunched over and panting with her hands braced on her knees, she held out her hand to get Roland to stop the music.

"Thank you, that was amazing," Roland said, clapping.

"I know," Polly said. "That's all I'm showing for now. On your drum part, after the first verse, you did a sweet left-hand right-hand paradiddle accent. Did you overdub that?"

"No, it was laid down in one take."

"Well, I'm impressed. You're very ambidextrous." From an end table, she picked up a sheet of paper. "I made a list of supplies and dancers. We can get Cornish students on the cheap, they're good and will follow my instructions. I mentioned some by name. Let me know if they need convincing. For the six-year-old ballerinas, they are generic, grab a random dozen from the ballet school at the strip mall. Got it?"

"Yes. I'll get our production coordinator on it. Can you be ready by Wednesday?"

"Sure. I'll call in sick a few more days."

"We have another song, the *B* side. Do you want to write a dance for that one too?"

"Let's see how this one turns out first."

"Right. Well, I'd better get busy," he said while fanning the production notes. "See ya."

She walked to the couch.

"Skootch over, I'm tired," she complained.

Mike and Lorenz scooted apart and made room for her. She dropped on the couch like a sack of onions. Mike's skin, where it touched the damp heat of her thigh, felt inflamed. He tried to ignore the sensation coming from those few square centimeters of flesh, but it was impossible.

Lorenz leaned over to make eye-contact with Mike.

"Tell me about your new weapon."

"It's a three-person job. One person generates the bubbles, one person bats them and the third activates them."

He slid the box toward himself and took out components.

"That looks like a cricket bat," Lorenz commented.

Mike looked ashamed. "I borrowed it. The owner played in Mexico. I dispersed a thin film of hexavalent

Cesium, then varnished over it."

He handed Polly a device that looked like a TV remote control.

"Shall we try it?" Mike asked. "I'll generate the bubble. Lorenz can knock it toward the target and Polly can pop the bubble with the infrared laser diode in the remote control. Ready?"

Polly and Lorenz nodded. Mike activated the trigger. An iridescent bubble, three inches in diameter, drifted in the air. Lorenz, barely missing Mike's head, tapped it with the bat. It drifted toward the front of the room. It got larger as it wafted. Polly pressed the *play* button on the remote. A beam of sunlight pierced the room from a hole in the heavy drapes. They walked over to take a look at a perfectly circular hole in the curtain. Cold air blowing though the glass made a breeze against their faces.

"That's great. Now I have a hole in my window," she complained. "There's duct tape in the junk drawer in the kitchen. Fix this. I'm going to take a nap."

"What happened to the window? The curtain and the glass? Matter can't disappear."

"It got randomized. Its coherency dissolved."

"If you say so," Lorenz said skeptically.

"So, what do you think? Cool?"

Unimpressed, Lorenz shrugged.

"When the A-Ks come for us, if nothing else, I can hit them with the cricket bat."

Madison Howard

Mike's beeper bleeped. In her desk's bottom drawer, Madison buried it under a stack of paper, but she could still hear it. Desperate for silence, she pulled it out and removed the battery. It still flashed and beeped until she smashed it with the heel of her shoe. She swept the remains into her waste basket.

"Is everything okay?" Rob asked, while standing and watching the scene from her doorway.

"Sure, I'm fine," she replied.

She smiled sweetly in a dangerous, passive-aggressive manner.

"I'm supposed to remind you about the Material Review Board meeting."

"I didn't forget. I'm waiting for my interview candidate. I'll take him to the meeting."

"Are you serious about hiring him?"

"Nah, it's a way of getting free labor as part of the qualification process. He's been unemployed for a few months, so he'll do it."

"Makes, sense, I guess," Rob said hesitantly.

It was a form of exploitation he'd not thought of.

Something they teach in MBA school?

"Are we still on for Friday?"

"Sure," Madison replied. "I expect a better date this time."

"So do I. Here they come, I'd better go."

Rob waddled toward his office.

Madison made eye-contact with her colleague, Annie

Kranston, to get a reading on Robert Marx, the applicant. The judgment was inconclusive; behind Robert's back, Annie shrugged and rolled her eyes.

"Have a seat, Bob. Is it okay if I call you Bob?"

"I prefer Robert, thank you."

Robert, a heavy-set man around forty, wore a haircut that looked self-imposed. Ragged swatches of gray hair cascaded over his ears.

"Okay, Robby, we have time for a few questions. Tell me a little more about why you left your last job."

"The division closed. Now, they buy circuit boards from a fabrication house in Malaysia."

"That sucks. I hate seeing good jobs exported to third world nations."

"If it serves the consumer, then that's the way it goes, protectionism doesn't work. With environmental regulations and taxation, we made a conscious decision to make domestic manufacturing expensive. We can't complain when our economy gets more virtual and service-oriented. This won't change until we decide an industrial job has higher value than the public cost of unquantified environmental hazards."

"You seem philosophical about being unemployed, though you've been out of work for a while…"

"I saved some money, so I can hold out until I find a job that fits my aptitude and experience. Freelance commercial photography pulls in a few dollars. I get by. Why get upset about being buffeted by the winds of global economics? I don't want to be on the wrong side of history."

"Sure, whatever you say."

Great, a worldly philosopher, just what we need around here.

"I'd like you to join me for a MRB meeting so I can get a feel for how you work. Let's head out."

They strolled toward the receiving area in the back of the warehouse. The MRB area was located inside a chainlink enclosure. The other members of the team waited. Madison introduced Robert around the table.

"Let's get started, shall we? Do we have any *code-red* materials?"

"Machine screws," Tom Wakefield said. He got up and removed a plastic bag from the cabinet. "Mike rejected them. 10-24 flat-head machine screws, Phillips head, zinc-plated steel."

"Why were they rejected?"

Tom read the hand-written note.

"Inclusions and poor plating adhesion."

Madison sighed. "How bad are they?"

She spilled a few on the table and moved them around with a painted fingernail.

Robert pulled a jewelers loupe from his jacket pocket and peered at a screw.

"I've seen worse," he commented.

He looked through the sheaf of engineering drawings.

"If we reject them, how quickly can we get more?"

"I talked to the buyer. There's no stock in the U.S. and it will take at least ten days to get a batch cleared through customs if we use the same supplier. Longer if we go with the alternate source."

"Let's not screw around, no pun intended," Madison said. "They're screws, buy them off and get the assembly line moving again. Do you agree with my decision, Robert?"

With all eyes on him, he pondered the situation.

"Without examining them under a microscope, I agree the problem seems tolerable, but I'd still reject the lot." He held up the bag. "A lot of the plating has come off. If there was a problem in the field, the FDA would be all over this ruling. I say it's not worth the risk."

"The drawing doesn't say anything about plating residue in the bag."

"You're right, it's a judgment call. You asked my opinion. That's my opinion."

"Duly noted. In my judgment, the batch meets the requirements of drawing so I'm going to sign them off," Madison said. "Anyone disagree?"

"You're in charge of mechanical design…" Tom said.

"Fine, what else do we have to disposition?"

"Pardon me for interrupting, but I'd like to be excused," Robert interjected.

"Give us a few more minutes and we'll be done," Madison said.

"No, you've got all the free advice you'll get from me. I'd like to leave. I can find my own way out."

"Company policy says visitors require an escort."

Nearby, a young shipping clerk poured foam peanuts from a huge overhead dispenser into a shipping box. Robert waved him over. The kid pulled off his earphones;

the volume was so high that tinny rap music could be heard.

"Would you mind escorting me to that exit?" Robert said, pointing.

After cautiously looking at the company managers for guidance, the kid spoke hesitantly. "Sure, I guess."

"Don't worry, I'll sign you out on the visitor's log," Madison called out toward Robert's retreating back. They watched him push through the exit.

"He'd be a pain in the ass to work with," Tom said.

"You got that right," Madison said, laughing. "Lots of people are looking for work, we can find someone more agreeable. Let's get back to it, shall we? I have another meeting at eleven. An hourly employee can sort the screws and pick out the bad ones. Then the production line starts up again and everybody is happy. Am I right or am I right?"

Lorenz and AK-18 Meet

Lorenz, peeking through the curtains, was unsurprised to see Agent AK-18 leaning against a light pole in the front yard.

"Who's that?" Mike asked, while peering over Lorenz's shoulder.

"The devil himself," Lorenz replied. "I should go talk to him."

Lorenz took deep breaths and held out his hands to evaluate his nervousness. They didn't quiver. Much. He buttoned his long coat and walked outside.

"I was wondering if you'd hide all day," AK-18 commented.

Pedro poked his mottled nose out of the AK's jacket, sniffed the air a few times and then disappeared.

"Ferret?" Lorenz asked.

"Ringtail cat," AK-18 replied. "Call me Artie." He held out his hand for a shake, but Lorenz waved it away.

"I'd rather not touch you, if you don't mind. My name is Lorenz Hartz and I'm not pleased to meet you."

"Ah, don't be that way, Lorenz. The universe tries to randomize you, but that doesn't mean it hates you. I don't hate you either."

"You don't hate me, but you'd kill me without remorse. Somehow, that seems worse. I'd rather die in a crime of passion. Have you accepted a contract to kill Mike?"

"We're debating the relative merits. He's a great agent of chaos, but, on the other hand, we could use the revenue. Where the matter settles, I don't know. As it is, we're in perfect balance. It's lovely. Neither dead nor alive, Mike is like Schrödinger's cat. Of course, there's no doubt about the final result. In the end we're all claimed by entropy, ashes to ashes, et cetera. Unless you believe in reincarnation? An afterlife? Some eternal essence to your coherency?"

"I'm agnostic, I don't claim to know. I've sworn to create beauty where I can for whatever it might be worth."

"Well, the randomness of the universe can be beautiful too. Dead meat is always fertilizer for something. Rust. Decay. The melting of the snow crystal into a transcendent drop of water. These are undeniable universal processes. Why not stop fighting and worship the inevitable, let yourself fall into the warm embrace of chaos."

"The embrace of chaos will be cold, not warm."

Artie chuckled. "You're right, but *the cold embrace of chaos* would be poor marketing. I love talking to your type; you turn random patterns of stars into constellations. You can't help yourself." He unwrapped a stick of gum and let the wrapper fly away in the wind. He held out the package. "Care for some?"

"I won't take anything from you. I suppose you've calculated the odds that I might choke on a piece."

Artie couldn't control himself. He laughed heartily.

"Yes, it's something like one in twenty-seven million that you'd choke to death. The odds stack against you more if you chew two pieces." Wiping tears from his eyes, he held the gum up and examined it. "An innocent, unaltered piece of gum. Damn it, that's funny."

"So, what's your evil plan?" Lorenz gestured around the neighborhood. "A tree falls and crushes the house? They look too far away. Give a kid bottle rockets and see if he can burn the place down? I know, maybe a propane truck could explode as it rolls by."

"Those ideas have merit, but I prefer something with better odds. Are you planning to hide out in the house forever?"

"Never you mind."

"The grand plan of the universe takes time to unfold. I have faith in the inevitable."

"Until then," Lorenz said.

"Yes," Artie replied.

Lorenz turned to walk back to the house. He saw Mike and Polly peering through the curtains; he waved them back. There was one step in the concrete walkway. He could see it coming and concentrated mightily, but, perhaps due to over-thinking, he stumbled. He easily caught his balance, so there was little danger of falling.

From behind, Artie laughed uproariously.

"Watch your step," he said. "Worldwide, almost eight-hundred people die every year after tripping on concrete stairs. Mostly old people of course, but still…"

In the house, Lorenz scowled at Mike and Polly.

"I hate those lousy A-K bastards," he said bitterly.

Mike Thomas

Sex, sex, sex. We're a sex-obsessed society. Endless streams of commercials use sex as a conduit directly to our subconscious to create the desire for fast food, liquor, cigarettes, clothing, automobiles and everything in-between. It's tawdry and cheap, but as long as it works, this crude tool will be used. Mike understood the dynamic of procreation; the species must reproduce or die. Hence, the metaphysical reward for copulation. But really, all the time and energy invested in achieving those few moments of bliss?

Then, without self-discipline, an hour after one orgasm, we're planning, plotting and strategizing to achieve the next one.

How efficient is all this waste of energy? What ultimate value comes from all the effort? At least we have a choice. We can defend ourselves by being conscious about what we allow into our minds. A sort of intellectual inoculation. It works.

If you'll allow me the conceit, I've done interesting work, creative work, even innovative work. Part of my success is due to channeling my sexual energy. I'm not distracted by women and their charms. I don't waste time chasing them, wooing them, or letting them divert me from my work.

Extreme, obsessive focus, that's the key to deep concentration and my mental exploration of the gravity-time continuum. I'm no freak—I have sexual feelings and desires, but I use this pent-up tension to drive my experiments. I'm no slave to flesh. What great man could be? And I confess, deep inside, I aspire to world-altering greatness. That's what gets me out of bed in the single-digit morning hours and motivates my mad exploration in the laboratory. I believe I can add something genuinely new to the world's intellectual property.

That's what I see when I stare into flickering plasmas—my mark on the world. There, I've said it. Buried deep inside, my ego is unbounded. The Thomas Effect, the confluence of standing microwaves and magnetic field lines of focused fluxions acting on marginally-stable radioactive ions. Beams and streams of unruly antiprotons flowing at my command. Convulsive expulsions of seminal gravity fluid. Gooey, musky effluvium ejaculated by productive, constructive channeling of primal sexual urges.

Mike pulled the curtains apart and idly rubbed his fingers

over the patch of duct tape that covered the hole in the front room picture window.

"Don't stand there, you're too-easy a target," Lorenz said while tugging at Mike's arm.

"Polly is a woman of amazing talents with a charming, multi-faceted personality."

"If anything, that's an understatement. She's a remarkable person. To top it all off, inexplicably, she likes you."

Mike turned and grasped Lorenz by the shoulders.

"You don't understand, I must possess this woman. I fear for my sanity, but I must conquer her, absorb and own her. You have to help me."

Lorenz laughed and brushed off Mike's hands.

"For such a grand intellect, you're slow on the uptake. What exactly do you think I've been doing besides saving your life and exposing your gifts of genius to the world? Leave it to me and you'll come out fine."

Polly came out of the kitchen. She wore a loose sweater over sweat pants.

"What are you geeks discussing so intently?"

"Nothing, just making chit-chat," Lorenz said smoothly.

"Well, make yourself useful and scratch my back. There's a spot in the middle I can't reach."

She turned and lifted her sweater to expose a pink expanse of smooth flesh. Maddeningly, the lower swells of her breasts were exposed. Lorenz pressed Mike forward.

"Lightly, I said," Polly scolded. "I don't need bloody gashes in my skin. Oh, that's good, thanks."

She pulled down her sweater and walked toward the back of the house. Mike and Lorenz looked at each other with mystified amazement.

CHAPTER NINETEEN

Charles 'CB' Barthre and Agent AK-18

CB WAS TIPSY, but not completely blotto. Over several hours at the sports bar, he'd consumed several pitchers of beer while the Trailblazers won an overtime basketball victory. He was in a good mood when the mishap occurred.

He found a place to piss in a dark corner of the parking lot. The need to relieve himself was urgent; he couldn't wait until he got home and he was too lazy to make the trek back to the bar. The grass was slippery with rain and he had trouble with footing. He had slipped and now something protruded from the left side of his chest. In darkness, he could not make out what it was. Air hissed from his lung and it hurt so much he couldn't gather a breath to shout for help.

"If you don't wriggle, you'll live a little longer," AK-18 said helpfully. "No one will believe this, but I didn't set this up. Who'd guess an ancient, bloodthirsty farm implement would patiently wait for you in the tall grass?

233

Its incomprehensible someone could fall so precisely and with such deadly effect. What are the odds? Astronomical. Perhaps forty-five million to one. On the other hand, you drink so much, over time, some sort of fatal incident due to car crash or other pratfall was likely. But right here and now, while I'm hanging around? As always, I'm amazed by the capricious, malicious beauty of chaos."

"Call 9-1-1," CB whispered.

"Oh, no, I don't think I will, that would be an insult to the cosmic destroyer. You won't be conscious much longer, so I should stop babbling. Remember Trent? He disappeared. Vanished. I fear unpleasantness might have overtaken him. He was an inept young man, but charming in his own way. I'd like to find him. Do you know what happened him?"

"No."

"When was the last time you saw him?"

"He ate my pizza." CB struggled to enunciate the words. "We talked. He invited me to join you guys."

"I'm sure he was simply making small talk. You don't measure up to agent standards. Besides, I don't think you'll be alive much longer, so that makes the question moot, wouldn't you say?"

"Unggh," CB groaned in complaint.

"I'm sorry, was that impolite? I suppose it was. Well, since you're useless, is there anything you'd like to say? Any momentous or profound last words?"

Pedro poked his head from the padded pocket. Artie held him out so Pedro could sniff at CB's face.

"You're an ugly fucking little man," CB hissed.

"That's interesting. Do you mean ugly in appearance or in deed?" He stood and eased Pedro back into his hidey-hole. "Will I heed a man with a ripped artery who irrationally refuses to stay still?" Succumbing to a flash of rage, he reared back and kicked CB in the head. "True enough, that was an ugly thing to do," AK-18 commented. "And now I have loser-blood on my Gila boots." He patted Pedro's head. "Shall we go back to the hotel and see what the escort service offers, my friend? I don't think it's too late for a thick steak, a nice Merlot and the intimate company of a woman."

He worked his feet in the grass to wipe gore off his shiny boots.

Madison Howard and Rob Perry

Rob ran up the stairs, and then stopped to look at his image reflected in a window. His clothes were wrinkled and his hair matted, he was a wreck. After pressing Madison's doorbell, he pounded on the door. She opened the door on its chain and looked out at him.

"Have you heard about CB?" Rob asked.

"Yes, Denise called. What a horrible accident. I'm sorry about your friend."

"Will you let me in?" Long seconds passed while she considered the question. "This is ridiculous. Open the door, will you?"

Sighing, she closed the door and lifted the chain. Leaving the door closed, she walked away. After a moment, Rob tried the door, and followed her after it opened. She settled on the couch and arranged her terrycloth bathrobe for as much cover as possible. Through a gap, a red-silk teddy and satin shorts were visible.

"I was getting ready for work," she said.

Rob perched on the edge of the couch and buried his face in his hands.

"He invited me to join him at the bar, but I was too tired."

"What happened? Denise said there was a freak accident."

"He slipped and fell on an old hay-baling machine. He bled to death. Alcohol thins the blood, he drained like a bathtub. He was my best friend," Rob said while trying not to be too obvious about staring at strips of soft flesh visible under her loosely-tied robe. "Please hold me," he said while leaning over her.

She patted him on the back. "I'm not very good with the comfort thing," she said. "Maybe you should take a pill and get some sleep."

"Make sweet love to me, Madison," Rob suggested while pulling her robe off her shoulders.

He gently kissed her neck under her ear.

"I knew it," she said, pushing him back. "This is a ploy to get me out of my panties. I have an interview with a candidate at nine. Get out of here so I can put myself together and get to work."

"This is no ploy. I need you. I can make it quick, I promise."

She stood and pointed to the door. "I can make it

quick, I promise," she repeated mincingly. "How romantic. If you shut up now, I'll give you a break and assume you're distraught and don't know what you're saying. Out."

Rob stood and walked toward the front door. He hesitated.

"Think carefully before opening your mouth," she warned.

"I was wondering if this counted toward the five dates?"

As she looked for something to throw at him, Rob hurriedly opened the door.

"I guess I'll see you at work then, Maddy," he said before scooting out.

Madison Howard and the Interview Candidate

"Throughput, efficiency, schedules, deadlines, turn-around time, expediency, cooperation, teamwork and focus," Madison said, while watching the candidate's face for his reaction.

"I inspect materials and make sure they meet the requirements of the drawings. It doesn't need to be any more complicated than that."

"Very well," Madison replied. "I don't have any more questions. Thank you for coming to see us. We'll get back to you once we've made a hiring decision."

They shook hands and Madison escorted him to the front lobby.

"We'll be in touch," she promised.

Loser, she thought.

Mike, Polly and Lorenz

Gathered around the breakfast table, Polly took delicate bites from a bowl of Grape Nuts while Lorenz and Mike took turns spearing frozen waffles from the toaster. All had mismatched cups of steaming coffee and sipped orange juice from old jam jars. Polly edited her rock ballet. Mike scribbled sketches in his lab notebook. Lorenz thought about things with alternating looks of worry and vacant concentration.

"Polly, as much as I love looking at you," Lorenz commented, "it would aid my concentration if you'd tuck yourself in."

Unconsciously, Polly rearranged the top of her wrap to cover her peeping breasts.

"Sorry about that," she mumbled.

Lorenz stood.

"Here's the bottom line. We need to get out of this house. There are no gas pipelines nearby, no railroad tracks or overhead wires, so the neighborhood seems safe, but I don't know what the A-Ks will come up with. They can be devilishly clever. As long as they know where we are, they have time to dream up something nasty. We need to slip away."

"I'm not leaving the city until filming is finished."

"I wouldn't suggest anything else. But, could we pack everything we need so when we leave this morning, we don't come back until the crisis blows over?"

"I can't fit everything into the Escalade," Polly said. "We'll have to make several trips."

"I thought of that. As a decoy, I want the Escalade parked out front. If we leave the music turned up, maybe they'll think we're holed up here for a couple of days. I called. A rental truck and movers will pull up on the street on the block behind us. One trip and they'll haul everything out. Five minutes and we're gone. I mapped a path; I don't think we'll be seen when we go out the back if we follow the neighbor's fence line. Sound like a plan?"

Mike raised a waffle fragment dripping with syrup and licked it off his fork.

"Works for me," he said.

"As long as the filming gets done, I'm willing to move out for a while," Polly said.

Lorenz clapped his hands briskly.

"I set up things for nine-thirty," he said. "Let's get our stuff boxed up."

The film crew took over the old King Theater in downtown Seattle. It was scheduled for demolition, so they were free to take liberties with sledge hammers, paint brushes and chainsaws to create a post-apocalyptic concert setting. Mike had the balcony to himself, so he had a good view of the stage activity.

Polly was firm and demanding. Her contract gave her complete control of sets, dancers and crew; she gave specific instructions and worked with each person until she got exactly what she wanted. Mike couldn't fathom the energy and patience she produced in endless supply, but, as viewed from his perch, the result was amazing. He could only imagine the complex-beautiful-precise-perfection that would be captured by the cameras.

Once the band began playing, Mike wandered until he found a sound crewman with a stash of foam earplugs. The music had delicate passages, but also hammering sections that filled his head and made his ears ring. Polly demanded all recording be performed live in front of an audience; she'd allow them to edit as they pleased, but each video image would have to match the live performance of the shot that was used. It took many takes.

A casting call for extras, spread via the band's website, announced the filming. They looked for audience members dressed like Australian road warriors. All seats were packed with leather-bound, wild-haired, rock-n-roll desert rats. The scene was surreal. Polly guided dancers firmly with pushes and shoves and directed the action. The dozen ballerinas had their section and Mike could see the effect Polly strived for; a molecular patchwork of pink, drifting snowflakes. Polly stamped her feet and argued until the band agreed to paste sweet chords on the end of the song. In spite of the song's anger and despair, she wanted a happy, optimistic ending for the video.

While watching Polly work, Mike realized how selfish he'd been. Sure, he'd done grand work by breathing life into building and controlling temporal-gravitational plasmas, but what was the point? Making weapons was fine; most new technologies were used for weapons, gambling or pornography before evolving into pride-worthy human achievements. It struck him while unconsciously absorbing the creative chaos unfolding on the stage below that his plasma could be used to create an engine. He racked his brain for details on the various thermodynamic engines.

Which is the closed-system gas engine?

Can I use helium in a Brayton turbine?

Entranced, he thought about the engine cycle. Create heat, expand gas, move a piston or turbine, recover as much heat as possible and start again. Inelegant. Strangely, Mike realized he'd been dreaming about this since he was a kid watching Westerns on TV. The locomotive hisses and groans and slowly the wheels begin to turn. A dirty, sweaty man heaves shovel-loads of coal into the firebox to heat the boiler. Mike's subconscious worked at the problem over and over, testing theories, running mental experiments and burning trillions of mental instruction cycles to solve the problem.

And there it was. Fully-formed and elegant. With a thin coating of hexavalent Cesium, the metal vanes of a turbine could be encouraged to spin as if sweet-talked by the persuasive influence of a low-temperature temporal-gravitational plasma. Room-temperature fusion. He wanted to run into the street and scream the news. Arrogantly, instinctively and irrationally, he knew he was the only one who could have put it all together.

Lorenz patted him on the shoulder. "Are you okay?" he asked with concern.

"I glimpsed the engine of the universe. It's beautiful."

"Oh, if that's all, then we're okay. From the look on

your face, I thought you'd completely gone around the bend. Listen, Polly needs you."

"What?"

"She dreamed up a role for an overweight, obsessive fanboy. We wonder if you'll do it?"

"I'm not that fat."

"Well, you're not thin either. If you're willing, we have to get you into makeup right away."

Mike shrugged. "For Polly, I'll do anything."

Lorenz tugged Mike's arm and led him down the balcony stairs. The next thirty minutes were a hustle-bustle of activity. They wrapped his torso in foam, and then enveloped him in a huge billowing flannel shirt covered by a flapping black overcoat. They ripped large gashes in his blue jeans and plastered his face with splashes of paint. Someone cropped huge, scary swaths from his hair with scissors as big as pruning shears. Polly appeared and asked him to spin. He'd never seen such an intense look of concentration as she looked him over.

"He'll do," she announced. "Get him onstage."

The stage lighting was lurid and dark with tendrils of smoke drifting like fog. Members of the band lolled in the wings watching and drinking coffee from huge paper cups. The drummer, high on his throne, idly slapped the skins creating a roar so loud that the air writhed in pain. Looking up, Mike recognized the kid from next door creating this percussive thunder.

"Mike? Can you hear me?"

Mike nodded and focused. Oddly, it seemed as if she was in his mind, it was as if he was tapped directly into her thoughts. The effect was created by the personal audio monitor system plugged in his ears.

"When the song enters the coda," she continued, "do you know what a coda is?" He nodded. "Good. When the drummer plays the vibe part, pull the bubble gun from under your overcoat and create as many bubbles as you can. Make them as big as possible. A stage tech will pop them with the remote. Do you understand? You're freaking out and worshiping the band, and then you pull out the bubble gun and begin firing. Do you follow? We've made stage marks for lighting and camera-angle sweet spots. Try to catch it all in one take, but if you screw up, don't worry, keep going; we'll roll until we get it right."

Mike knew from the hours of watching that she told the truth, they'd work until the end of time to capture her ideas perfectly.

Experiencing self-doubt and weakness, he said, "I don't know if I can do this."

"And I'm telling you that you can. No bullshit. Follow your instinct but remember the stage marks. Do this and I'll be yours forever? Do you understand?"

Mike nearly collapsed on the stage, but somehow his knees held him up.

"I will do anything for you."

"Good, use that emotion. You love this band more than you love life itself, more than you love your momma, more than you love the ethereal cosmic winds of the subquantum universe. You'll do anything for the band. Let it all fly. Ready? When I say action, release everything, don't hold anything back."

"I love you, Polly," Mike said.

"Don't tell me, show me," she said while pushing him into the center of the stage.

Stumbling and turning to face the drummer, he stood up straight and still. Polly screamed *action* and the music roared like an angry earthquake. Initially frozen, he slowly came to life, gyrating like a dervish and rotating like an out-of-balance top.

Feeling the stir of paganism take control, the band became his mother, father, lover, life and soul. When the loud music faded into echo and heavenly vibes rang like bells, he pulled out the bubble gun and let loose a stream of gleaming, mesmerizing bubbles. Oily rainbows roiled on their surfaces.

Then, one-by-one, the bubbles burst. The guitarist, Raz, pressed pickups against his amp—evoking a soul-stealing shriek of screaming feedback. A bubble ate the head of the guitar and the strings released and slashed his arm. Immediately, vivid stripes of blood welled. A digital delay echoed the feedback in coiling swirls while Raz tripped backward in shock and fell on his ass.

"Keep everything going," Polly shouted. Finally, the last cascade of notes faded and the scene was quiet. "Cut," Polly said, nearly whispering. "That's a wrap, folks. Pack it up."

Exhaustion, strain and effort were etched on her face. She collapsed onto a folding chair. A tech brought her a bottle of icy water and a large, fluffy towel. No one approached for several minutes while she wiped her face and guzzled great draughts of bottled water. Finally, in groups of two or three, the band and crew walked by and congratulated her with worshipful awe. The injured guitar player introduced himself and showed off the bloody welts.

"At first, I didn't see why you wouldn't work with recorded music, but I get it now."

"You'll carry scars. I'm sorry about that."

"I'll wear them with pride the rest of my life. Thank you. I'm going to be world-famous, maybe you'd like to join my journey?"

Polly looked into his eyes and felt a tidal pull.

"Yes, I see it. You'll be famous, but I'm taking a different path."

Raz smiled and patted her cheek. "We'll meet again," he said.

"Wait," Polly said, "isn't there already a famous guitar player named Raz?"

"He's my father," Raz said with an enigmatic smile before wandering off.

The keyboard player stopped by.

"We have another, even better, song we're working on."

"I can't go through this again, there's nothing left. I'm done."

"Once the world sees this video, there will be no respite."

"We'll see."

The next person, a tall Puerto Rican wearing an

elaborate Latino zoot suit, handed her a business card.

"You need an agent. Call me," he said.

Dancers, stage crew and management spoke kind words and patted her arm or kissed her cheek. All were eager to work with her again. Her mind was blank and empty, like a flaccid balloon. The ballerinas gathered onstage and waved for her to come up. Slowly, with muscles made of liquid, she climbed the stairs and dropped to her knees. Like butterflies, the unruly girls kissed her cheeks, ruffled her hair and hugged her.

By chance, from a scaffolding, a photographer using a zoom lens captured the picture that made Polly internationally famous.

Bliss was the caption of the poster they made of it.

The girls flitted away and Polly sat on the edge of the stage and watched the sets being dismantled. Lorenz, approaching quietly as if not wanting to spook her, sat beside her.

"Thank you. That was incredible," he said.

"You're welcome," she said. "Where'd Mike disappear to?"

"I don't know." Lorenz stood and offered his hand to help her up. "I suppose we should find him."

It was not easy. He was not on the balcony, nor in the reception area or the backstage green room. After asking a few people, a technician carrying a large roll of audio cable gestured toward a door that led to the basement.

"I think I saw someone go down there," he said, pointing.

The stairway was well-lighted and the paint was

surprisingly fresh. The vast cool space was filled with old theater chairs and racks of stage clothing. Mike, sitting on a spring-sprung couch under a bank of fluorescent lights, scribbled in his notebook. He was a mess. With smeared makeup and his hair standing up in tufts, he looked like a rabid leprosy victim.

"Why are you hiding down here? Are you okay?" Lorenz said.

"I needed a quiet place to think. I had ideas I wanted to get on paper, that's all. When you said *cut*, I assumed you were done with me. I'm not a dancer or an actor, so I don't think I could do any better."

"It was fine. You'll be amazed when the video gurus splice the whole thing together. Thanks for being a good sport."

"I'm glad to help. Besides, remember what you said."

"I said a lot today. What are you talking about?"

"I made a note for the record." He thumbed through a few pages of his notebook. "*Do this and I'll be yours forever*, you said."

"Oh that? I was just trying to get a performance out of you. I'm sorry about that."

"What? Shit. I'm the one who's sorry. My mind jumped to conclusions."

"Mike, relax. That's not what I meant." To Lorenz, she said. "Guys can be so dense." Continuing, she said, "What I meant was, I'll be yours forever even if you don't get on stage. I'm not ready to marry you or anything, but we're headed in that direction, so chill. Need I say more?"

"I guess not," Mike said with his forehead crinkled in

extreme concentration. "I want to write that down too."

"Sure," Polly said, laughing. She leaned over and gave him a kiss on the forehead. "Don't dawdle. We should carb up on burgers and beer. Tonight we've earned decadence and gluttony." Turning to leave, she said, "Come on Lorenz, let's leave the mad genius to his scribbling."

Agent AK-18

The afternoon slipped into gray Seattle murk—the day died with a soggy whimper. Artie was morose. The short days and dark skies oppressed him. He walked the block around Polly's house several times, looking for anything that might work against his enemy's fortune. Even Pedro was no comfort, he would occasionally poke his nose out, sniff the humid air with disapproval, and then hide again in his nest.

Nothing held promise. The neighborhood rested on a flat parcel of land and there were no water towers to topple or chemical plants to sabotage. The street was constricted with turnabouts and parked cars. There was no room for a careening semi truck to get out of control. It seemed hopeless.

On Artie's last lap around the block, it occurred to him that the house, though the stereo blared, seemed empty. His suspicion was not raised because Polly's Mazda and Lorenz's Escalade were present and accounted for. He walked up the sidewalk, pounded on the door and leaned on the doorbell. Except for cats, there was no sign of life from inside.

Slipped by me, did you? Very clever. Let's see if you found a safer place.

Shaking his head, he walked a few steps away from the door, then on impulse, turned back to try the knob. He was surprised when it turned. Walking in the house, the first thing he did was turn off the stereo. The house turned quiet. The austerity of the living room surprised him; it was outfit as a dance studio with hardwood floors, a ballet barre and large wall-mounted mirrors. He poked his head in the rooms and dumped clothes out of the hampers. Her underwear was plain and small. Pedro poked his head out and wanted a sniff, so Artie let him.

"Do you approve?" Artie asked.

Pedro always approved of soiled underwear, so the question was rhetorical.

Artie turned out the garbage can on the kitchen floor and inspected the contents as if divining secrets from aardvark entrails. In the refrigerator, a bottle of Chardonnay cooled. Artie found a corkscrew and a glass and helped himself. The wine was middling-good and Artie approved. Carrying his glass, he looked in the sunroom that held the bubbling hot tub.

Very nice.

He walked around the edge. His foot slipped on a patch of wet linoleum and flew from under him. Unbidden statistics came to mind. Twenty-nine Americans died every year in household falls, usually people under the influence of drugs or alcohol. This seemed ironic to Artie as he watched the wine glass cascade through the air.

One sip, that was all he had. He grabbed a corner of a cabinet and steadied himself just before he would have received a nasty blow to the head. His heart raced, but he was okay. He slipped to the floor and caught his breath.

Someone should do something about the hazard.

Stepping more carefully, he walked to the back door and noticed the many footprints in a patch of mud.

They slipped out the back door.

Fiendishly clever.

CHAPTER TWENTY

The Skeleton and Crossbones Society

BARRY ROTHSCHILD, DRESSED in a silk robe and wearing woolly slippers on his feet, walked into the dining room.

"Pull the drapes," he said, while covering his eyes to block the glare reflecting off Lake Starnberg.

The meeting convened in the Bavarian town of Tutzing; the last stop on the S6 train from Munich. Will Mellon wanted to lease Kehlsteinhaus—the Eagle's Nest, Hitler's mountain getaway—but he was overruled due to the expense of closing the popular restaurant for a week and the general tackiness of the idea. After closing the drapes, Barry's rented supermodel, Xena, flopped in a chair and poured coffee into a delicate china cup. Barry lifted it out of her fingers and sipped.

"Thanks," he said, while idly kneading the silicon implant in her breast.

"You're welcome," Xena said sarcastically while pouring herself another cup.

Ralph Rockefeller's twins sashayed down the stairs holding hands. Dressed identically, they were topless—wearing spandex riding shorts and blonde hair pulled into pigtails. Their small breasts jiggled.

"Come and give me a kiss, girls," Barry said.

They kissed the top of his head while he nuzzled their bosoms.

"Get your filthy mouth off my girls' titties," Ralph said.

"Like you give a shit," Barry said.

"Well, I do. I paid a fucking fortune to rent those things for the weekend and I don't want your slobber all over them." To the girls he said, "Go take a shower."

"We're hungry, Ralphy," Brigitte said.

"Shower off, then you can have breakfast."

"Grump," Bambi complained as, hand-in-hand, the girls flounced upstairs.

"And put some damned clothes on," he shouted after them as he poured a cup of coffee.

Barry reached over the table and dragged over a crystal bottle of cognac. He poured a stiff shot into Ralph's cup.

"Have a drink and mellow-out, will you? You're such a cunt in the morning."

"Blow me," Ralph replied, sipping his coffee.

Marty Bilderberg walked in the dining room. "Blow me first," he said.

"You'd like that, wouldn't you, faggot?" Ralph groused.

"Knock it off. We're *all* hung over and grouchy. Let's

have breakfast and cheer up. Hey, I know what we need." To Xena, he said, "Baby, share your Vicodins, they will take the edge off our headaches. Break them in half; we don't want anyone passing out before we finish our business."

"I'm getting low," Xena said.

"Then buy more. With what I pay you, you can afford it. Besides, I know I'll see them on your invoice with a big markup."

She carefully cut the pills with a silver butter knife and passed the pieces around.

"Ah, man, what happened to us?" Ralph asked, looking around the table at his friends.

"What?" Marty grunted after tossing back his pill fragment and following it with a sip of fresh-squeezed orange juice.

"We used to party down. Remember the girls we used to bring? Marty, you brought Siamese twins and midgets. Barry brought the legless-armless girl; she was a lot of fun. I couldn't believe it when you hauled her out of that duffel bag. She had a nasty bite when she was upset, but you took out her dentures so all she could do was lisp and complain. It was classic. Remember Nicole? It's a shame AIDS took her so young. Now look at us. Marty just got out of rehab and the best Barry can come up with is a slutty Midwest cheerleader."

"Hey," Xena protested.

"No offense," Ralph said, waving her away. "I'm just saying, are we over the hill? We used have memorable parties, now we don't even do much dope. Look," he said, holding up his piece of pill for examination, "we're taking crummy little pieces of Vicodin."

"I still do a line of coke on New Year's Eve," Marty said.

"Yeah, I remember Eve, she was hot," Ralph said with enthusiasm.

"Maybe this isn't the right time to bring this up, guys, but I'm getting married," Marty said.

"You can't get married, you're gay," Ralph said.

"I'm not gay, I'm bi, asshole. Look it up in the dictionary."

"Who's the girl?"

"I don't know her well, my uncle set it up. She's the daughter of a Russian politician. I like her, she's hot and not all hung up like American women. Plus, it's good for business, so I said I'd do it."

"I thought you learned a lesson with your first two wives," Ralph said.

"Knock it off. Where will the wedding go down?" Barry asked.

"I don't know, maybe Kiev."

"Your love life is fascinating, but can we get to the point of our meeting?" Barry complained. "My dad says we need to get serious about getting completely out."

"Shit. We can't all sell everything at once or the market will go to hell. I'll lose my ass," Marty said.

"You've been selling little-by-little for the last five years, haven't you?"

"The returns were too sweet—I couldn't bear to get out. What's the problem? Can't we ice a few more eggheads and keep the lid on for a while longer?"

"Dad says no. We have six months, max."

Ralph groaned.

"I'm going to take a bath on my Lukoil holdings."

"Honestly, how much money do you need?" Marty asked. "Not even married into the KGB and he's turning into a damned Commie."

"Stop it. I say we go back to our families and convince them to hold out for a couple more years. We've been milking the petroleum economy for seventy-five years, there has to be juice left in it."

"Dad says it's really over this time. The fundamentalist Muslims went too far. We're unleashing the Physicists to topple the Royal families and start the energy revolution. We'll stop killing eggheads; that's the final word from the syndicate. If you didn't sell when you should have, that's your problem. Maybe you'll have to drive last year's Maserati."

"I switched to Saleen's."

"Will you guys stop it? This is serious."

"Cars *are* serious."

"Shut the fuck up. The world is turning upside down and all you guys care about are your hotrods."

"Okay, you don't have to get bitchy. The families locked up the mines and refineries. What's that shit again?"

"Hexavalent Cesium."

"What exactly is it? Is it like the stuff in my radio-controlled car batteries?"

"No, that's Nickel-Cadmium. Hexavalent Cesium is a

radioactive rare earth."

"I'm afraid to ask, but where are the mines?"

"God-awful cold places. Siberia and Alaska."

"I knew it would be something like that. So much for warm destinations. Does anyone want to buy my Mercedes dealership in Abu Dhabi? Dad says we should grow up, take real jobs and make ourselves useful."

"Now that it's settled, does anyone want to take over the twins?" Ralph asked. "They're sweet and open-minded, but getting tedious, if you follow my drift," he said, making a chitter-chatter gesture between his two hands.

"Sure, I'll take them, since this is as close as I'm going to get to a bachelor party," Marty said.

Agent AK-18

Artie walked around the King Theater—disgusted with the lost opportunity. There were so many potential hazards, it was hard to know where to begin. A lighting scaffold could come loose and crush a dozen. With all the wiring strewn around, there were plenty of opportunities for electrocution. A stack of speakers could topple or a person could take a wicked header into the orchestra pit. In fact, he, himself, nearly fell over the balcony after leaning on a dodgy section of railing. He'd missed his targets by a couple of hours and no one knew where they were headed. Back to Polly's house? That didn't seem likely.

What had gone on here?

He caught scattered conversation among the crew about the filming of a music video.

What to do?

He considered visiting the morons at Pacific ElectroMed, but couldn't gather sufficient enthusiasm. He couldn't think of anything other than going back to the hotel, ordering in an escort girl and a Kobe beef hamburger and waiting for Lorenz and his protectorate to show themselves. They weren't clever enough to avoid the questing tentacles of the Agents of Karnage forever.

Mike, Polly and Lorenz

Lorenz parked the borrowed truck in front of a run-down building in the industrial section of South Seattle. Traffic was heavy and the scene was chaotic. Trains, trucks and airplanes provided a constant background bustle. The building had gaping broken windows and was covered with balloon-lettered graffiti.

"What's this?" Mike asked.

"It will be our home for a while," Lorenz said with an indecipherable look on his face. "Shall we take a look around?"

The gravel parking lot was decorated with clumps of unruly weeds and greasy patches of oil. Trucks and vans, parked near a set of sliding doors, bore jazzy slogans like *Meridian Electric: Let us remove your shorts* and *Johnny on the Spot Plumbing*.

Deafening banging and raucous sawing echoed from within.

"I hope you like it," Lorenz commented as he braced himself to slide open heavy doors.

Inside, bright overhead lights illuminated a vast open area. Large machines were being installed: milling machines, lathes, a drill press, a vacuum chamber and a clean room. Stacks of microwave ovens on shipping pallets were moved by a pair of forklifts.

"Holy shit, what is all this?" Mike asked.

"I think I get it," Polly said with the hint of a grin. "There's a dance studio being installed in a corner somewhere?"

Lorenz smiled broadly. He gestured vaguely toward a loft at the north end of the building. Weaving around workers and equipment, she walked off to take a look. A man, incongruously wearing a hard hat with a suit and tie, walked over with rolls of engineering drawings. He wore a tarnished brass nametag that said *Warren*. Every other sentence was spoken into a radio so it was hard to follow the flow of his conversation.

"Are you the boss-man? Tell Brad to move the circuit breaker box to section SA-5 like I told him yesterday or I'm going to kick his ass around his shoulders. It's about time you got here, we need to figure out the stainless steel, do you really need Austenitic Forged & Bored Pipe for High Temperature Service or can you get by with Welded Austenitic Alloy? Call Pat over, the big-wigs are here, we can get the ion-emitter situation straightened out."

Mike looked around with wonder when he realized a group had assembled. They stared at him expectantly.

"Um, excuse me?" he said.

"Look, chum, we don't have all day. Time is money like Einstein said, am I right? We're using lead to seal the seams on the radioactive chamber, but it would be easier if we could use alloy solder. At sixty-three percent lead, how much thicker would it have to be? We have to get enamel on it so the guys can work without masks. Bob, do you hear me? Bob? Don't turn on the servers until the air conditioning is working and the air filters are in place. Make those yuppie assholes wait, I want to see BMWs in the parking lot all night if that's what it takes. And you, are you useless like the other executive brass? I need answers."

"What's going on?" Mike asked Lorenz plaintively.

Warren grunted. "We did the best we could from your sketches and notes, but there are always details that need to be ironed out. Am I getting help here, or what?"

Turning to Warren with an irritated look, Mike said "Give me a minute to think, will you? The welded stainless is fine. The solder will have to be thicker, let's pick an easy number to work with, say fifty percent to get the same radiation shielding if you're using sixty-three percent lead. You have my permission to use your best judgment on construction changes. Document everything in detail so I can review it later."

Something hauled by on a handcart caught his eye. He waved at the laborer to stop so he could read the shipping paperwork. Unsteady on his feet, it appeared he might pass out.

"The model PK-1998 Gallium-Heisenbach N-ray Diffractometer, that's great." To Lorenz, he asked: "Did you get the sub-ion manipulator feature?"

Lorenz nodded.

"It was expensive, but we bought all the options. I took liberties, I hope you don't mind."

He waved at a couple of workers on a scaffold unfurling a huge banner. In large block letters, it proclaimed:

PollyPhase Turbine Engine Company, LLC

The logo was a pair of P's surrounded by magnetic field lines.

"Fine, whatever," Mike said.

"You're adapting to the situation better than I thought you would."

"The shipping manifest says the PK-1998 has been sitting around since last Thursday. I can't believe it hasn't been installed and calibrated. That pisses me off. What a waste. I don't have time to chat, but we'll talk later, believe me. I have to get this facility moving in the right direction." To Warren, he said, "You, follow me."

Warren whispered to Lorenz before he scurried off to follow Mike's retreating back.

"Don't worry, he and I will get along fine."

Lorenz nodded and watched them walk away. He ambled toward the dance studio where Polly lectured three huge men who towered over her like monsters.

They were covered in glue and pieces of foam. Lorenz got close enough to hear the end of their conversation.

"Make sure to use foam padding on the struts. It needs to be like a basketball court, springy. Got it? Okay? Thanks, guys."

"Is everything in order?"

"They almost laid down oak flooring without the padding which would have been a disaster. They'd of had to tear the whole thing up."

Lorenz gestured around the large room at the mirrors, ballet bars and sound system.

"Will you be able to work here?" he asked.

"I can work anywhere as long as the floors are right," she replied.

Madison Howard and Rob Perry

Madison reviewed her next-quarter budget while sipping a steaming cup of Chai in the employee dining room. There were more people than usual milling around, gossiping in quiet clumps around the cavernous room.

"What have you heard?" Rob asked.

"Excuse me? I've been away from email for a while. I need to figure out how to cut eight percent from my budget or I'm not going to make my management objectives."

"The rumor mill says the contract manufacturer is buying our production operation."

"Wow, let me think about that. Manufacturing is a pain in the butt, so I don't care."

"If we don't have captive manufacturing, then there's no need for receiving inspection, is there? I'm all right because I'm in engineering, but part of your job goes bye-bye."

"I didn't think of that. I wonder if management has thought through the ramifications? We developed a world-class FDA-approved facility with dedicated and highly-skilled employees. Surely outsourcing will impact our product quality and long-term reliability. This could be a bad move."

"Who cares? They'll have someone to blame and can threaten to move the business elsewhere. That gets results. Management loves the idea and we don't have to expense the production line worker's medical and retirement plans. Efficiency, that's all anyone cares about."

"I don't want to work for a CM, that's like a sweatshop. They pay crap and work their employees like dogs."

Rob tapped his index finger on her desk.

"You'd better come up with a plan, Get into engineering or marketing or something safe. Maybe we could get together for a quick bite after work and go over your options."

Madison did not like the way power had shifted between them. On the edge of desperation, she needed to process the shocking news.

There's no reason to panic, she hoped.

She felt confident, she'd at least have a job until returning from her illicit get-away with Emmett. He was, after all, the company president.

Can I gather enough blackmail credit to get some job security?

The way things worked in the modern business world, this was questionable. She'd have to sign legally-binding non-disclosure agreements and various pre-intimacy disclaimers before they'd let her on the plane. Sighing, she decided to hedge her bet.

"Sure, Rob, you're sweet. That would be nice, thank you," she said breathily.

CHAPTER TWENTY-ONE

Polly and Mila

POLLY FINISHED STRETCHING and warm-up exercises at the barre and worked through dance sequences from her notebook. Interrupting her movements to twiddle the sound system equalizers, it took time before she was satisfied. The equipment was well-selected and even included vacuum tube amplifiers and electrostatic speakers, but setting the equalizers to compensate for the brightness of the large, hard-surfaced room took time. She worked on center floor combinations until she realized she had an audience. A slender, older woman quietly watched from a folding chair in a corner. Polly walked over.

"Hello?" she said.

"You didn't like the shoes?"

Polly shrugged. "My old ones are broken in. You're responsible for all this?" she asked, gesturing around the studio.

"Yes. It was an interesting contract, unique in my

experience. It came together nicely for such a tight schedule. I hope you approve."

"Yes, it's nice, but will take time to get used to it."

"You've had professional schooling?"

"I studied for a few years with Pacific Northwest Ballet, but I'm more interested in developing my own style. I don't expect to go professional or anything."

"How much did the rock band pay you?"

"I don't know. Five thousand after expenses, I think."

"So, you are a professional whether you want to be or not. You have an interesting mix of ballet and jazz dance language. A little wild, but pleasant. I like your chops, but…"

"But?"

"From your batterie and pirouettes, you are obviously a virgin."

"You can tell?"

"By the tightness in your groin. However, you have a lovely figure and beautiful rhythm, style and grace. I'm rarely impressed."

"Might I ask? Who are you?"

The woman tilted her head back and laughed. "My name is Mila, but that doesn't mean anything. Perhaps a more proper introduction would be a demonstration? Give me a minute to warm up, dear."

She took off her jacket and approached the barre. With eyes closed, she stretched and worked on loosening her muscles. Polly reappraised Mila's age, she was in great physical condition, but very old for a dancer, at least forty. She started by standing with her feet in parallel, then with a click of her fingers, splayed her feet into the classic ballet first-position, then launched into a staged sequence of poses, pirouettes, allegro-adagio combinations, grand plies, glissades and ended with a cascade flourish of sweeping bows. She curtseyed and then broke into a roaring-twenties flapper dance.

Polly clapped politely. "I recognize your knowledge of Balanchine, but it doesn't answer my question about who you are."

The woman cupped Polly's chin. "I can dance, my dear, so it doesn't matter who I am, does it? If you'll have me, I'll be your teacher and assistant."

Polly noticed a group of construction workers hovering; some leaned against a pile of sheetrock while others sipped coffee on a suspended scaffolding.

As she slid the door closed, she addressed them.

"Show's over guys. We girls need to talk." She ignored the grumbling. "This is interesting," Polly said, "what's your role?"

"In a contract addendum, I included eight hours of one-on-one instruction. No one complained, so here I am."

"In other words, you are in my service for eight hours?" Polly asked.

"I suppose you could look at it that way, the check didn't bounce. I'd like to start you off with pointe exercises and see if I can get you up on your toes more smoothly."

"And I'd like to get you started on a new dance suite, a duet. I'm calling it *The Flowering*." She made quick slashes in her notebook. "We'll rig you up with a prosthetic stomach that expands into a full pregnancy as the dance develops. Have you used props and special effects in your work?"

"No, dear, just tights, tutus, shoes and me," Mila said, laughing.

"Well don't worry, I'll make sure the moves and jumps are appropriate for your age. Let me know if something presses you too much and I'll write around it. Music from Béla Bartók, Concerto for Orchestra, will be pressed into service. We'll start with a dark stage and a still figure in solitary spotlight. Are you with me so far?"

"You're a unique young woman," Mila commented.

"Are you comfortable with a wire harness? I will want to see you fly in the first movement," Polly said, while concentrating and distractedly brushing a wisp of hair from her forehead.

Mike and Lorenz

The unfinished conference room held bundles of wires and conduit. Safety hazards, but tables and chairs were present, so the room was useful. Warren, the construction supervisor, went over blueprints with Mike while Lorenz looked on with a look of wry amusement on his face.

"Look, Mike," Warren said, "you're paying me a lot of money. If you help me understand, we can build for you, but some of this does not make sense. Let's go over this alternator. I understand the wiring, but there are errors in the wire gauges. We can hold that until later.

What I don't understand is what makes it turn? You need magnetic materials, line voltage and coils of wire."

"Oh, I see the confusion," Mike said. "This is a generator, not an alternator."

"Don't talk down to me. I have a degree in electrical engineering, but I took up construction because I didn't want to be trapped behind a desk all day. I know a generator and an alternator are the same thing depending on whether you're using mechanical energy to create electrical energy or vice versa."

"Sorry, I didn't mean to patronize you. You want to know what makes it turn? That's simple enough, we're making a gated quantum-atomic room-temperature superconducting gravitational-temporal laser- and microwave-stimulated fluxion plasma with hexavalent Cesium vapor. The plasma gating acts as a bridge rectifier for temporal-gravitational dark-matter currents. As to what makes it turn, well, the clearest I can explain it, it turns because it wants to and we simply release the resistive stiction and friction forces that stop it."

Warren had trouble breathing. His cheeks flushed and he blinked rapidly.

"Right. Okay, what about the wire, this can't be right. Silver buss bars and quadruple-aught wire?" he said nervously. "It doesn't make sense for something this small. You don't need conductors like that unless you're talking about hundreds of amps, which is absurd, of course."

"Pardon my ignorance, but is there a kind of wire that is made of tiny individually-insulated conductors?

Hundreds or even thousands of strands? I'd like to maximize skin area for a given conductor size."

"Yes," Warren said, "it's called Litz Wire."

"Cool! Then the quad-aught wire stubs can be made from that. And we'll need to design a transformer because the output voltage will only be a fraction of a volt."

Warren worked through a quick calculation in his head. "A generator the size of a matchbox rated at almost 150 watts? The buss bars and the wire will take up a lot of space. It's impractical. The bulk of the wire is many times larger than the generator itself."

"Dammit," Mike grunted. "Do I have to do everything myself?" He rubbed his eyes. "I'm sorry. I'm worn out, I didn't mean that." He walked to a whiteboard and scribbled a sketch. "We'll use a Tesla waveguide to couple high-frequency energy to the transformer. We'll need more pure silver. Can you mill silver forms?"

"Yes, sure we can, but this is incredible. Can the generators be made bigger?"

"Sure."

"Okay, you're scaring me. What do you use for fuel? What gets burned?"

"We're taking advantage of an intrinsic field bias in the black matter fluxion fabric radiated from the center of the universe."

"You crazy assholes are spending millions to create a perpetual motion machine?"

Mike laughed uproariously.

When he caught his breath, he said, "First of all, the bearings will wear out, but beyond that, when the universe goes into its contraction cycle, the turbines will spin in the reverse direction. There is nothing here that Isaac Newton would have any trouble with, believe-you-me. Perpetual motion, that's a good one. You raise a good question, however. How is all this being paid for? What's our initial debt load?" Mike asked Lorenz.

"Do you mind if I stay around to hear this?" Warren asked.

Mike shrugged.

"The SUVs did an angel and VC seed-capital round, so we have something like forty million to work with. If that's not enough, we can get more. When we get a minute, I have papers for you to sign and we can go over the details. It's a great deal. We're taking good care of you, don't worry about that."

"Okay, whatever. Right now, I want to start making quantum turbines."

"Um, I hope you'll excuse me for asking," Warren interjected, "but is the initial funding round closed? I have savings I'd like to kick in."

Lorenz smiled kindly.

"We'll get you in, but the investment will be worthless if we don't finish the facility, see what I'm saying?"

"Sure, yes, absolutely, I'm on it, sir," Warren said while scurrying from the room with bundles of drawings under his arms.

Agent AK-18

Blind with insane, irrational fury, Artie, sitting in his hotel room, pounded his hands on his laptop keyboard. Logged onto the A-Ks secure Virtual Private Network, he looked at the flashing icons for instant messages, emails, alerts and bulletins that communicated the same urgent instruction.

His mission was aborted.

He was to disconnect, break off, disengage, sever and truncate all project activities. Reading between the lines, those who once were once foes would now be friends.

Artie often argued with Agents of Karnage Central Command that contracts were great things to fund global chaos, but when conflict occurred, they had to favor their central mission. They should never subvert chaos to make money. Making money should always serve the cause of chaos. Their founder, AK-47, smiled at this argument, but never defined his central philosophy when conflicting missions occurred.

"We'll burn that bridge when we get to it," he'd said.

Don't they know how close to the edge I am? How much I need random acts of violence to maintain a semblance of control? How hard it is, holding off slitting my skin with a razor blade? And, once I start cutting, how hard it will be to stop? How overwhelming is the self-hate that wells from my core? Well, of course they don't. As mad and as evil as the A-Ks might be, they insist on following central tenets.

Employing an undisciplined, mass-murdering serial killer

might bring unwanted attention to the group. How serious are they about the cause of chaos when they insist that expense report spreadsheets balance properly, that withdrawals from the petty cash drawer are fully accounted for? Sometimes I think about getting out and taking a job with some soulless corporation where I can express my angry creativity. Be a snake in a suit. Or, better yet, politics. A clever, driven politician could wreak havoc. Would the satisfaction of sending young people to far lands to die and stealing cash from future generations be enough to satisfy an eternal craving to crush and destroy? It was enough for others.

The AK rules were constrictive, like wearing death itself. There is only one thing to do. I must kill someone. But who? I could kill the escort service girl, but that would be too easily traceable back to me.

He wandered the halls of the hotel, scoping the sight lines of the security cameras. An idea hit him. It wasn't creative or original, but Artie was in no position to be picky. On the third floor where the lower-cost rooms were located, a smirking ice machine sat, leaking water. The floor in the alcove was tile and the only security cameras in the hallway were in the elevator area around the corner. Artie filled an ice bucket with water and wetted down the floor more thoroughly, then waited inside the fire stair doorway while peeking through a gap.

A man, scratching his belly and wearing unzipped slacks and a white undershirt, came from Room 307. He walked to the Coke machine where he spent three dollars for a soda. Then, placing his feet carefully to avoid getting his socks wet, he put his ice bucket in the machine and pressed the button. While the dispenser ground out mangled hunks of ice, Artie came up from behind and hit him in the back of the head as hard as he could with a steel pole he'd borrowed from an artistic reading lamp in his room. The man hit the floor with a satisfying thump. Breathing hard, Artie watched blood pool as the man gasped his last few breaths. Then he walked toward the fire stairs and back to his room.

Yes, that's better. My head is clear and I can think. Most people don't get the beauty of chaos and murder. If murder is not sublime, then why does God do it so often?

Am I not worshiping God by emulating his work?

Most people describe a dead rose as ugly, but desiccated decay is perfectly natural. The bulb, the sprout, the flower and the wilting, discarded corpse were all part of the continuum of God's system.

Who are we to judge which part is attractive and which is not? Should we be so arrogant?

The loser from Room 307 would eventually die and rot. So, he was struck down. Perhaps this was a favor, who knows who he might have hurt or what other painful, lingering way he might have died. We share the same fate. Only time, place and method are variable. God is the ultimate Agent of Karnage. *AK-0.* We're his disciples, doing the best we can with the paltry tools at our command.

In his room, AK-18 petted Pedro and looked out over the city. While he watched the snarled traffic on I-5, an old Jeep Cherokee, covered with ugly swatches of primer paint, ran up the bumper of an Audi A8 with dealer stickers decorating the windows. The Audi driver emerged from his car, red-faced and screaming. Without warning, he was flattened by the Mexican-looking Jeep driver wielding a baseball bat. Artie was too far away to hear the screaming voices, but the scene soothed, mellowed and amused him. With patience, life rewarded one with beautiful things to make it all worthwhile. He allowed Pedro to pick a peanut off his palm.

Am I right, Pedro?

Of course I am.

Madison Howard and Rob Perry

The restaurant was good, but not fancy. Outside, the brake lights of commuter traffic were diffused by misty rain and low clouds. The menus stood on the table, held vertical by salt and pepper shakers. Rob ordered glasses of red house wine and slid a jewelry box across the table.

"I'm not a girl won over by shiny baubles."

"It's no big deal, something to mark our fourth date."

Inside, Madison seethed.

Third date, moron. Stopping at my place for a sympathy screw does not count as a date.

She smiled, though strain was evident in her lips and the stiff way she held her head.

"Our fourth date, how sweet," she said, while ignoring the flash of victory Rob could not stifle.

Now, no sex until our sixth date.

Unwrapping the shiny paper, she found an opal on a delicate silver chain.

$19.99 at JC Penney's, she thought uncharitably.

"Let me put it on you," Rob suggested.

"I'm already wearing a necklace, in case you didn't notice."

Jerk.

Ham-handed, he fumbled with her hair hanging loosely on her shoulders, but got the necklace clasped.

"Stunning," he said, "I can't wait for the night we light candles and that's all you're wearing."

Will I wear conflicting necklaces then too?

"Thank you for thinking of me," she said.

"Have you heard about the president?"

"Emmett? What about him?"

"He resigned. There are rumors, some say he was caught doing insider trading. The bottom line? He took a buy-out deal. He's gone."

There goes the weekend in the Bahamas and leverage with executive management. Was there ever a worse day in my career?

"Shit. Who will replace him?"

"A corporate drone from the holding company. They say he's a Mormon," Rob whispered.

She visualized a soulless corporate bean-counter with a bad toupee and a cheap suit. The horror.

Madison examined Rob closely. Maybe he was as good as she would get. He had a boyish charm in the vulnerability of his crooked lower teeth. There was a hint of hunter-gatherer breeding in the squareness of his shoulders.

He was shallow and simple, what guy is not? He couldn't be completely dumb. After all, he made it through engineering school where social promotion didn't work; where you couldn't slide through on glib business school bullshit.

Could she bear his children and wash his filthy underwear?

What was she thinking? This was the 21st century, he could wash his own slimy shorts.

Who am I fooling? I am the very definition of expensive, expendable middle-management. Jobs like mine are moved to India as fast as corporate America can unload them.

What are my real, long-term job prospects?

Succumbing to Rob's charm might be her easiest path. What's the downside beyond the fact that he'd stop calling and she'd never get another bauble, not even a cheap necklace bought for a former girlfriend on impulse when he was at the mall and was too clueless to return after she dumped him?

What would he look like with a fresh haircut and new clothes? Would I be comfortable introducing him to my girlfriends?

Can I train him to stop picking his teeth at the dinner table with a fingernail? Can he be converted into something classy and smooth? Do I have the energy and patience to take on this project?

She smiled as warmly and sweetly as she could, and, with a coquettish tilt to her head, placed her hand on his.

"A Mormon, how interesting," she said, while batting her lashes over the wineglass.

Mike, Polly and Lorenz

Outside, the city quieted. The construction workers had left for the day. Street lights poured through plastic film stretched over broken windows. A security guard walked around shining his flashlight into corners.

"Man, could I use a shower. It's been a hell of a long day," Mike said, yawning and running his fingers through his ragged hair.

"Yeah, what's the deal? We can't go home. Are we staying in a hotel or something?" Polly asked.

"No, we're all set here. We have clothes and plumbing and bedding and everything. We can call for pizza on a cell phone," Lorenz said, while herding them toward a small room in the corner of the building. "Voila," he said after ushering them in.

The room was sparsely furnished with a couple of mismatched easy chairs and three cots. Through an unfinished doorway, a toilet and shower were visible.

"Order Thai or Vietnamese, I don't care as long as there is rice and a spicy vegetarian dish of some kind. I'm taking the shower first," Polly said while peeling off her clothes. She rooted through a box and found makeshift pajamas: a bathrobe, sweat pants and a t-shirt. As she walked to the shower, she said, "Stop staring at my ass and order food."

Lorenz and Mike looked at each other.

"Busted," Lorenz said.

"Right away," Mike said, embarrassed.

After the food arrived, Polly appeared in her pink

bathrobe with her wet hair wrapped in a towel.

"I have wine," Lorenz said.

He brought out a bottle and three plastic cups. For lighting, he gathered and lighted butane torches which hissed and flickered. He turned out the overhead fluorescents and filled the room with dancing shadows.

"I propose a toast," Lorenz said while raising his cup, "to good friends and interesting lives."

"That's a good one," Polly agreed.

They tapped cups together and drank deeply.

While Mike coaxed a last slice of water chestnut from the bottom of his takeout container, Lorenz slipped under the blankets on his cot and rolled over, leaving Polly and Mike in relative privacy.

"Back in the theater, you said…" Mike looked through his notebook and recited: "*I'm not ready to marry you or anything, but I think we're headed in that direction.*"

"Yes?"

"I want to make sure I understand. Are we engaged?"

"No."

"Oh, sorry. I don't mean to get ahead of things."

"First of all, stop writing things down. Second, when you ask me the big question and give me the ring, then we'll be engaged. Because you're dense, let me tell you a few things. I studied you for a couple of years, so I know you better than you know yourself. I don't believe in sex before marriage, so erase any thought of shacking-up from your horny little mind. No rock, no rock-n-roll, if you follow my analogy. If you betray me, there will be no divorce, with the dullest knife I can find, I'll cut you from groin to jawbone and that will be that. We'll have several kids. I don't need a fancy house or a shiny car, but I demand every cubic centimeter of your loyalty and passion."

"You're amazing," Mike commented.

"It damned well took you long enough to figure it out."

"I'll buy you a ring tomorrow."

"Right, like I want a department store diamond." She picked up her jeans and from the front pocket pulled out a small paper packet. She handed it to Mike. "This was my grandmother's engagement ring."

Mike looked flustered. He brought out the ring and examined it in the torch lighting.

"It looks small."

"It fits. Shut up and put it on me."

With shaking hands, Mike slipped the ring on her slender finger.

"Now what?" he asked.

"Don't get fancy, just ask the question," she said.

"Will you be my wife?"

"Yes," Polly said.

They sat and looked at each other for several long seconds.

"I don't know what your rules are," Mike said.

He held his notebook as if ready for dictation.

"My rules say put down the damn pen and kiss me."

"Um, okay," Mike said. "I think I will."

"And shut the hell up," Polly said, while leaning forward and puckering.

279

CHAPTER TWENTY-TWO

Madison Howard

MADISON LOGGED ONTO the company intranet and looked over the corporate organizational chart. All the connection trees related to manufacturing, including the series of boxes where her job as Manager of Manufacturing Engineering resided, were dead ends, one-way trips to sweat-shop jobs or the unemployment line. She was assigned to the dust bin of corporate history.

What safe job am I remotely qualified for?

She decided to walk by Emmett's office and see if she could learn anything useful.

Emmett's admin was already gone; her cubicle was barren. The only things left on her desk were a company-approved mouse pad and a scattering of colorful plastic paperclips. Emmett, with his feet propped on his desk, stared out the window and chewed on a massive wad of nicotine gum.

"Madison, come in. I suppose you've heard the news." She nodded. "Well, I don't care, I guess. I've been thinking of retiring for a long time. I have the money. I could move to my weekend place at the San Juan Islands, grow out my hair and cultivate a shaggy, old-geezer hipster beard. Raise organic barley and brew my own beer. You're probably wondering about our trip to the Bahamas? I'll be joining my wife and daughters in Italy. Too bad, we coulda' had a lot of fun. My wife won't even let me take Viagra. She likes it better when I leave her alone, I guess."

Madison spread the org charts on Emmett's desk.

"How about helping me out before you go?"

Emmett sighed. "Corporate dictates, office politics, market position, return on investment and quarterly earnings reports. Overnight, none of that means anything to me." He sighed and scanned the charts. "It's a stretch, but what about Harris Stanwood's position in Marketing? He inherited a butt-load of money and isn't happy. He'll probably resign."

Marketing has a nice ring to it. I'm not exactly sure what they do on a day-to-day basis, but the travel and expense allowances are great. Marketing could work.

"I could put in a good word for you with the V-P," Emmett said.

"What would you want in return? We could book a cozy room with a fireplace for a long weekend at Whistler…"

"No, I'd better not. As great as that sounds, I'd better be good. If my wife divorces me, my retirement nest egg flies out the window. I thought I had a few years left with the company, but I was wrong. Sad day."

Standing, Madison put a comforting hand on his shoulder.

"Thanks for the career advice," she said.

"Think nothing of it," Emmett replied.

Polly and Mila

Polly held up her hand so Mila would stop talking. Concentrating on dance notations, Polly moved her arms and worked through the sequence in her mind. Once she captured the movements that filled the dance cycle, she looked up.

"Yes, Mila, what is it?"

"I enjoy our experiments, but I must get back to my work. I hate to be crass, but we've gone way over the eight hours you paid me for."

"Oh, that," Polly said.

Ignoring the construction worker audience sitting on a scaffold eating donuts and sharing drinks from an insulated container, she walked to the loft railing over the main work area. She spotted Mike and yelled out to him.

"Hey, Mike, aren't we rich?"

Mike, confused, turned and looked around until he found her.

"What?" he yelled back.

"Aren't we rich?"

"Yeah, pretty much, I think," he replied.

"Okay," Polly said to Mila. "Submit an invoice and I'll make sure you get paid. Will that do it?"

"Sure," Mila responded.

Polly got on her hands and knees and placed Mila's feet for the start of a movement. Standing, she arranged Mila's arms and pushed her into a balanced position. Then she was distracted by one of the construction workers.

"Polly."

She looked around, and then walked to the point where the loft was closest to the scaffolding.

"What?"

"Wouldn't an *aerial* be nice after the *cross body with inside turn* move?"

"No. If you don't shut up, I'll close this door."

"Hey, you damned apes, break time is over," Warren called up to them. "Get your lazy asses back to work."

The workers complained.

"Paul, you're such a prick. If you get us banned from watching, you'll have an unfortunate on-the-job accident."

"Shut your trap. I'm right, an aerial maneuver would be pretty neat."

"All fucking welders think they're artists."

Polly went back to work with Mila.

"Can I ask what we're doing? Are you thinking of a public performance?"

"Yes, we'll perform a once-only show as a duet. Do you know people who do costumes and prosthetics?"

"Sure, of course. What do you have in mind?"

"To start with, I want aerial harnesses like Cirque de Soleil. Multimedia. Now hush and let me think this through."

Agent AK-18

The Pacific ElectroMed facility, embedded in a hillside, overlooked farmland evolving into Suburbia with tract houses on cul-de-sacs surrounding a sprawling golf course. The building was designed as if asking to be fired into the stratosphere by a bomb. The contour of the hillside would naturally create a shaped charge.

Diesel from the emergency generator buried in the ground outside the loading dock area could be vaporized into the enclosed under-building and ignited. The building would launch like a rocket. Artie, sitting in his car, examined the facility with field glasses while petting Pedro and plotting. Tired of stacking odds, he craved the direct action of mass-murder. A hundred feet of PVC pipe fed by a high-pressure pump connected to fuel injectors from an auto parts store would deliver and create the fuel-air vapor. An igniter from a gas furnace, connected to a cell phone, would make a lovely remote-controlled detonator. After forty-five minutes of sneaking around, laying plastic pipe and wiring things up, everything was ready.

"Kaboom, Pedro, wouldn't you like to see that?" he mumbled. "Yes, you would. Let's kill some yuppie assholes."

Madison Howard and Harris Stanwood

Madison walked straight to Harris's office. He repetitively threw darts at a map push-pinned to the wall. She plopped down in his guest chair and watched him with curiosity.

"I'm trying to hit Tasmania but I keep hitting Perth or

Manila. I don't want to go to Perth or Manila."

She reached over the desk and plucked a dart from his hand. She stabbed it into Tasmania.

"Okay, now you can go to Tasmania."

"Thanks," he said.

"What's it like working in marketing?"

"It seems glamorous with travel and unlimited expense accounts, but it's a drag. You hump equipment to trade shows, pull booth duty, and then there's all the tedious talking to doctors and nurses and writing requirements documents for last year's product that engineering will deliver next year, long after anyone cares. I'm sick of it."

"If you quit, will you help me get your job?"

"Why would I?"

She sat up straight and fluffed her hair. "There are fringe benefits to teaching me what I need to know. We'll spend a lot of time together. With late nights studying, it might be better for me to sleep over at your place," she said, while picking an imaginary fleck of lint off the front of her blouse.

"My girlfriend dumped me, but that doesn't mean I'm pathetic and desperate."

"Yes it does."

Harris's shoulders slumped. "You wouldn't be sitting here if I didn't have something you wanted."

Madison shrugged.

"So what?"

Harris brightened as an idea struck him.

"Would you be interested in joining me on my

retirement trip?"

She wrinkled her nose. "I'm getting a headache. Let's get out of here and get a drink. We can talk it over."

"Okay," Harris said.

Madison leaned over and pulled an errant dart out of Antarctica. She stabbed it into the map just east of Seattle.

"Meet me at the Lucky Seven in half an hour."

Mike and Lorenz

Peering through a magnifying lamp, Mike concentrated on assembling the final part of a Pollyphase Turbine when he noticed the building was quiet and empty. He stretched his back and glanced around; tools were scattered, it looked like the workplace had been hastily abandoned. Lorenz, wearing a sour look on his face, walked over.

"Where is everyone?" Mike asked.

"We have a problem with the money," Lorenz said, rubbing his forehead. "Teams in Shenzen, Shanghai and Mexico are trying to duplicate your design and nothing works. Our lead investor lost confidence. He thinks you're a fraud."

Mike laughed. "Does my contract give you permission to copy my design?"

"Well, no, but close enough," Lorenz replied. "You granted an exclusive license in exchange for stock and the money to build this place. However, you'll spend the rest of your life in courtrooms if the turbine doesn't actually spin. The company copied your drawings and followed your notes precisely. What's the problem?"

"I didn't document a few key details. If you understand the inner motivation and desire of hexavalent Cesium vapor, the standing-microwaves and temporal-gravitational fluxions, then it's obvious what's missing. Can't your eggheads figure it out?"

"Given time, probably."

"This one is ready to test. Let's see how big of a fraud I am."

Mike, using a jeweler's screwdriver, torqued tiny stainless steel screws and placed the turbine on a bench. He flipped a toggle switch. The machine sat quiet and inert.

"Is it going to work, or not?"

"You should have more faith after all we've been through," Mike said calmly. "It needs a nudge, that's all." He tapped the rotor with his finger and it slowly started spinning. As it accelerated, a smell of ozone filled the air; an annoying high-pitched whine raised in pitch until becoming supersonic. Mike pointed at the readout on a wattmeter.

"See, just like I said. One-hundred and fifty-three watts. It will run until the bearings seize or the universe collapses on itself, whichever comes first."

"Will you disclose the details?"

"Look at the violet glow in the vacuum bulb, doesn't that give you a hint? Sublimation of iodine vapor plays a part in the reaction. Halogen series, atomic number fifty-three, seventy-four neutrons, and you never noticed iodine's enthalpy of fusion rating and its unique crystalline structure?"

With a scowl, Lorenz pulled out his cell phone. "Iodine," he said, before slapping his phone shut. Slowly, workers came back and picked up their tools. "The team of investors is led by one of the Mellon heirs. He's irritated, but I don't blame you for protecting yourself. Don't forget, this technology liberates mankind and is bigger than any of us."

"Is this Mellon-fellow someone I would like?"

"No."

"Here's the bottom line, when I feel safe, then and only then, I will tell you about all of my tweaks. But, if anything happens to me now, you can count on years of expensive research, because some of the key concepts are devilishly subtle."

"I'll order iodine from Element Sales. Is there anything else?"

Mike smiled enigmatically. "I'll let you know," he said. "Now, let's build bigger versions and generate more-manly power."

Agent AK-18

Artie noticed a curious boy about four-years-old sitting on a plastic potato. The potato had a steering wheel, a goofy face and large yellow wheels. Artie shook his head with the absurdity of it. He got out of the car and walked to the boy, who wore a suspicious expression on his face.

"Would you like to pet my ringtail cat?" Artie asked.

He lifted his jacket. Pedro poked his nose out to sniff the air.

Solemnly, the boy shook his head.

"Looks like a skunk," the boy said.

"Do you know the company down there?" Artie asked, gesturing down the hill toward the Pacific ElectroMed building.

The boy shrugged.

"By chance, does your mommy or daddy work there?"

"No," the boy said firmly. "My daddy works for the phone company and Mommy works for Microsoft. I stay home with Nana, but she's with her boyfriend. She told me to go outside and play. I'm not supposed to leave the yard," he said with a defiant tone.

"Can't have everything," Artie grumbled.

He slipped on gloves, and then brought out the prepaid cell phone he'd bought at a drugstore. There was no way he'd touch this phone with his bare hands, so it was completely untraceable.

"Would you like to play with my cell phone? It has Froggyville."

"Okay," the boy said after consideration.

Artie handed it over.

"Whatever you do, don't press the green phone-icon."

"I know about the *send* button."

"Of course you do, silly me. Do you understand? Play Froggy as much as you want, but never, ever press the send button. Do you promise?"

The boy nodded. Artie got back in his car and drove until he found a vantage point several blocks away. Settling in, he watched the Pacific ElectroMed building while sipping cold coffee and listening to NPR on the radio.

Would anything happen?

Only if the lords of chaos willed it.

He ran the engine to keep the windows unfogged. Ten minutes elapsed, then there was flash.

Good boy. I knew the temptation would be irresistible.

He was gratified. The main part of the building launched twenty feet in the air and then collapsed. A cascade of rubble avalanched down the hillside while a billow of black smoke soared into the sky. The car shook with a wind that roared by. Something large flew into the valley and embedded in the soggy fifth green of the golf course. Artie's body flushed with the warm pleasure of mass destruction. The sound of sirens in the distance roused him from his trance. After starting the car, he drove slowly to the west.

God must love explosive destruction, otherwise why would he make it so breathtakingly beautiful?

Rob Perry

One of Rob's direct reports, Mary Wilson, poked her head in his office. "Doesn't the smell bother you?" she asked. "Was there a fuel spill? It's giving me a headache."

"Maintenance is checking it out," Rob replied, distracted.

"I can't take it," she said, "I'm going home. Call me when the place airs out."

"Fine," Rob replied.

He worked on a spreadsheet called GettingIntoMadisonsPants. It was nearly worked out, though the budget for the fourth date was questionable, forty dollars allotted for hamburgers and a Hugh Grant chick flick. He hoped Madison would not want a ten-dollar tub of greasy theater popcorn. Her figure was trim; it seemed worth the gamble.

He needed to save money for the penultimate fifth date, his big-money shot. A limousine charged on his MasterCard, a romantic candle-lighted dinner charged to one of his Visa cards and finally, a hotel room with hot tub charged on his American Express card. He budgeted sixty-eight dollars in cash for incidentals. The plan seemed viable until he realized there was no money for flowers and only roses would be appropriate. He thought of strolling the gardens at the University of Washington Arboretum and rustling blooms. That would take care of the flowers.

There's no margin for error, but the plan has a good chance of working, Rob thought as the floor buckled and he was crushed by a steel I-beam.

Madison Howard and Harris Stanwood

After being seated at a booth at the Lucky Seven, Madison excused herself to use the restroom. She tugged on the arm of their server so she could talk without Harris seeing them. She waved a folded bill.

"This twenty is for you if, no matter what I order, you bring me ginger ale on the rocks, got it?"

"Whatever you say, dearie," the server replied while efficiently tucking the money in her pocket.

In the restroom, Madison checked her makeup and ran her fingers through her hair. Back at their booth, the waitress waited.

"What are you drinking?" Harris asked.

Madison thought about it and said, "I'd like a gin and tonic and make it a double, please." She settled on the bench seat and began playing with a coaster. "I won't dance around. There's talk that you're quitting the company and I want your job. Your help and endorsement would be appreciated."

"I thought that would be it. You're not the first to ask. Everyone's in a panic with the production work moving to India and China."

The waitress placed drinks in front of them, Harris made a small gesture in toast and took a deep drink.

"Bring us another round," he said.

"Have you committed your help to anyone else?" Madison said.

"Nothing I can't back out of," Harris replied. "Look, about my little problem, does everyone know?" Madison shrugged noncommittally. "It's not like I'm sterile, I have a daughter by one of my high-school girlfriends. She's twelve and I don't ever see her."

Madison sipped her drink.

Do guys really think women care how large the penis is? What trauma was caused by the guys in his prep school locker room?

She allowed him a small comfort.

After placing her hand on his, she said "I only care about the size of a man's heart."

As if God was displeased with her white lie, there was a deep rumble, glasses behind the bar rattled. The lamp hanging over their booth swung like a pendulum.

"What the hell was that?" Harris said.

"Earthquake, I guess. I hope that was all of it," she said while looking around the room for reassuring signs.

"Instead of slaving away at the company, come with me. I inherited a one-hundred and thirty-seven foot boat and crew. I'm taking a year off and sailing around the world. Hawaii, Tahiti, Fiji, New Zealand, the Philippines, Hong Kong, Sri Lanka, the Suez Canal, the Mediterranean, Bahamas, the Panama Canal, the whole shebang. It will be great. We'll see the whole world, including Tasmania."

"I'd never recover from the damage to my career," she said.

"You don't need a career if you have a rich boyfriend."

A rude thought flashed through her mind before she could squelch it.

A rich boyfriend with a midget penis.

She rotated the round-the-world cruise idea in her mind.

"I'm not a fan of boats and open water."

"This is not just a boat, it's more like a floating luxury condo with satellite TV, theater-grade audio/video system, microwave ovens, washer/dryers, a full wait staff and cook, wine cellar, computer-controlled stabilization, high-speed Internet, work-out room, everything. Please say you'll join me."

"I'd want a contract in case you change your mind about me. I need security for the future."

"Anything. You'll be set for life."

Over the beeps of video games and the clatter coming from the pool tables, they heard sirens howling outside.

"The fancy equipment is nice, but what I'll really need is a medicine cabinet filled with Dramamine for motion sickness," she sighed. "Very well, I'll have my lawyer draft something for you to review."

"Fine," Harris said. He raised his glass and they toasted to their agreement. The waitress brought fresh drinks. "Keep them coming," Harris said. "We're celebrating good fortune."

"You still drinking doubles, or do you want to switch to single-shots?" the waitress asked Madison with an inscrutable look in her eyes.

"No, keep bringing doubles, thanks," Madison said.

Caller X

The streets north of Boeing Field were confusing. Caller X cursed his TomTom GPS, which told him to turn the wrong way under the Spokane Street overpass. Finally, by traveling along an alley past an abandoned steel plant, he found the hustle-bustle of the PollyPhase Turbine Engine Company. He backed up to the loading dock and got out of his Suburban. A pimply kid, wearing an Opeth t-shirt and large black disks in his earlobes emerged from the receiving area office.

"Pardon me, Harold, you can't park there."

"Harold?" Caller X said.

The kid shrugged. "You look like a cop."

"Ah, I see. I'm looking for Mike Thomas."

"Okay, I'll find him."

Mike looked as if he'd been sleeping in his clothes. Wearing a greasy plaid shirt, his belly strained against the buttons. He scratched his head vigorously as he approached.

"What?"

"Are you Mike?"

"Yeah, what do you want? I'm in the middle of something."

"I want to invest in your company. Can you use palladium?"

"I'd rather have hexavalent Cesium, got any?"

"No."

"Okay, Hartz handles investors. I'll send him out."

"Lorenz Hartz?"

"Yeah, hang on."

Lorenz was talking into a cell phone when he appeared. With the phone still chattering, he held it away from his head to address Caller X.

"First round financing is in place. Leave a card and I'll call you when the next round opens," he said.

"Lorenz, it's great to meet you face-to-face. My name is Carlton, but you can call me Caller X."

Lorenz studied Carlton's face. Into the phone he said, "I'll call you back." He folded the phone and dropped it in the pocket of his heavy coat. "Okay, what've you got?"

Carlton gestured to the rear of the Suburban. He flipped the latches on a flight case and pulled the lid open.

"Palladium," he said. "Lots of it."

Lorenz thought for a moment.

"Okay, you're in," he said.

CHAPTER TWENTY-THREE

Agent AK-18

ARTIE, SURROUNDED BY scattered newspapers, sat by himself in his room. He drained the last of a superb bottle of Spanish Rose Cava into his glass and scraped the vestiges of caramelized Burnt Cream from the shallow ceramic bowl it was baked in. The initial fatality count from the explosion was disappointing; only eighty-eight dead were confirmed. Fifty were still missing, so breaking one-hundred was still possible. Local hospitals treated two-hundred and forty-eight, some seriously injured.

Not bad for a few hours of plotting and $107 spent at an auto parts store.

He basked in the self-satisfied glow of accomplishment, then noticed a small article in the business section.

New Company to Produce Turbine Generators

According to public records, a start-up company in South Seattle called PollyPhase Turbine Engine Company collected $44M in first-round capital from investors including Paul Allen's Vulcan Ventures, Sequoia, Sand Hill Capital and unnamed angel investors rumored to be connected to multinational oil companies. Little is known about COO Lorenz Hartz who did not return phone calls or answer repeated requests for an interview.

"We're delighted they chose Seattle for the development of post-petroleum energy machinery," Seattle Mayor Leon Salyer said at a press conference. "Seattle's progressive nature makes it a natural fit for modern, clean energy technologies."

Artie smiled.

I knew I'd find you sooner or later.

The Grand Finale

Artie watched the last of the construction workers drive away in company vans and pickup trucks. As the sun set, he sipped wine from a paper cup and enjoyed the sight of business jet landing lights glittering on approach to Boeing Field. With an empty mind, he shuffled a deck of cards and waited for the goddess of chaos to show him the way.

After dusk, he watched a slight-framed Vietnamese teenager, driving a microscopic Indian car, pull into the parking lot.

I thank the undergods of mayhem. Turn a face card and you

can live, kid.

He turned over a card. A King mocked him.

One more try to be sure.

He flipped another card and turned up a Jack. Angry now, he flipped another and was gratified to see a three of hearts.

Too bad, kid, the odds went against you, so tonight you'll die.

Toying with a loop of diamond wire in his pocket, Artie waved the boy over. Wary, the kid walked into bright area of the parking lot, under overhead lighting.

"You come over here," the boy called out.

Artie cursed the boy's streetwise caution. The parking lot was open to the street and the floodlight would expose him to witnesses.

Smart kid.

In spite of the command of the card, eradicating the boy would compromise the central mission. He made a note of the restaurant name emblazoned on a magnetic sign stuck to the car door.

Perhaps I can come by later and finish my business with you.

He walked to the pool of light.

"Thanks for coming so quickly," he improvised, "what do I owe you?"

"Thirty bucks," the young man said.

"Here's fifty, keep the change," Artie said.

"Thanks a lot. That's very generous."

"Think nothing of it," Artie replied with a wide, toothy grin.

He took the bag back to his car and sampled each of

the take-out boxes. He liked the curry, spring rolls and squid, but the crabmeat-tofu-watercress-mushroom soup was nasty, so he tipped it into the gravel of the parking lot. Under the wan parking lot lighting, it glistened like aardvark entrails.

While chewing, he watched the darkened building. From roaming flashlights, he deduced that two security officers patrolled the building. He went to the darkest corner and placed the remaining food by the rear door. When the flashlight approached, he tapped on the door.

"Food delivery," he said.

When the guard came out, Artie slipped fine wire around his neck. The man grabbed at it.

"Do you want your fingers in there?" Artie asked.

He loosened the wire slightly and the man, desperate, slipped gloved fingers inside the loop. Artie pulled hard on Kevlar handles. The man's fingers and head effortlessly separated from his body. Artie kneeled and rotated the head. He waggled one of the severed fingers.

"Feel stupid now, don't you?" he whispered. The eyes blinked and Artie was sure that the man understood him before slipping into death. "Moron. That's diamond wire."

He pulled the body into the shadows, sat on the torso and drank wine from the bottle while patiently waiting for the other guard to look for his partner. When the flashlight drew near, he stood beside the door. The guard poked his head out.

"Charlie?" he said, while Artie slipped the wire over his head.

This'd be more fun if it was a bigger challenge. I hope

Lorenz and the rest put up more of a fight.

Artie dragged the second guard's body parts to join the first. He arranged the heads so they appeared to be kissing.

He took the guard's heavy revolver and checked the cylinder to make sure it was loaded, and then picked up the bag of Vietnamese food. Walking through the darkened building, he wished he'd thought to steal a flashlight. Slowly his eyes adjusted and he weaved around machinery that filled the building. Light poured from under a doorway. He stopped and listened to the voices. A man and a woman. He knocked.

"Dinner is served," he said.

When Lorenz opened the door, Artie poked the pistol in his face.

"Hello, Lorenz."

"Hello, Artie."

"Keep your hands where I can see them and back up."

"Okay."

Polly sat on a camp stool with a notebook splayed on her lap. Her mouth was open with surprise.

"Where's the genius?" Artie asked.

Lorenz jerked his head toward the bathroom. "He's taking a dump. We heard about your work at Pacific ElectroMed. You're a sick fucking bastard."

Gesturing with the revolver, Artie herded them toward the wall.

"Sit down and shut up," he commanded.

"I had a lot of friends there," Polly said.

"What part of *shut up* confuses you?" Artie said as he

pressed the barrel of the gun into her cheek.

"The *why* part, since you're going to kill us anyway."

"No one likes a mouthy bitch. Let's quietly wait for the boy wonder to wipe his ass and come out, shall we?"

Artie backed up and flicked his eyes from the prisoners to the bathroom door. Pedro poked his nose out to smell the air, and then pulled back into his lair.

"What was that?" Polly asked.

"Do I have to shoot you to shut you up?" Artie said.

Mike was startled by a tap on his shoulder. He stretched his back and removed headphones. Tired and hungry, he'd been working in the dark. He turned to see the delivery boy. The boy held his finger before his lips to silence him.

"Vu, we've been waiting for you," Mike said.

"There's a man," the boy whispered. "A dangerous man, I think."

Mike turned toward their living quarters.

"Have you seen the guards?" he asked.

"No," the kid whispered.

"Okay," Mike said, thinking.

He walked toward their makeshift apartment and heard an unfamiliar voice talking about shooting.

"That damned Agent of Karnage," he mumbled. "Now what?"

Quietly fumbling in the dark, he found one of the latest bubble guns. He created a big bubble and watched it drift into their room.

Artie turned as a large bubble drifted through the doorway. Four feet in diameter, its surface glistened with color like water floating on oil, diffracting light. The random patterns hypnotized him. It drifted toward Lorenz who slowly stretched his hand up the wall and grabbed the modified cricket bat.

"Sit down," Artie said, while waving the gun between his prisoners and the open door.

Lorenz tapped the bubble toward Artie, who was distracted by a remote control sliding through the doorway. Polly grabbed the remote while Artie fired at the bubble, the report was deafening in the small room. The bullet passed through the bubble without effect, though the bullet's trail seemed to attract it. It moved toward Artie as though connected by a wire.

Polly, aiming the remote control, waited until the bubble passed through Artie's lower body, and then pressed the *play* button. Artie's legs vaporized and his upper body fell to the floor with a sickening thump. His midriff ended with a curved, black, cauterized edge. Pedro crawled out of the coat and sniffed Artie's face. His furry tail was truncated by several inches, otherwise, he appeared undamaged.

Artie scrabbled for leverage to aim the gun still clasped in his fist. Mike walked through the door and stepped on his wrist. He bent over and removed the weapon from Artie's grasp. Artie looked at the missing part of his body with shocked wonder.

"It doesn't hurt," he said.

He dragged himself across the floor.

Polly picked up Pedro. "You're a cute little guy," she said, stroking his black and white speckled fur. "What's his name?"

"Pedro," Artie said, while futilely trying to pull his wrist from under Mike's heel. "You assholes randomized me," he commented bitterly.

"Almost," Lorenz said.

He tugged the revolver from Mike's hand.

"You guys don't want to see this, you should leave the room."

Mike took Polly's hand.

"Can I keep Pedro?" she asked.

Lorenz and Mike exchanged a look.

"Sure, if you want to," Mike said. "Will he get along with your cats?"

After they left the room, a gunshot echoed through the vast building. Lorenz walked out.

"Sorry, I'm old-school," he said, apologizing. "Loan me the bubble gun and I'll clean up the mess."

The police searched the building, took away the guard's bodies and towed Artie's car. Then came endless, probing questions, which Lorenz, with a lawyer's evasive smoothness, deflected. Exhausted, Mike slipped into his cot and, snoring and drooling into his pillow, soundly slept.

Polly tapped Lorenz's shoulder.

"Are you asleep?"

"Almost," Lorenz replied.

"Would you do me a favor?"

"Sure."

"Pronounce Mike and me to be man and wife."

Lorenz swiveled and sat up.

"It won't have the power of law."

"I know, we'll take care of the legal formality later," she said.

She gently freed Mike's hand from his blankets. He shifted his weight but did not wake. She cupped his hand in hers.

"Okay, I pronounce you man and wife," Lorenz said solemnly. "You may now kiss the groom."

Polly laughed. "Sure, thanks," she said. She leaned over and kissed Mike's forehead. "Goodnight, Lorenz," she said before slipping back into her bedding.

"Goodnight, Mrs. Polly Thomas," Lorenz whispered, while laughing quietly to himself.

Saudi Royal Family Declares Jihad against Wahabi Clerics

ZBS News – North American Herald-Star - Riyadh

King Abdullah Fahd, the recently crowned monarch of the Royal Saudi ruling family, declared the fundamentalist Wahabi sect a terrorist organization and promised to track down and arrest Imams preaching violence against the West.

"We must embrace a new partnership with Western countries," he said at a meeting of OPEC nations.

He also recommended an immediate reduction of the crude oil spot price to ten-dollars per barrel.

CHAPTER TWENTY-FOUR

The Flowering

THE HALL WAS packed with enthusiastic fans because Polly called in a favor. Nabokov's Hammer agreed to open the show with acoustic versions of a few of their songs. Word spread over the Internet.

"If you guys behave yourselves, we'll come out after the dance and do another song," Raz announced.

This announcement was greeted with cheers and raucous clapping.

Polly was more nervous than she thought she'd be, her stomach roiled and a massive headache threatened to split her skull. She asked Mila to rub tension from her neck and shoulders. From experience with overstressed ballerinas, Mila expertly kneaded Polly's neck with strong fingers; the headache retreated.

For the fifth or sixth time, Polly checked the backstage room she'd set up. A mattress on the concrete floor was covered with a colorful comforter. Candles decorated every flat surface. She'd prepared everything with precise planning. For her first scene, the stage crew hooked her to a harness and she took position on an overhead catwalk with the tiny, fragile ballerina that represented the child as an infant. She watched the lighting brighten and was gratified when the crowd quieted. Beyond quiet conversation and occasional catcalls, the audience was attentive as Nabokov's Hammer finished their short set and exited the stage.

As Mila danced, her prosthetic stomach expanded with simulated pregnancy. Her moves, as practiced, became awkward and off-balance. With a flash of red light and stage smoke, a tiny ballerina descended from heaven. They danced in synchronization until slowly, the little girl moved with increasing independence. After that sequence, with strobe lights creating a hallucinogenic scene, the girl dashed off stage and Polly pendulumed across the stage, slowly descending until her feet touched the stage.

Unconscious, she performed a section called *Teenage Rebellion* until the short intermission. She ran to her improvised bedroom as fast as she could and arrived out of breath and sweaty. The candles were lighted and the room smelled of musky incense. As ordered, Mike waited. Polly gave him a kiss on the neck.

"We don't have much time. Get nekkid," she said.

"What? Are you sure?" Mike said.

Polly laughed heartily while peeling off tights. In seconds she was stood naked except for ballet shoes. She rose on her toes and struck a teasing pose.

"Yes, I'm sure," she said.

"Lorenz gave me the ring," Mike said, showing off his

finger. "It fits."

"Get those clothes off and we'll see what else fits," Polly said with a hoarse voice.

"Okay," Mike said.

Polly, on top, straddled him and quickly initiated penetration. She athletically undulated her loins and Mike experienced a heaving, spasmodic and blissful orgasm.

"Sorry Mike, we'll take time to do this right later," she whispered. "I have to go."

She tossed a lacy, flowing dress over her head and patted it into place, then leaned over to give him a full and passionate kiss on the lips. In an instant, she was gone. Drifting in post-coital harmony with the universe, Mike, moving slowly, got up and pulled his clothes back on. Something in the back of his mind distracted him; something complex and elusive. He walked back to his place in the audience and sat next to Lorenz. Polly, on stage, performed elaborate jumps with rubbery, loose-limbed precision.

Lorenz patted him on the shoulder. "Everything go as planned?" he asked.

"She's an angel."

"I know," Lorenz replied, "you're a lucky guy."

"Luck, there's something I just realized," Mike whispered.

"What is it?" Lorenz asked.

"Time and gravity unification. They are reversible. We can't see it because of the sequential nature of our brain's biochemical machinery. I touched the secret mind of God. Time is an illusion, luck can be materialized and everything is simultaneous." He grasped Lorenz's arm and squeezed with painful pressure. "It's beautiful," he said with mad intensity.

As if synced with his thoughts, the crowd surged to its collective feet and roared with approval. The stage lights came up and Polly, Mila and the ballerina skipped to center stage and bowed.

"Mike, this is important," Lorenz said. "Stop thinking about your stupid time machine." He pressed elaborate rose bouquets into Mike's hands. Gesturing, he said, "Go through that doorway and follow the hallway. You'll come out in the orchestra pit. Don't worry, the guards will let you pass. Hand these flowers to the ladies. You get one chance, do you understand? Give Polly the largest bundle. Go now!" he commanded.

Grinning with fatherly pride, Lorenz watched as Mike followed instructions and delivered the flowers. After a full minute of enthusiastic applause, the ladies, laughing, waved their bouquets and bowed one final time. Then, hand-in-hand, they skipped offstage.

EPILOGUE

ON A COMPUTER screen, Barry Rothschild studied his bank balance and tried to figure out how to make his salary stretch until payday.

Work, he thought bitterly. *I don't know how the little people stand it.*

From his desk on the 98th floor of the Sears Tower, he could see Soldier Field, the marina and a wide blue swath of Lake Michigan. Daydreaming, he stared out the window. His phone bleeped. He pressed the button for the intercom.

"I said no calls."

"I'm sorry, sir. It's Prince Mutaib bin Abdullah Bin Abdl-Aziz Al-Saud. He says the matter is urgent."

Fucking Saudis, why can't they fathom the message? They're obsolete.

"Sir?"

"Tell him I'm out of the office and you don't know when I'll be back."

"Yes, sir."

Barry sighed. Leaning back in his chair with his feet on his desk, he returned to staring through the window.

www.ingramcontent.com/pod-product-compliance
Lightning Source LLC
Chambersburg PA
CBHW022136170626
46807CB00005B/1962